SEAROAD

Chronicles of Klatsand

Ursula K. Le Guin

HarperPrism
An Imprint of HarperPaperbacks

This is a work of fiction. The characters, incidents, and dialogues are products of the author's imagination and are not to be construed as real. Any resemblance to actual events or persons, living or dead, is entirely coincidental.

HarperPaperbacks *A Division of* HarperCollins*Publishers*
10 East 53rd Street, New York, N.Y. 10022

A trade paperback edition of this book was published in 1992 by HarperCollins*Publishers.*

Cover illustration by Kirk Reinert

First HarperPaperbacks printing: November 1994

Printed in the United States of America

HarperPaperbacks, HarperPrism, and colophon are trademarks of HarperCollins*Publishers*

❖ 10 9 8 7 6 5 4 3 2 1

BOOKS BY URSULA K. LE GUIN

Praise for Ursula Le Guin
and **SEAROAD**

"A winning example of Le Guin's best writing ... Another triumph."
—*Kirkus Reviews*

"Idiosyncratic and convincing. Le Guin's characters have a long afterlife."
—*Publishers Weekly*

"Extraordinary ... absorbing ... brilliantly wrought. This is what the best science fiction does best—and this is one of the best."
—*The Village Voice*

"SEAROAD shows a more personal and intimate side of Le Guin's talent, akin to her lovely poetry. This woman can do anything! Long may she continue to do it all."
—Carolyn Kizer

"Her writing is remarkable. . . .Le Guin's characters are complex and haunting."
—*Time*

"Like all great writers of fiction, Ursula Le Guin creates imaginary worlds that restore us, hearts eased, to our own."
—*Boston Globe*

"Le Guin is the only author who has won three Nebulas and four Hugos (the major science fiction prizes) as well as the National Book Award. . . .Le Guin's books tap both the technology of the future and the resonant archetypes of fairytale."
—*Life*

"She wields her pen with a moral and psychological sophistication rarely seen in science fiction circles, and while science fiction techniques often buttress her stories, they rarely take them over. What she really does is write fables: splendidly intricate and hugely imaginative tales about such mundane concerns as life, death, love, and sex."
—*Newsweek*

ACKNOWLEDGMENTS

CONTENTS

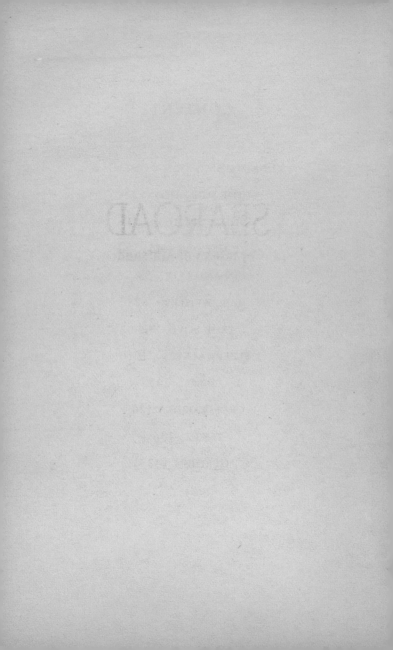

SEAROAD
Chronicles of Klatsand

Foam Women, Rain Women

The foam women are billowy, rolling, tumbling, white and dirty white and yellowish and dun, scudding, heaving, flying, broken. They lie at the longest reach of the waves, rounded and curded, shaking and trembling, shivering hips and quivering buttocks, torn by the stiff, piercing wind, dispersed to nothing, gone. The long wave breaks again and they lie white and dirty white, yellowish and dun, billowing, trembling under the wind, flying, gone, till the long wave breaks again.

The rain women are very tall; their heads are in the clouds. Their gait is the pace of the storm-wind, swift and stately. They are tall presences of water and light walking the long sands against the darkness of the forest. They move northward, inland, upward to the hills. They enter the clefts of the hills, unresisting, unresisted, light into darkness, mist into forest, rain into earth.

The Ship Ahoy

The White Gull was the really nice motel in town. The Brinnesis had run it since 1964, and they kept it up, with white trim renewed every few years on the sixteen shingled cabins, firewood for the fireplaces, a flower box by every doorstep, good stoves and refrigerators in the kitchenettes. The last few years, they were asking sixty dollars a night for the ocean-view cabins, and on weekends in the season taking reservations only for two-night occupancy, and still filled up every weekend. Mrs. Brinnesi wore dresses, never pants; she was a religious-minded woman, attending Sunday mass at St. Joseph's up the coast and various retreats and Catholic women's meetings. Mr. Brinnesi would tell people right to their faces that if they wanted to have loud drinking parties or behave immorally they could go to another motel in another town. They were strict people, the Brinnesis. Their son had not turned out well. He had raised hell in high school, and run off to Portland and become some kind of hippie, and they did not even know where he lived now. Somebody told Tim Merion at the gas station that he had AIDS and was in San Francisco. But the

2

Brinnesis were good neighbors, and the White Gull was a place people in town could be proud of.

Then across the loop road, up in the spruce and alder woods, was Hannah's Hideaway. Most people thought Hannah was a woman it was named for, but people like Mr. Voder could tell you that the man who built it way back in the Depression years had been named John Hannah, an eccentric Portlander with lumber money. He had started out building a cabin for himself there in the woods above Klatsand Creek when there wasn't anything much in town but an old falling-down hotel and the General Store and a few houses and summer cabins scattered around between the road and the beach; the loop road was the main road then, before they built the coast highway. John Hannah built his wife a second cabin, a sort of tower, two rooms one on top of the other. He said she got on his nerves sitting knitting in his cabin. Then some friend of his came to visit, and John Hannah built a cabin for him. And some more friends came to visit. It ended up with seven different cabins sitting there in the woods on two and a half acres. After the Hannah estate sold it, there were times the Hideaway had been, as Mr. Voder said, "a very shady retreat," rented out to parties of men who brought their liquor by the case and their women by the carload and never came into town at all. Other owners had cleaned up the old cabins and made it almost a private club kind of resort. In the seventies it had changed hands again and run down into an on-again-off-again second-rate seasonal motel. Now that the Shotos had it, it was doing a lot of week-long and even month-long summer rentals, and a nicer kind of people stayed there, although there was still something a little queer about the place, all those cabins with their gables and dormers and ladder lofts in the thick woods, compared to the White Gull right in town at the top of the beach, with its white trim and sunny marigolds.

And then there was the Ship Ahoy. The Tuckets took over the Ship Ahoy in the mid-eighties, when it was pretty badly run down. It never had amounted to much: a double row of jerry-built cabins with a carport between each pair, on a U-shaped driveway with a grass plot in the middle. The office and apartment were on the right coming in, and a storage building connected the two rows at the west end. The four cabins on the left had kitchens and could sleep five apiece; the three on the right were duplexes, a room and bath with one queen or two twin beds. All the showers were some kind of plastic unit made for motels, installed when the place was built in the fifties, and they were really decrepit by now, cracked through, with dirt in the cracks, and leaking. The faucets were cranky and the plumbing was explosive. The TV sets were huge old things fixed on imitation wood stands; in the smaller rooms you could barely get between them and the foot of the bed. Most of the sets picked up three or four of the five cable channels available, but none of them got all of them. The bedspreads and curtains and carpets of all the rooms smelled of cigarettes and mildew, and the equipment in the kitchens was sorry: groaning refrigerators, stoves with dead burners, a couple of thin pots, a scratched no-stick frying pan that stuck, table knives and forks from the Goodwill, one dull serrated cutting knife, and odd plastic plates and cups that had been scraped and scorched and battered and worn till their aggressive pink and orange and aqua and chartreuse colors had gone whitish-grey. But then, the Tuckets seemed a little run down, too.

He had been in the Marines, how long and how long ago nobody knew, but it was about all anybody did know about him. His first name was Bob, and this was his second marriage. People learned that from Mrs. Tucket. She joked that when she married Mr. Tucket she ought to have changed her name to Nan. But it was

Rosemarie; and she had been married before, too; but she didn't say more about it than that. She was friendly enough, and pleasant mannered, but people knew her only in the stores and from when she chatted with Tim at the filling station or had to have Bigley come out for the plumbing, that kind of thing; she did not get to know any women in town well, for the motel kept her on a short chain. She hired no help to run it, and did almost everything herself. Mr. Tucket had some kind of health condition that got worse soon after they bought the Ship Ahoy. He could not move furniture or do any heavy work. He wheezed and looked shaky even when he ran the heavy old vacuum cleaner. Mostly he sat in the apartment living room and watched NBC, and answered the bell when anybody telephoned or came to the office to ask for a room. Nobody ever made reservations at the Ship Ahoy except maybe on the really big weekends: Memorial Day, Sandcastle Day at Cannon Beach, the Fourth, and Labor Day. People just saw the sign up on the highway as they drove by, or the Gull and Hannah's filled up and sent people to it. It was on the loop road a little out of town to the south. It didn't have a sea view, but was only one block of sandy road and a bit of dune grass away from the beach. It could have been a nice little place, and no doubt Rosemarie and Bob Tucket had meant to make it nicer; or anyway Rosemarie had, since he seemed to be one of those men who never meant anything they did but just got angry when it didn't come out right.

Rosemarie had talked with people in town about some of the things she hoped to do with the Ship Ahoy to fix it up and make it more attractive. She did plant petunias in front of the office, first thing. She made a good deal on weekly linen and towel rental with a nice young couple starting an agency in Astoria. The first week they had the place she threw out the old bedspreads that were fit for nothing but furniture packing

and hounds to lie on in the back of pickups. She bought
pale green fiber-filled coverlets that served both as blanket and bedspread and were fireproof. All a cigarette
could do to them was melt a hole with hard brown edges.
Several guests with cigarettes did so pretty soon. It took
more money than she had figured on to buy the six
queen, four double, and twelve twin spreads for the ten
units (she kept the best of the old bedspreads for the
rollaways and sofa beds). She bought good curtain material, beige with wide pale green stripes, and sewed the
drapes for the front kitchen units, the best ones, 1 and 2;
but putting in the hooks for the drapery installation
took so long, it would take forever to make curtains for
all the units, hundreds of hooks to be sewn in. When
was she to do it? At night the light wasn't good enough
to sew by. Cleaning up the units to be ready by two P.M.
took the whole morning, and there was their own apartment to keep clean, and meals to cook and clear, and she
had to have some time to herself. Hadn't they looked
for a motel in a small town, a beach town, so that they
could have some time free?

She had never minded being alone; indeed, she
would have enjoyed it, if she had had time to enjoy it.
Certainly she hadn't planned to socialize with the
guests. That might be what people wanted at these fancy
bed-and-breakfasts where there was champagne and
orange juice and everybody used first names. But most
people at motels wanted to be left alone, she thought;
and all she wanted was to greet them in a nice way so
they felt at home, take their money and give them their
key, and then clean up after them next morning. And
she knew what that involved. Working at her first husband's service station in Tucson years ago she had
learned how people use public facilities, not only peeing
on the floor and strewing paper around, but scraping off
paint, unscrewing fixtures, uprooting toilets even, like
crazy monkeys wrecking their cage. She didn't expect

the cleaning to be pleasant, and sometimes it was disgusting, you wanted to rub their noses in it. But then some people left things neat, the wet towels in a pile, trash in the wastebaskets, sometimes even a dollar bill under the ashtray, as if she was a maid, but they meant well. And nobody came here for big wild parties, like in city motels. Mostly they were just driving through on the Coast Highway and pulled off for the night—single men, a good many elderly couples, some families with young children. Sometimes women staying with their families in the kitchen units for a couple of nights liked to talk with her while the children were down playing on the beach. Mostly they started out with a complaint about the refrigerator or the shower or they wanted extra cups, but sometimes they also got to talking about their lives; and that was interesting. In some of them she recognized right away the pain and strangeness she felt in her own life, but others interested her because they seemed to be so dull and so familiar, and the women living these lives complained about them comfortably, feeling no strangeness at all. Such conversations usually took place in the front office or at the doorway of the units. Once, an elderly lady staying alone for the weekend for a church conference up in Seaside invited her in for a glass of iced tea. Rosemarie did not feel that she should accept the invitation, and did not want to accept it, but she appreciated it.

The apartment kitchen was cramped. The living room was dark, because Bob kept the blind down and the TV on, and it smelled like his socks. Since he was always there to answer the bell, Rosemarie took to spending a good deal of time that fall in the storage room. It had the only west window in the motel, looking down through some big old black Sitka spruce trees to the grassy dunes. You couldn't see the sea, but you could hear it, if you wanted to. Or she would lie down on one of the twin beds in No. 10, a unit they had never rented even in the summer, saving it till last because its TV and heating unit both acted funny. She would lie down on the bed farther from the door and look at a mail-order catalogue or doze and think at the same time. Sometimes she read science-fiction books or magazines from the secondhand paperback book store in Astoria. She had never liked what they called women's books. She did not like most of these, either, the ones that were about wars and drugs and killing like the newspapers and everything else, but some of them told stories about places that were different from here. She wondered where the writers got their ideas from. She spread the untouched pale green coverlet back across the bed and went back to the storage room to put the wash in the dryer. She looked out at the edge of the land, the dune grass bowing in the sea wind, and pretended that if you walked down the sandy road past the spruce trees and the empty lots and stood there on the edge you would see something entirely different—not the long, wide, brown beach and the breakers and the grey horizon, but another world. A city with glass towers, maybe. Pointed green glass towers like thin church steeples. A person came up from that green city towards her. He shone, with a kind of shimmering and sparkling at the edges and in his hair, because he was an energy person. Not flesh and blood, not earthly. She did not dare take his hand, although he held it out. She was afraid the touch would destroy her, until he smiled and said, "It's all right."

Then she smiled at him, or at herself daydreaming, and finished loading the dryer. But she remembered him. He was sad, in trouble, she thought, another day, after she had cleaned 2 and 6 and put new blue deodorant blocks in the toilet tanks and emptied the vacuum for Bob and was opening a box of plastic glasses for the bathrooms. It was raining and the rain beat on the window of the storage room. Through the water-wavery glass the old black spruces moved their stiff arms. Beyond them the top of the dunes was pale against grey-black cloud. She thought what it would be like if he came up over the edge of the dunes and down the sandy road. He needed help. He was in trouble. He had been driven out of the green city because the other energy people did not understand him. He had enemies, and was in danger, perhaps because he could talk to people in her world. She went to No. 10 and dusted the lamps and the TV before she took off the coverlet and her shoes and lay down on the twin bed farther from the door. If she could take him in and let him stay here, he would be safe. He could stay in No. 10. "You can come in," she whispered.

Bob never looked in the units any more. It was easy enough. She told him not to put anybody in 10 till she could get the TV fixed, and she fiddled with the fine tuning and the vertical hold till it was completely out of whack, in case Bob got a fit of trying to fix it himself. He had used to be pretty handy with repairs, but it seemed that since they bought the motel, instead of fixing it up like they had planned, he only wanted to sit and watch TV like one of the guests instead of the owner. And there was so much to do, she could never catch up. In a way it was lucky so few people were coming now, in the rainy fall. The shower in 2, their best unit, had kind of split right down the back wall. The family with the teenagers from Illinois had spilled what must have been beer on the queen bed in 4. Even after she poured scented deodorant disinfectant right on the mattress the beery smell came back, only with a sort of bubble-gum flavor to it. Once it dried, probably people wouldn't notice. But she had wanted the place to be nice. Not fancy, but homey. So that nice families would come back, with little kids. She didn't mind little kids, the way some motel managers did. She loved getting the old crib out of the storage room. Kids of six or seven were hard on the TVs, but there really wasn't anything else they could hurt, and what did it matter, anyway?

"If I used my energy," her friend said, with his lovely smile, and she said, "If you used your energy—?"

"All the rooms would be painted white, to start with."

"Oh, no," she said. "I wanted each unit different, see—1 pink, and 2 peach, and 3 aqua blue, and 4 daffodil . . ."

He smiled, shaking his bright head. "All pure white," he said. "Energy white. But with different-colored carpets. And curtains—red and white checked, blue and white, yellow and white. . . . "

"Oh, curtains," she said, her heart sinking at the thought of that huge bolt of material, green and beige striped, but he laughed again, laughed at her so kindly that she had to laugh at herself, too.

"It's all right. I'll handle the curtains," he said. And he did, for the time being, anyhow.

She was not foolish about him. When she read in the *Sun* or the *Enquirer* about Space Aliens and flying saucer visits, she enjoyed the stories, but they were just like the science fiction. If you began to believe all that, you'd be in trouble. Her friend was different, because he was only a kind of game of make-believe or a gift to her, and because he needed her. It wasn't like the saucer people, who always knew everything and were sent to save people. Although he helped her in her daydreams, it was because he needed her help, because he was in trouble.

Bob had a gallbladder attack after Christmas. He thought it was his heart and was terrified. But it was so much like his first attack two years ago that she was pretty sure it was gallbladder and was not too frightened, though the drive at night up the coast to the hospital was very like a nightmare, in the hard black rain, with Bob gasping for air, panicked. He would not listen to her trying to reassure him, or even to the doctor. Even after he was home, though he did stop eating so much potato chips and pork skins and boughten pop-corn while he watched TV, he went on saying it had been his heart. She heard him say it to a guest checking in at the front desk. "Had some heart trouble lately, can't get around much for a while." He would talk with some of the guests, she never could figure out which ones or why, and then with the next ones be as sour and mean as an old hyena.

"It was all right in January when you weren't well and hardly anybody came anyway, but if you're going to be in the office registering guests you *got* to *shave*," she said to him in March, after the family of four from Washington looked at No. 3 and then said, "Thank you," embarrassed—they were nice young people with pretty children—and got back in their car and drove on south.

"I'll shave when I damn want to," he said. "Quit your damn nagging!" As if she had said one word to him from the night she drove him to the hospital to this day, one word anything but cheerful. She hadn't even felt cross with him, only sorry for him, even when he sort of boasted about his "heart trouble." But now his rudeness turned her against him, like the slam of a door. She could not bear the sight of his grey-stubbled chin. She wanted to cry, looking at it, it was so ugly. She went off to the storage room without a word, though when she got there she did not know what she had meant to do there. It was late afternoon and there was only one unit occupied. A young man had come in before noon yesterday. He had a junk-food complexion and a dull look, like the photos in newspapers of the man whose neighbors say, "He was always real quiet," after he kills his wife, the four-year-old, the baby, the baby-sitter, and finally gets around to himself, which he would much better have tended to in the first place. Rosemarie was not at all afraid of this young man, but she thought him creepy, and she put him into 9, where the TV only picked up two channels, because it seemed the right room for him. And she never could talk herself out of the notion that all the better units should be held for the nice families that were going to come later in the day. The young man paid cash and made no complaints. He stayed shut up with his two-channel TV all afternoon, as far as she noticed what he did. Later in the afternoon a couple in their fifties from Montana wanted a kitchen unit. She gave them Unit 1, still saving 3 for the nice family (and when they did come, Bob scared them off). The Montana couple paid with Visa, and Rosemarie could tell that they would leave the room clean. Then past eight last night a man in a pickup with Canadian license plates came in with a crunch of gravel and a slam of the car door and was in the office before she could get there, saying in a big, booming, beery voice, "All I want's a bed, lady. Dead on my feet!" Bob had taken over from her and had put the man in 3, which she wouldn't have done, twenty dollars extra for a kitchen he wouldn't use. But he didn't complain, either. His light went off five minutes after he went into the unit. He had left before sunrise. She had heard the pickup's wheels on the gravel, and then the crows began their morning cawing, and the singing birds tuned up inland in the alder woods.

She had got up early and had breakfast by herself. She cleaned 3, and then after she had made Bob's breakfast and saw the Montana car leave, she cleaned 1, which they had left clean, as she expected. As she was coming out of the unit with the mop bucket and plastic bags, the young man in 9 had come across the gravel towards her, not looking at her.

"Thought I might stay another night," he said in a kind of mumbling, sneering tone. It probably was shyness—young men did such strange things to disguise their shyness—but it was unpleasant all the same, the way he looked past her.

She nodded and said, "Just tell Mr. Tucket, he's in the office. Just pay him. You need towels, or anything?"

He turned away without response. It annoyed her. Even if they didn't have to be all over each other friendly, people could have manners, not just cut each other off. Even if he was young he didn't have to be rude. Some men treated every woman over thirty like their mother, like dirt. She wasn't his mother, thank God. Even if he was young he could start noticing other people existed. Probably he was a lonely person himself, or else why would he be here, a man in his twenties by himself not doing anything, not even going down to the beach, as far as she knew, just going into town for dinner and back by nine last night, but he wasn't going to make any friends by cutting people off like that. Not even "No thanks," just turning away.

She stood in the storage room at the window, looking down the sandy road to the edge, but she could not think about her friend. Only of what had to be done so that nice people wouldn't look at the units and go on to another motel. Because it wasn't just Bob's fault. But there were so many, many, many things that had to be done to each one of the units, and they could not get more in debt. They were spending Bob's Marine pension to eat on and it was still three years before she could start Social Security. She had the green and beige material and the sewing machine and the hooks. She could make new curtains. That was the first thing she could do. She ought to do it. The material had been expensive. But she could not bear it, sewing in those endless hooks for the out-of-date fixtures. She went to 10 and let herself in with the passkey. The little room was dim and stuffy. It did not smell clean.

"I'll just lie down a moment first," Rosemarie thought, distinctly, as if the words were saying themselves and she was listening to them. She took the new coverlet off the bed farther from the door, folding it on the other bed, and pushed off her shoes, and lay down. She lay still and began to see the sandy road. There was someone on it, but his back was turned; and she heard something terrible, and did not know what it was. It was a crying. The young man was in his room and he was crying. There was nothing but the thin wall between the head of this bed and the head of his bed. She could hear or feel his bed shake and hear him crying, not stifled sobbing but terrible, hoarse, short screams of pain or grief or fear.

"I can't stand this, I can't bear this, what shall I do?" said the words in Rosemarie's mind. She got up, slipped on her shoes, replaced the coverlet with shaky hands, and hurried out of the room. She stood in the pale, foggy sunlight on the rutted gravel in front of 9 and 10. She could not hear the crying from outside. There was no sound at all but the low undertone that was always there of the sea and the wind and the cars up on the highway. She wanted to knock on the door of 9, but she could not do it. She could not use the passkey. She did not deserve to. She was afraid. She thought as hard as she could, trying to send the energy through the door, to send the words to him: "It's all right. It will be all right. You're young, it will get better. Don't cry!" But it was no good. Like her friend, she could not help him.

Hand, Cup, Shell

The last house on Searoad stood in the field behind the dunes. Its windows looked north to Breton Head, south to Wreck Rock, east to the marshes, and from the second story, across the dunes and the breakers, west to China. The house was empty more than it was full, but it was never silent.

The family arrived and dispersed. Having come to be together over the weekend, they fled one another without hesitation, one to the garden, one to the kitchen, one to the bookshelf, two north up the beach, one south to the rocks.

Thriving on salt and sand and storms, the rosebushes behind the house climbed all over the paling fence and shot up long autumn sprays, disheveled and magnificent. Roses may do best if you don't do anything for them at all except keep the sword fern and ivy from strangling them; bronze Peace grows wild as well as any wild rose. But the ivy, now. Loathsome stuff. Poisonous berries. Crawling out from hiding everywhere, stuffed full of horrors: spiders, centipedes, millipedes, billipedes, snakes, rats, broken glass, rusty knives, dog

15

turds, dolls' eyes. I must cut the ivy right back to the fence, Rita thought, pulling up a long stem that led her back into the leafy mass to a parent vine as thick as a garden hose. I must come here oftener, and keep the ivy off the spruce trees. Look at that, it'll have the tree dead in another year. She tugged. The cable of ivy gave no more than a steel hawser would. She went back up the porch steps, calling, "Are there any pruning shears, do you think?"

"Hanging on the wall there, aren't they?" Mag called back from the kitchen. "Anyway, they ought to be." There ought to be flour in the canister, too, but it was empty. Either she had used it up in August and forgotten, or Phil and the boys had made pancakes when they were over last month. So where was the list pad to write *flour* on for when she walked up to Hambleton's? Nowhere to be found. She would have to buy a little pad to write *pad* on. She found a ballpoint pen in the things drawer. It was green and translucent, imprinted with the words HANK'S COAST HARDWARE AND AUTO SUPPLIES. She wrote *flour, bans, o.j., cereal, yog, list pad* on a paper towel, wiping blobs of excess green ink off the penpoint with a corner of the towel. Everything is circular, or anyhow spiral. It was no time at all, certainly not twelve months, since last October in this kitchen, and she was absolutely standing in her tracks. It wasn't *déjà vu* but *déjà vécu,* and all the Octobers before it, and still all the same this was now, and therefore different feet were standing in her tracks. A half size larger than last year, for one thing. Would they go on breaking down and spreading out forever, until she ended up wearing men's size 12 logging boots? Mother's feet hadn't done that. She'd always worn 7N, still wore 7N, always would wear 7N, but then she always wore the same kind of shoes, too, trim inch-heel pumps or penny loafers, never experimenting with Germanic clogs, Japanese athletics, or the latest toe-killer fad. It came of having had to dress a certain way, of course, as the Dean's wife, but also of being Daddy's girl, small-town princess, not experimenting just knowing.

"I'm going on down to Hambleton's, do you want anything?" Mag called out the kitchen door through the back-porch screen to her mother fighting ivy in the garden.

"I don't think so. Are you going to walk?"

"Yes."

They were right: it took a certain effort to say *yes* just flatly, to refrain from qualifying it, softening it: *Yes, I think so; Yes, I guess so; Yes I thought I would. . . .* Unqualified *yes* had a gruff sound to it, full of testosterone. If Rita had said *no* instead of *I don't think so,* it would have sounded rude or distressed, and she probably would have responded in some way to find out what was wrong, why her mother wasn't speaking in the mother tongue. "Going to Hambleton's," she said to Phil, who was kneeling at the bookcase in the dark little hall, and went out. She went down the four wooden steps of the front porch and through the front gate, latched the gate behind her, and turned right on Searoad to walk into town. These familiar movements gave her great pleasure. She walked on the dune side of the road, and between dunes saw the ocean, the breakers that took all speech away. She walked in silence, seeing glimpses between dune grass of the beach where her children had gone.

Gret had gone as far as the beach went. It ended in a tumble of rusty brown basalt under Wreck Point, but she knew the ways up through the rocks to the slopes and ledges of the Point, places where nobody came. Sitting there on the wind-bitten grass looking out over the waves bashing on Wreck Rock and the reef Dad called Rickrack and out to the horizon, you could keep going farther still. At least you ought to be able to, but there wasn't any way to be alone any more. There was a beer can in the grass, a tag of orange plastic ribbon tied to a

stake up near the summit, a Coast Guard helicopter
yammering and prying over the sea up to Breton Head
and back south again. Nobody wanted anybody to be
alone, ever. You had to do away with that, unmake it, all
the junk, trash, crap, trivia, David, the midterms, Gran,
what people thought, other people. You had to go away
from them. All the way away. It used to be easy to do
that, easy to go and hard to come back, but now it was
harder and harder to go, and she never could go all the
way. To sit up here and stare at the ocean and be thinking about stupid David, and what's that stake for, and
why did Gran look at my fingernails that way, what's
wrong with me? Am I going to be this way the rest of
my life? Not even seeing the ocean? Seeing stupid beer
cans? She stood, raging, backed up, aimed, and kicked
the beer can in a low, fast arc off the cliff into the sea
unseen below. She turned and scrambled up to the summit, braced her knees in soggy bracken, and wrenched
the orange-ribboned stake out of the ground. She hurled
it southward and saw it fall into bracken and salal scrub
and be swallowed. She stood up, rubbing her hands
where the raw wood had scraped the skin. The wind felt
cold on her teeth. She had been baring them, an angry
ape. The sea lay grey at eye level, taking her immediately
now into its horizontality. Nothing cluttered. As she
sucked the heel of her thumb and got her front teeth
warm, she thought, My soul is ten thousand miles wide
and extremely invisibly deep. It is the same size as the
sea, it is bigger than the sea, it *holds* the sea, and you
cannot, you cannot cram it into beer cans and fingernails and stake it out in lots and own it. It will drown
you all and never even notice.

But how old I am, thought the grandmother, to
come to the beach and not look at the sea! How horrible! Straight out into the backyard, as if all that mattered
was grubbing ivy. As if the sea belonged to the children.
To assert her right to the ocean, she carried ivy cuttings

to the trash bin beside the house and after cramming them into the bin stood and looked at the dunes, across which it was. It wasn't going to go away, as Amory would have said. But she went on out the garden gate, crossed sandy-rutted Searoad, and in ten more steps saw the Pacific open out between the grass-crowned dunes. There you are, you old grey monster. You aren't going to go away, but I am. Her brown loafers, a bit loose on her bony feet, were already full of sand. Did she want to go on down, onto the beach? It was always so windy. As she hesitated, looking about, she saw a head bobbing along between the crests of dune grass. Mag coming back with the groceries. Slow black bobbing head like the old mule coming up the rise to the sagebrush ranch when? old Bill the mule—Mag the mule, trudging obstinate silent. She went down to the road and stood first on one foot then the other emptying sand out of her shoes, then walked to meet her daughter. "How are things at Hambleton's?"

"Peart," Mag said. "Right peart. When is whatsername coming?"

"By noon, I think she said." Rita sighed. "I got up at five. I think I'm going to go in and have a little lie-down before she comes. I hope she won't stay hours."

"Who is she, again?"

"Oh ... damn ... "

"I mean, what's she doing?"

Rita gave up the vain search for the lost name. "She's some sort of assistant research assistant I suppose to whatsisname at the University, you know, doing the book about Amory. I expect somebody suggested to him that maybe it would look odd if he did a whole biography without talking to the widow, but of course it's really only Amory's ideas that interest him, I believe he's very theoretical the way they are now. Probably bored stiff at the idea of actual *people*. So he's sending the young lady into the hencoop."

"So that you don't sue him."

"Oh you don't think so."

"Certainly. Co-optation. And you'll get thanked for your invaluable assistance, in the acknowledgments, just before he thanks his wife and his typist."

"What was that terrible thing you told me about Mrs. Tolstoy?"

"Copied *War and Peace* for him six times by hand. But you know, it would beat copying most books six times by hand."

"Shepard."

"What?"

"Her. The girl. Something Shepard."

"Whose invaluable assistance Professor Whozis gratefully . . . no, she's only a grad student, isn't she. Lucky if she gets mentioned at all. What a safety net they have, don't they? All the women the knots in the net."

But that cut a bit close to the bones of Amory Inman, and his widow did not answer his daughter as she helped her put away the flour, cornflakes, yogurt, cookies, bananas, grapes, lettuce, avocado, tomatoes, and vinegar Mag had bought (she had forgotten to buy a list pad). "Well, I'm off, shout when she comes," Rita said, and made her way past her son-in-law, who was sitting on the hall floor by the bookcase, to the stairs.

The upstairs of the house was simple, rational, and white: the stairs landing and a bathroom down the middle, a bedroom in each corner. Mag and Phil SW, Gran NW, Gret NE, boys SE. The old folks got the sunset, the kids got dawn. Rita was the first to listen and hear the sea in the house. She looked out over the dunes and saw the tide coming in and the wind combing the manes of the white horses. She lay down and looked with pleasure at the narrow, white-painted boards of the ceiling in the sea-light like no other light. She did not want to go to sleep but her eyes were tired and she had not brought a book upstairs. She heard the girl's voice below, the girls' voices, piercing soft, the sound of the sea.

"Where's Gran?"

"Upstairs."

"This woman's come."

Mag brought the dish towel on which she was drying her hands into the front room, a signal flag: I work in the kitchen and have nothing to do with interviews. Gret had left the girl standing out on the front deck. "Won't you come in?"

"Susan Shepard."

"Mag Rilow. That's Greta. Gret, go up and tell Gran, OK?"

"It's so lovely here! What a beautiful place!"

"Maybe you'd like to sit out on the deck to talk? It's so mild. Would you like some coffee? Beer, anything?"

"Oh, yes—coffee—"

"Tea?"

"That would be wonderful."

"Herbal?" Everybody there at the University in the Klamath Time Warp drank herbal tea. Sure enough, chamomile-peppermint would be wonderful. Mag got her sitting in the wicker chair on the deck and came back in past Phil, who was still on the floor in the hall by the bookcase, reading. "Take it into the *light*," she said, and he said, "Yeah, I will," smiling, and turned a page. Gret, coming down the stairs, said, "She'll be down in a minute."

"Go talk to the girl. She's at the U."

"What in?"

"I don't know. Find out."

Gret snarled and turned away. Edging past her father in the narrow hall, she said, "Why don't you get some *light*?" He smiled, turned a page, and said, "Yeah, I will." She strode out onto the deck and said, "My mother says you're at the U," at the same time as the woman said, "You're at the U, aren't you?"

Gret nodded.

"I'm in Ed. I'm Professor Nabe's research assistant for his book. It's really exciting to be interviewing your grandmother."

"It seems fairly weird to me," Gret said.

"The University?"

"No."

There was a little silence filled by the sound of the sea.

"Are you a freshman?"

"Freshwoman." She edged towards the steps.

"Will you major in Education, do you think?"

"Oh, God, no."

"I suppose having such a distinguished grandfather, people always just expect. Your mother's an educator, too, isn't she?"

"She teaches," Gret said. She had got as far as the steps and now went down them, because they were the shortest way to get away, though she had been coming into the house to go to her room when Sue Student drove up and she got caught.

Gran appeared in the open doorway, looking wary and rather bleary, but using her politically correct smile and voice: "Hello! I'm Rita Inman." While Sue Student was jumping up and being really excited, Gret got back up the steps, past Gran, and into the house.

Daddy was still sitting on the floor in the dark hall by the bookcase, reading. She unplugged the gooseneck lamp from the end table by the living-room couch, set it on the bookcase in the hall, and found the outlet was too far for the cord to reach. She brought the lamp as close to him as she could, setting it on the floor about three feet from him, and then plugged in the plug. The light glared across the pages of his book. "Oh, hey, great," he said, smiling, and turned a page. She went on upstairs to her room. Walls and ceiling were white, the bedspreads on the two narrow beds were blue. A pic-

ture of blue mountains she had painted in ninth-grade
art class was pinned to the closet door, and she recon-
firmed with a long look at it that it was beautiful. It was
the only good picture she had ever painted, and she
marveled at it, the gift that had given itself to her, unde-
served, no strings attached. She opened the backpack
she had dumped on one bed, got out a geology textbook and a highlighter, lay down on the other bed, and
began to reread for the midterm examination. At the
end of a section on subduction, she turned her head to
look at the picture of blue mountains again, and
thought, I wonder what would it be like?—or those are
the words she might have used to express the feelings of
curiosity, pleasure, and awe which accompanied the
images in her mind of small figures scattered among
great lava cliffs on the field trip in September, of jour-
neys, of levels stretching to the horizon, high deserts
under which lay fossils folded like tissue paper; of
moraines; of long veins of ore and crystals in the darkness underground. Intent and careful, she turned the
page and started the next section.

Sue Shepard fussed with her little computer thing.
Her face was plump, pink, round-eyed, and Rita had to
make the interpretation "intellectual" consciously. It
would not arise of itself from the pink face, the high
voice, the girlish manner, as it would from the pink face,
high voice, and boyish manner of a male counterpart.
She knew that she still so identified mind and masculini-
ty that only women who imitated men were immediately recognizable to her as intellectuals, even after all these
years, even after Mag. Also, Sue Shepard might be dis-
guising her intellect, as Mag didn't. And the jargon of
the Education Department was a pretty good disguise
in itself. But she was keen, it was a keen mind, and perhaps Professor Whozis didn't like to be reminded of
it, so young, so bright, so close behind. Probably he
liked flutter and butter, as Amory used to call it, in his

graduate-student women. But fluttery buttery little Sue had already set aside a whole sheaf of the professor's questions as time-wasting, and was asking, intently and apparently on her own hook, about Rita's girlhood.

"Well, when I was born we lived on a ranch out from Prineville, in the high country. The sagebrush, you know. But I don't remember much that's useful. I think Father must have been keeping books for the ranch. It was a big operation—huge—all the way to the John Day River, I think. When I was nine, he took over managing a mill in Ultimate, in the Coast Range. A lumber mill. Nothing left of all that now. There isn't even a gravel road in to Ultimate any more. Half the state's like that, you know. It's very strange. Easterners come and think it's this wild pristine wilderness and actually it's all Indian graveyards underfoot and old homesteads and second growth and towns nobody even remembers were there. It's just that the trees and the weeds grow back so fast. Like ivy. Where are you from?"

"Seattle," said Sue Shepard, friendly, but not to be misled as to who was interviewing whom.

"Well, I'm glad. I seem to have more and more trouble talking with Easterners."

Sue Shepard laughed, probably not understanding, and pursued: "So you went to school in Ultimate?"

"Yes, until high school. Then I came to live with Aunt Josie in Portland and went to old Lincoln High. The nearest high school to Ultimate was thirty miles on logging roads, and anyhow it wasn't good enough for Father. He was afraid I'd grow up to be a roughneck, or marry one. . . . " Sue Shepard clicketed on her little machine, and Rita thought, But what did Mother think? Did she want to send me away at age thirteen to live in the city with her sister-in-law? The question opened on a blank area that she gazed into, fascinated. I know what Father wanted, but why don't I know what she wanted? Did she cry? No, of course not. Did I? I don't think so.

I can't even remember talking about it with Mother. We made my clothes that summer. That's when she taught me how to cut out a pattern. And then we came up to Portland the first time, and stayed at the old Multnomah Hotel, and we bought shoes for me for school—and the oyster silk ones for dressing up, the little undercut heel and one strap, I wish they still made them. I was already wearing Mother's size. And we ate lunch in that restaurant, the cut-glass water goblets, the two of us, where was Father? But I never even wondered what she thought, I never knew. I never know what Mag really thinks, either. They don't say. Rocks. Look at Mag's mouth, just like Mother's, like a seam in a rock. Why did Mag go into teaching, talk, talk, talk all day, when she really hates talking? Although she never was quite as gruff as Gret is, but that's because Amory wouldn't have stood for it. But why didn't Mother and I say anything to each other? She was so stoical. Rock. And then I was happy in Portland, and there she was in Ultimate. . . . "Oh, yes, I loved it," she answered Sue Shepard. "The twenties were a nice time to be a teen-ager, we really were very spoiled, not like now, poor things. It's terribly hard to be thirteen or fourteen now, isn't it? We went to dancing school, they've got AIDS and the atomic bomb. My granddaughter's twice as old as I was at eighteen. In some ways. She's amazingly young for her age in others. It's so complicated. After all, think of Juliet! It's never *really* simple, is it? But I think I had a very nice, innocent time in high school, and right on into college. Until the crash. The mill closed in '32, my second year. But actually we went right on having a good time. But it was terribly depressing for my parents and my brothers. The mill shut right down, and they all came up to Portland looking for work, everybody did. And then I left school after my junior year, because I'd got a summer job bookkeeping in the University accounting office, and they wanted me to stay on, and so I did, since everybody else in the family was out of work, except Mother finally got a job in a bakery, nights. It was terrible for men, the Depression, you know. It killed my father. He looked and looked for work and couldn't find anything, and there I was, doing what he was qualified to do, only of course at a very low level, and terrible pay—sixty dollars a month, can you imagine?"

"A week?"

"No, a month. But still, I was making it. And men of his generation were brought up to be depended on, which is a wonderful thing, but then they weren't allowed ever *not* to be depended on, when they had to depend on other people, which everybody actually does. It was terribly unrealistic, I think, a real whatdyoucallit. Double time?"

"Double bind," said young Sue, sharp as tacks, clicketing almost inaudibly away on her little lap computer, while the tape recorder tape went silently round and round, recording Rita's every maunder and meander. Rita sighed. "I'm sure that's why he died so young," she said. "He was only fifty."

But Mother hadn't died young, though her husband had, and her elder son had drifted off to Texas to be swallowed alive so far as his mother was concerned by a jealous wife, and her younger son had poured whiskey onto diabetes and died at thirty-one. Men did seem to be so fragile. But what had kept Margaret Jamison Holz going? Her independence? But she had been brought up to be dependent, hadn't she? Anyhow, nobody could keep going long on mere independence; when they tried to they ended up pushing shopping carts full of stuff and sleeping in doorways. Mother hadn't done that. She had sat here on the deck looking out at the dunes, a small, tough, old woman. No retirement pension, of course, and a tiny little dribble of insurance money, and she did let Amory pay the rent on her two-room apartment in Portland, but she was independent to the end, visiting them only once or twice a year at the University, and then always for a full month here, in summer. Gret's room now had been Mother's room then. How strange it was, how it changed! But recently Rita had wakened in the deep night or when it was just beginning to get light and had lain there in bed thinking, not with fear but with a kind of frightened, lively thrill, It is so strange, all of it is so *strange!*

"When were you able to go back to college?" Sue Shepard asked, and she answered, "In '35," resolving to stick to the point and stop babbling.

"And then you met Dr. Inman when you took his class."

"No. I never took a class in Education."

"Oh," Sue Shepard said, blank.

"I met him in the accounting office. I was still clerking there half-time, paying my way. And he came in because he hadn't been paid his salary for three months. People used to be just as good at mistakes like that as computers are now. It took days and days to find out how they'd managed to lose him from the faculty payroll. Did he tell somebody that I'd taken his class and that's how we met?" Sue Shepard wasn't going to admit it; she was discreet. "How funny. It was one of the other women he went out with, and he got his memories crossed. Students were always falling in love with him. He was *extremely* attractive—I used to think Charles Boyer without the French accent."

Mag heard them laughing on the front deck as she came through the hall, edging around her husband. A gooseneck lamp standing on the floor near him glared in his eyes, but he was holding his book so that its pages were in shadow.

"Phil."

"Mm."

"Get up and go read in the living room."

He smiled, reading. "Found this . . . "

"The interviewer's here. She'll be staying for lunch. You're in the way. You've been in the way for two hours. You're in the dark. There's daylight six feet away. Get up and go read in the living room."

"People . . . "

"Nobody's there! People come through *here.* Are you—" The wave of hatred and compassion set free by her words carried her on past him, though she had checked the words. In silence, she turned the corner and climbed the stairs. She went into the southwest bedroom and looked for a decent shirt in the crowded closet; the cotton sweater she had worn from Portland was too warm for this mild coastal weather. The search led her into a rummage-out of summer clothes. She sorted, rehung, folded her clothes, then Phil's. From the depths she pulled out paint-stiff, knee-frayed blue jeans, a madras shirt with four buttons gone which had been stuffed into the closet unwashed. Even here at the beach house, her father's clothes had always been clean, smelled clean, smelled of virtue, *virtú.* With a violent swing she threw the madras shirt at the wastebasket. It draped itself half in, half out, a short sleeve sticking up pitifully. Not waving but drowning. . . . But to go on drowning for twenty-five years?

The window was ajar, and she could hear the sea and her mother's voice down on the front deck answering questions about her husband the eminent educator, the clean-bodied man: How had he written his books? When had he broken with John Dewey's theories? Where had the UNICEF work taken him? Now, little apple-cheeked handmaiden of success, ask me about my husband the eminent odd-job man: how did he quit halfway through graduate school, when had he broken with the drywalling contractor, where had his graveyard shift at the Copy Shop taken him? Phil the Failure, he called himself, with the charming honesty that concealed a hideous smugness that probably but not certainly concealed despair. What was certain was that nobody else in the world knew the depth of Phil's contempt for them, his absolute lack of admiration or sympathy for anything anybody did or was. If that indifference was originally a defense, it had consumed what it had once defended. He was invulnerable, by now. And people were so careful not to hurt him. Finding that she was Dr. Rilow and he was an unemployed drywaller, they assumed it was hard for him; and then when they found that it wasn't, they admired him for being so secure, so unmacho, taking it so easily, handling it so well. Indeed he handled it well, cherished it, his dear failure, his great success at doing what he wanted to do and nothing else. No wonder he was so sweet, so serene, so unstrained. No wonder she had blown up, teaching *Bleak House* last week, at the mooncalf student who couldn't see what was supposed to be wrong with Harold Skimpole. "Don't you see that his behavior is totally irresponsible?" she had demanded in righteous wrath, and the mooncalf had replied with aplomb, "I don't see why *everybody* is supposed to be responsible." It was a kind of Taoist koan, actually. For Taoist wives. It was hard to be married to a man who lived in a perpetual condition of *wu wei* and not to end up totally *wei;* you had to be very careful or you ended up washing the ten thousand shirts.

But then of course Mother had looked after Father's shirts.

The jeans weren't even good for rags, even if they would sell in the Soviet Union for a hundred dollars; she threw them after the shirt, and knocked the wastebasket over. Faintly ashamed, she retrieved them and the shirt and stuffed them into a plastic bag that had been squirreled away in a cranny of the closet. An advantage of Phil's indifference was that he would never come downstairs demanding to know where his wonderful old jeans and madras shirt were. He never got attached to clothes; he wore whatever was provided. "Distrust all occasions that require new clothes." What a prig Thoreau was. Ten to one he meant weddings but hadn't had the guts to say so, let alone get married. Actually Phil liked new clothes, liked to get them for Christmas and birthdays, accepted all presents, cherished none. "Phil is a saint, Mag," his mother had said to her shortly before they were married, and she had agreed, laughing, thinking the exaggeration quite forgivable; but it had not been a burble of mother love. It had been a warning.

She knew that her father had hoped that the marriage wouldn't last. He had never quite said so. By now the matter of her marriage, between her and her mother, was buried miles deep. Between her and her daughter it was an unaskable question. Everybody protecting everybody. It was stupid. It kept her and Gret from saying much to each other. And it wasn't really the right question, the one that needed asking, anyhow. They were married. But there was a question. No one had asked it and she did not know what it was. Possibly, if she found out, her life would change. The headless torso of Apollo would speak: *Du musst dein Leben ändern.* Meanwhile, did she particularly want her life to change? "I will never desert Mr. Micawber," she said under her breath, reaching into yet another cranny of the closet and discovering there yet another plastic bag, which when opened disclosed rust-colored knitted wool: a sweater, which she stared at dumbly till she recognized it as one she had bought on sale for Gret for Christmas several years ago and had utterly forgotten ever since. "Gret! Look here!" she cried, crossing the hall, knocking, opening the door of her daughter's room. "Merry Christmas!"

After explanations, Gret pulled the sweater on. Her dark, thin face emerged from the beautiful color with a serious expression. She looked at the sweater seriously in the mirror. She was very hard to please, preferred to buy her own clothes, and wore the ones she liked till they fell apart. She kept them moderately clean. "Are the sleeves kind of short, a little?" she asked, in the mother tongue.

"Kind of. Probably why it was on sale. It was incredibly cheap, I remember, at the Sheep Tree. Years ago. I liked the color."

"It's neat," Gret said, still judging. She pushed up the sleeves. "Thanks," she said. Her face was a little flushed. She smiled and glanced around at the book lying open on the bed. Something was unsaid, almost said. She did not know how to say it and Mag did not know how to allow her to say it; they both had trouble with their native language. Awkward, intrusive, the mother retreated, saying, "Lunch about one-thirty."

"Need help?"

"Not really. Picnic on the deck. With the interviewer."

"When's she leaving?"

"Before dinner, I hope. It's a good color on you." She went out, closing the door behind her, as she had been taught to do.

Gret took off the orange sweater. It was too hot for the mild day, and she wasn't sure she liked it yet. It would take a while. It would have to sit around a while till she got used to it, and then she would know. She thought she liked it; it felt like she'd worn it before. She put it into a drawer so her mother wouldn't get hurt. Last year when her mother had come into her room at home and stared around, Gret had suddenly realized that the stare wasn't one of disapproval but of pain. Disorder, dirt, disrespect for objects caused her pain, like being shoved or hit. It must be hard for her, living, in general. Knowing that, Gret tried to put stuff away; but it didn't make much difference. She was mostly at college now. Mother went on nagging and ordering and enduring, and Daddy and the boys didn't let it worry them. Just like some goddamn sitcom. Everything about families and people was exactly like some goddamn sitcom. Waiting for David to call, just like a soap opera. Everything the same as it was for everybody else, the same things happening over and over and over, all petty and trivial and stupid, and you couldn't ever get free. It clung to you, held on, pinioned you. Like the dream she used to have of the room with wallpaper that caught and stuck to you, the Velcro dream. She reopened the textbook and read about the nature of gabbro, the origins of slate.

The boys came back from the beach just in time for lunch. They always did. Still. Just as when her milk would spurt and the baby in the next room cried at the exact same moment. Their clomping in to go to the bathroom finally got Phil off the hall floor. He carried out platters to the table on the front porch and talked with whatsername the interviewer, who got quite pink and pleased. Phil looked so thin and short and hairy and vague and middle-aged that they never expected it till whammy! right between the eyes. Wooed and won. Go it, Phil. She looked like an intelligent girl, actually, overserious, and Phil wouldn't hurt her. Wouldn't hurt a fly, would old Phil. St. Philip, bestower of sexual favors. She smiled at them and said, "Come and get it!"

Sue Student was being nice to Daddy, talking with him about forest fires or something. Daddy had his little company smile and was being nice to Sue Student. She didn't sound too stupid, actually. She was a vegetarian. "So is Gret," Gran said. "What is it about the U these days? They used to live on raw elk." Why did she always have to disapprove of everything Gret did? She never said stuff like that about the boys. They were scarfing up salami. Mother watched them all loading their plates and making their sandwiches with that brooding hawk expression. Filling her niche. That was the trouble with biology, it was the sitcom. All niches. Mother provides. Better the dark slate levels, the basalt plains. Anything could happen, there.

She was worn out. She went for the wine bottle; food later. She must get by herself for a while, that bit of a nap in the morning hadn't helped. Such a long, long morning, with the drive over from Portland. And talking about old times was a most terrible thing to do. All the lost things, lost chances, all the dead people. The town with no road to it any more. She had had to say ten times, "He's dead now," "No, she's dead." What a strange thing to say, after all! You couldn't *be* dead. You couldn't *be* anything but alive. If you weren't alive, you weren't—you had been. You shouldn't have to say "He's dead now," as if it was just some other way of being, but "He isn't now," or "He was." Keep the past in the past tense. And the present in the present, where it belongs. Because you didn't live on in others, as people said. You changed them, yes. She was entirely different because Amory had lived. But he didn't live on in her, in her memory, or in his books, or anywhere. He had gone. He was gone. Maybe "passed away" wasn't such a what-dyoucallit, after all. At least it was in the passed tense, the past tense, not the present. He had come to her and she had come to him and they had made each other's life what it had been, and then he had gone. Passed away. It wasn't a euphemism, that's what it wasn't. Her mother . . . There was a pause in her thoughts. She drank the wine. Her mother was different, how? She came back to the rock. Of course she was dead, but it did not seem that she had passed away, the way he had. She went back to the table, refilled her glass with the red wine, laid salami, cheese, and green onions on brown bread.

She was beautiful now. In the tight, short, ugly fashions of the sixties, when Mag had first looked at her from any distance and with any judgment, she had looked too big, and for a while after Amory's death and when she had the bone marrow thing she had been gaunt, but now she was extraordinary: the line of the cheek, the long, soft lips, the long-lidded eyes with their fine wrinkle-pleating. What had she said about raw elk? The interviewer hadn't heard and wouldn't understand if she had heard, wouldn't know that she had just been told what Mrs. Amory Inman thought of the institution of which her husband had been the luminary, what indeed she thought, in her increasing aloofness, her old-womanhood, of most human institutions. Poor little whatsername, trapped in the works and dark machinations of that toughest survivor of the Middle Ages, the university, ground in the mills of assistantships, grants, competitions, examinations, dissertations, all set up to separate the men from the boys and both from the rest of the world, she wouldn't have time for years yet to look up, to look out, to learn that there were such bare, airy places as the place where Rita Inman lived.

"Yes, it is nice, isn't it? We bought it in '55, when things over here were still pretty cheap. We haven't even asked you indoors, how terrible! After lunch you must look round the house. I think I'm going to have a little lie-down, after lunch. Or perhaps you'd like to go down on the beach then—the children will take you walking as far as you'd like, if you like. Mag, Sue says she needs an hour or two more with me. She hasn't asked all . . . " a pause, "the professor's questions yet. I'm afraid I kept wandering off the subject." How sternly beautiful Mag was, her rock-seam mouth, her dark-waterfall hair going silver. Managing everything, as usual, seeing to everything, the good lunch. No, definitely her mother was not dead in the same way Father was dead, or Amory, or Clyde, or Polly, or Jim and Jean; there was something different there. She really must get by herself and think about it.

"Geology." The word came out. Spoken. Mother's ears went up like a cat's, eyebrows flickering, eyes and mouth impassive. Daddy acted like he'd known her decision all along, maybe he had, he couldn't have. Sue Student had to keep asking who was in the Geo depart-

ment and what you did with geology. She only knew a
couple of the professors' names and felt stupid not
knowing more. She said, "Oh, you get hired by oil companies, mining companies, all kinds of land-rape companies. Find uranium under Indian reservations." Oh, shut
up. Sue Student meant well. Everybody meant well. It
spoiled everything. Softened everything. "The grizzled
old prospector limps in from twenty years alone in the
desert, swearing at her mule," Daddy said, and she
laughed, it was funny, Daddy was funny, but she was for
a moment, a flash, afraid of him. He was so quick. He
knew that this was something important, and did he
mean well? He loved her, he liked her, he was like her,
but when she wasn't like him did he like it? Mother was
saying how geology had been all cut-and-dried when she
was in college and how it was all changed now by these
new theories. "Plate tectonics isn't exactly new," oh,
shut up, shut up. Mother meant well. Sue Student and
Mother talked about academic careers in science and got
interested comparing, colleaguing. Sue was at the U but
she was younger and only a grad student; Mother was
only at a community college but she was older and had a
Ph.D. from Berkeley. And Daddy was out of it. And
Gran half asleep, and Tom and Sam cleaning up the platters. She said, "It's funny. I was thinking. All of us—the
family, I mean—nobody will ever know any of us ever
existed. Except for Granddaddy. He's the only real one."

Sue gazed mildly. Daddy nodded in approval.
Mother stared, the hawk at bay. Gran said in a curious,
distant tone, "Oh I don't think so at all." Tom was
throwing bread to a seagull, but Sam, finishing the
salami, said, in his mother's voice, "Fame is the spur!"
At that, the hawk blinked and stooped to the prey:
"Whatever do you mean, Gret? Reality is being a dean
of the School of Education?"

"He was important. He has a biography. None of
us will."

"Thank goodness," Gran said, getting up. "I do hope you don't mind, if I have just a bit of a lie-down now I'll be much brighter later, I hope."

Everybody moved.

"Boys. You do the dishes. Tom!"

He came. They obeyed. She felt a tremendous, a ridiculous surge, as warm and irresistible as tears or milk, of pride—in them, in herself. They were lovely. Lovely boys. Grumbling, coltish, oafish, gangling, red-handed, they unloaded the table with efficiency and speed, Sam insulting Tom steadily in his half-broken voice, Tom replying on two sweet notes at intervals like a thrush, "Ass-sole. . . . Ass-sole. . . . "

"Who's for a walk on the beach?"

Mag was, the interviewer was, Phil was, Gret surprisingly was.

They crossed Searoad and went single file between the dunes. Down on the beach she looked back to see the front windows and the roof above the dune grass, always remembering the pure delight of seeing it so the first time, the first time ever. To Gret and the boys the beach house was coeval with existence, but to her it was connected with joy. When she was a child they had stayed in other people's beach houses, places in Gearhart and Neskowin, summerhouses of deans and provosts and the rich people who clung to university administrators under the impression that they were intellectuals; or else, as she got older, Dean Inman had taken her and her mother along to his ever more exotic conferences, to Botswana, Brasilia, Bangkok, until she had rebelled at last. "But they are interesting *places*," her mother had said, deprecating, "you really don't enjoy going?" And she had howled, "I'm sick of feeling like a white giraffe, why can't I ever stay home where people are the same *size?*" And at some indefinite but not long interval after that, they had driven over to look at this house. "What do you think?" her father had asked, standing in the small living room, a smiling sixty-year-old public man, kindly rhetorical. There was no need to ask. They had all three been mad for it from the moment they saw it at the end of the long sand road between the marshes and the sea. "My room, OK?" Mag had said, coming out of the southwest bedroom. She and Phil had had their honeymoon summer there.

She looked across the sand at him. He was walking at the very edge of the water, moving crabwise east when a wave came washing farther in, following the outwash back west, absorbed as a child, slight, stooped, elusive. She veered her way to intersect with his. "Phildog," she said.

"Magdog."

"You know, she was right. What made her say it, do you think?"

"Defending me."

How easily he said it. How easy his assumption. It had not occurred to her.

"Could be. And herself? And me? . . . And then geology! Is she just in love with the course, or is she serious?"

"Never anything but."

"It might be a good major for her. Unless it's all labs now. I don't know, it's just a section of Intro Sci at CC. I'll ask Benjie what geologists do these days. I hope still those little hammers. And khaki shorts."

"That Priestley novel in the bookcase," Phil said, and went on to talk about it, and novelists contemporary with Priestley, and she listened attentively as they walked along the hissing fringes of the continent. If Phil had not quit before the prelims, he would have got much farther in his career than she in hers, because men got farther easier then, of course, but mainly because he was such a natural; he had the right temperament, the necessary indifference and passion of the scholar. He was drawn to early twentieth century English fiction with the perfect combination of detachment and fascination, and could have written a fine study of Priestley, Galsworthy, Bennett, that lot, a book worth a good professorship at a good school. Or worth at least a sense of self-respect. But self-respect wasn't a saint's business, was it? Dean Inman had had plenty of self-respect, and plenty of respect, too. Had she been escaping the various manifestations of respect when she fell for Phil? No. She still missed it, in fact, and supplied it when she could. She had fallen for Phil because she was strong, because of the awful need strength has for weakness. If you're not weak how can I be strong? Years it had taken her, years, until now, to learn that strength, like the lovely boys washing the dishes, like Gret saying that terrible thing at lunch, was what strength needed, craved, rested in. Rested and grew weak in, with the true weakness, the fecundity. Without self-defense. Gret had not been defending Phil, or anybody. Phil had to see it that way. But Gret had been speaking out of the true weakness. Dean Inman wouldn't have understood it, but it wouldn't have worried him; he would have seen that Gret respected him, and that to him would have meant that she respected herself. And Rita? She could not remember what Rita had said, when Gret said that about their not being real. Something not disapproving, but remote. Moving away. Rita was moving away. Like the gulls there ahead of them, always moving away as they advanced towards them, curved wings and watchful, indifferent eyes. Airborne, with hollow bones. She looked back down the sands. Gret and the interviewer were walking slowly, talking, far behind, so that she and Phil kept moving away from them, too. A tongue of the tide ran up the sand between them, crosscurrents drawing lines across it, and hissed softly out again. The horizon was a blue murk, but the sunlight was hot. "Ha!" Phil said, and picked up a fine white sand dollar. He always saw the invaluable treasures, the dollars of no currency; he went on finding Japanese glass netfloats every winter on this beach, years after the Japanese had given up glass floats for plastic, years after anyone else had found one. Some of the floats he found had limpets growing on them. Bearded with moss and in garments green, they had floated for years on the great waves, tiny unburst bubbles, green, translucent earthlets in foam galaxies, moving away, drawing near. "But how much Maupassant is there in *The Old Wives' Tale?*" she asked. "I mean, that kind of summing-up-women thing?" And Phil, pocketing his sea-paid salary, answered, as her father had answered her questions, and she listened to him and to the sea.

Sue's mother had died of cancer of the womb. Sue had gone home to stay with her before college was out last spring. It had taken her four months to die, and Sue had to talk about it. Gret had to listen. An honor, an imposition, an initiation. From time to time, barely enduring, Gret lifted her head to look out across the grey level of the sea, or up at Breton Head towering closer, or ahead at Mother and Daddy going along like slow sandpipers at the foam-fringe, or down at the damp brown sand and her grotty sneakers making footprints. But she bent her head again to Sue, confining herself. Sue had to tell and she had to listen, to learn all the instruments, the bonds, the knives, the racks and pinions, and how you became part of the torture, complicit with it, and whether in the end the truth, after such efforts to obtain it, would be spoken.

"My father hated the male nurses to touch her," Sue said. "He said it was woman's work, he tried to make them send women nurses in."

She talked about catheters, metastases, transfusions, each word an iron maiden, a toothed vagina. Women's work. "The oncologist said it would get better when he put her on morphine, when her mind would get confused. But it got worse. It was the worst. The last week was the worst thing I will ever go through." She knew what she was saying, and it was tremendous. To be able to say that meant that you need not be afraid again. But it seemed like you had to lose a good deal for that gain.

Gret's escaping gaze passed her mother and father, who had halted at the foot of Breton Head, and followed the breakers on out to where the sea went level. Somebody had told her in high school that if you jumped from a height like Breton Head, hitting the water would be just like hitting rock.

"I didn't mean to go on telling you all that. I'm sorry. I just haven't got through it yet. I have to keep working through it."

"Sure," Gret said.

"Your grandmother is so—she's a beautiful person. And your whole family. You all just seem so real. I really appreciate being here with you."

She stopped walking, and Gret had to stop, too.

"What you said at lunch, about your grandfather being famous."

Gret nodded.

"When I suggested to Professor Nabe about talking to Dean Inman's family, you know, maybe getting some details that weren't just public knowledge, some insights on how his educational theories and his life went together, and his family, and so on—you know what he said? He said, 'But they're all quite unimportant people, aren't they?'"

The two young women walked on side by side.

"That's funny," Gret said, with a grin. She stooped for a black pebble. It was basalt, of course; there was nothing but basalt this whole stretch of the coast, outflow from the great shield volcanoes up the Columbia, or pillow basalts from undersea vents; that's what Mother and Daddy were clambering on now, big, hard pillows from under the sea. The hard sea.

"What did you find?" Sue asked, over-intense about

everything, strung out. Gret showed her the dull black pebble, then flipped it at the breakers.

"*Everyone* is important," Sue said. "I learned that this summer."

Was that the truth that the croaking voice had gasped at torture's end? She didn't believe it. Nobody was important. But she couldn't say that. It would sound as cheap, as stupid, as the stupid professor. But the pebble wasn't important, neither was she, neither was Sue. Neither was the sea. Important wasn't the point. Things didn't have rank.

"Want to go on up the Head a ways? There's a sort of path."

Sue consulted her watch. "I don't want to keep your grandmother waiting when she wakes up. I'd better go back. I could listen to her talk forever. She's just amazing." She was going to say, "You're so lucky!" She did.

"Yeah," Gret said. "Some Greek, I think it was some Greek said don't say that to anybody until they're dead." She raised her voice. "Ma! Dad! Yo!" She gestured to them that she and Sue were returning. The small figures on the huge black pillows nodded and waved, and her mother's voice cried something, like a hawk's cry or a gull's, the sea drowning out all consonants, all sense.

Crows cawed and carked over the marshes inland. It was the only sound but the sound of the sea coming in the open window and filling the room and the whole house full as a shell is full of sound that sounds like the sea but is something else, your blood running in your veins, they said, but how could it be that you could hear that in a shell but never in your own ear or your cupped hand? In a coffee cup there was a sound like it, but less, not coming and going like the sea-sound. She had tried it as a child, the hand, the cup, the shell. Caw, cark, caw! Black heavy swoopers, queer. The light like no other on the white ceiling boards. Tongue and groove, tongue in cheek. What had the child said that for, that Amory was the only real one of them? An awful thing to say about reality. The child would have to be very careful, she was so strong. Stronger even than Maggie. Because her father was so weak. Of course that was all backwards, but it was so hard to think the things straight that the words had all backwards. Only she knew that the child would have to be very careful, not to be caught. Cark, ark, caw! the crows cried far over the marshes. What was the sound that kept going on? The wind, it must be the wind across the sagebrush plains. But that was far away. What was it she had wanted to think about when she lay down?

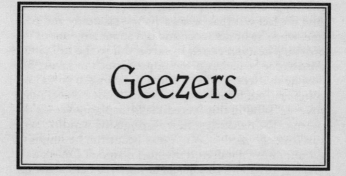

Geezers

The idea of driving over to the coast for the weekend came to him as a revelation—what his English professor used to call an epiphany. Actually it came to him from Debi, his personal secretary. "You look *so* tired, Warren," she had said. "Last weekend, I left the kids with Pat and went over to Lincoln City and found a motel, and I just sat there with a dumb novel for a whole afternoon, and went to bed at nine, and in the morning I had this long walk on the beach. I must of gone a mile. It made all the difference. In case you noticed how cheerful and brilliant I've been all week." Although he did not always get the details, he generally listened to Debi; and this time what she had said, even the words, came to him, as an epiphany, while he was driving home.

Saturday was lunch with the Curry County commissioner about south county development, but a phone call put that off till Tuesday. He got back into the car in jeans and windbreaker, with pajamas, running shoes, sweats, and a toothbrush in his briefcase, and took off.

He knew he was a creature of habit, stuck in every

rut he got into. He knew that was why he was effective, got things done. But Debi was right, he needed a break. And the fact was that because he was so steady and routine, when he broke loose and did something out of the ordinary he *appreciated* it, savored it to the full. Since the divorce he hadn't given himself much to savor. But now he was free, and he wasn't even going to go to Lincoln City, but farther, to find some hidden place, a discovery. "I found this incredible little place over on the coast. . . ." The Cutlass flew through the winding Wilson River gorges—God, it was beautiful, he ought to get out of town more often—to Tillamook Junction. A toss-up, 101 south to Tijuana or north to Fairbanks. He did not hesitate. Fancy free, he sped north.

He had forgotten that 101 ran inland for a good way north of Tillamook. By the time he got back out to the coast the sun had set and motel signs in the little towns said NO and SORRY. When he saw the sign for KLATSAND, POP. 251, PLEASE DRIVE CAREFULLY, he took the chance and turned off the highway. There'd be something down in town.

There was: the White Gull, VACANCY, marigolds in wooden boxes brightening the twilight.

"You're lucky," said the short woman at the desk, with a smile that grudged him his luck. "They booked the whole place. But they're two short, and they only pay for what they get. It's two nights minimum. Fourteen's the end one, across there." She pushed the key at him with no questions about what he wanted and no information concerning the cost. He was lucky. He accepted the luck and the key and put down his credit card. A lot of people in Salem would have recognized his name, but not over here in the boonies. The woman (JOHN AND MARY BRINNESI, YOUR HOSTS, ARE PLEASED TO WELCOME YOU) ran the imprinter over the card with a heavy hand. "Have a nice day," she said, although it was nearly nine at night. "Park anywhere. They're all in the bus."

What she meant, evidently, was that the other people staying at the White Gull had all come on the huge bus that loomed across four or five parking spaces. Walking along beside it on his way to No. 14, he read the sign that ran along under its windows:

THE SIGHTSEEING SENIORS OF CEDARWOOD
A CHRISTIAN COMMUNITY

It'll be a quiet night at the White Gull, he thought with amusement. He looked over the clean room, its king-size bed, its gypsy dancer on black velvet and schooner in the sunset, smelled its bubble-gum disinfectant, and went out to dinner. Coming into town he had noticed a place called Mayfield's, a promising name; he had a flair for little places.

Mayfield's was bigger than it looked from outside, and rather elegant, with white tablecloths and hurricane-lamp candles. It was also quite full, voices crowding warmly under the beamed ceiling. A boy hurried to seat him: "Are you with the group, sir?"

"No, no," Warren said, smiling.

"I thought you were kind of late if you were," the boy said, ingenuous, leading him to a small dark table under a Boston fern. "They're mostly on dessert. I'm Josh. Would you like something from the bar?"

Rose Ellen, who looked like she might be Josh's mother, brought Warren a glass of Chardonnay. While he waited for his grilled Chinook he watched the Sightseeing Seniors. They sat by fours and sixes; they were merry, convivial, grey and white and bald heads bobbing in the candlelight. They shouted stories from table to table and laughed aloud. There wasn't a wineglass on any table but his own. Strong in their numbers, they acted like they owned the place, but they were having such a good time, who could blame them? And suddenly his sleeve was plucked; a nice-looking old lady at the next table was leaning over and smiling. "If you'd like to join us, you know, you just do that. We're terribly noisy!"

"Oh, no, thanks so much," Warren said, with his fund-raising smile. "I'm just enjoying listening to you all."

"Well, you looked so lonesome sitting there, and I just didn't like to think you might feel left out," the old lady said, and nodded reassuringly, and turned away.

These are the salt of the earth, Warren said to himself as his salmon arrived. These are Americans.

A few of them left while he was eating. They stopped by one table or another to say good night and make more jokes. There seemed to be an infallible subject of hilarity, something to do with Wayne and trout fishing, and when Wayne himself left, shouting, "See you at the fishing hole!" gales of laughter swept the room. Most of them were still there, some still eating cake and drinking coffee, when Warren slipped out with a nod to the nice lady at the next table. She smiled and said, "You take care, now."

His room had no sea view, but he could hear the breakers just over the dunes. He had stuffed a folder on the Amonson committee in his briefcase under the running shoes, but after looking at it for five minutes he turned on the big TV set and watched the last half of a detective show. Finding he had slept right through the gunfire, he brushed his teeth and went to bed. Faint sounds of Seniors parting before their doors blended with the long in—out, in—out of the sea. He slept.

He woke, where? Banging on the door—what door?—"Oh, excuse me! Gee, I thought Jerry and Alice were in this one. Ex-cuse us!" Retreating laughter.

It was a little before seven. He lay a while luxuriating, then got up ready for a run on the beach. He thought of Debi, so proud of walking a mile. Most women past a certain age didn't keep themselves fit. He felt tremendously fit this morning.

After the dim motel room with its lined curtains, the sweep of the morning sky dazzled him. Shadows of the dunes lay cool and blue across the sand, but the foaming breakers and the sea burned like salt fire in the summer light. All up and down the beach, though it wasn't seven-thirty yet, people walked and jogged in pairs and groups. As he trotted by they nodded and greeted him: "Morning!" "Morning!" They were bald or grey, in purple sweats and flowered shirts. They were the Seniors, keeping fit.

A young man and woman flashed by at a run, running like deer. He jogged after them. Their double footprints in the sand were at twice the interval of his own. As he kept on, the Seniors began to thin out. By the time he was halfway to the big rock that closed off the beach at the south he had it all to himself, except for the young couple, who sped back past him without a glance, talking continuously in clear, unwinded voices.

It was a long way to the rock. He got his breath there, sitting on a black boulder over tide pools, and then jogged back slowly. No need to push it. The beach was now empty as if new-created, made for him alone, the first man. He was grateful.

He showered and went to find breakfast.

Tom's Seaside Grill looked like the place for breakfast, red-checked tablecloths, bustling waitresses.

"Your party's in the garden room, sir," said the fair, plump girl with the menus.

"I'm not with them," Warren said with a flash of irritation.

"I see. This way, then," said the girl, woundingly uninterested, and took him to a front window table. From it he watched all Klatsand pass.

As the occupants of the garden room left in pairs and groups and stood about in front of Tom's, it appeared that all Klatsand consisted of Sightseeing Seniors; but of course, Warren thought, these small beach communities had a large percentage of retired population year-round. Thinking about taxation demography, he was relieved to see a young woman with two toddlers go by. And there was a couple, not exactly young but anyway not old. And dogs—large, free, joyous dogs, beach dogs—went by, stopping now and then politely to greet a Senior.

The menu had a Senior Special across the top: one piece bacon or sausage, no-cholesterol Eggo, wheat toast, lo-cal spread, and prunes.

Warren ordered two over easy with home fries. The coffee was warm brown bitter water, but the food was hot and succulent, hi-cal.

I'll work this morning and sit on the beach this afternoon, he told himself. He liked to know what he was going to do, to dig his rut, even for a day. He strolled back to the White Gull, happy. The marigolds blazed. "Hey there! Terrific day!" somebody greeted him. He tried to place him—county? state?—this imposing old man with a broad, bald, brown head, then realized it was Wayne, the trout fisherman.

"Well, hi!" he said. He almost added, "Going fishing?" but did not. It would have pleased the old geezer, but he wanted, he did not know quite why, he wanted not to be *involved* with them.

He read, made notes, drafted a proposal. Though the light in the room was annoyingly dim, the work went fast and easily here, with no distractions, and all at once it was one o'clock. He had worked off that big breakfast and was hungry. He went back up to Main Street and walked up one side and down the other of its three commercial blocks, appreciating the sunlit, salt-bitten, grey-shingled shops and houses, all one-storyed; no neon; no fast-food chains. They had a smart town council here, with a policy. Edna's Dory Diner looked like a good bet for lunch. He checked through the window first. Edna's was nearly empty: a couple with a baby at one table. No grey, white, or bald heads. There were only six tables. He went in. A woman shaped like a section of log covered with a short dress and apron greeted him from the kitchen doorway: "Your group's over at the Dancing Sand-Dab," she said sternly.

"I don't have a group," he answered equally sternly.

"Oh, sorry," she said, not sounding sorry. "I just thought. Well, sit anywhere." She vanished into the kitchen. He sat.

The sole was heavily breaded and had been fried in grease for a long time. He knew in his heart that the Dancing Sand-Dab had light, delicate, lo-cal sole.

After lunch he walked around town, happy again, conscious of being happy. He looked at souvenirs in windows. He would come back and get one of those sand-castle ashtrays for Debi. She still smoked, though not on the job, of course. He played with the idea of buying one of the little houses east of Main, serene in their weedy gardens and grey paling fences, sunlight on their silvery shake roofs. It wasn't old money, of course, like Gearhart, or a prestige location, like Salishan, but it had a kind of quiet class. A house in Klatsand would be an interesting statement. Independent. That's my trademark, he thought, independence. I don't go with the group.

Wandering astray, he found he had to cross a strange, marshy area and skirt a black wood of heavily drooping trees to get back to the dunes. The dunes were higher here south of the main part of town. He climbed; his shoes filled instantly with sand. He came out above the broad sweep of beach, already familiar: the big rock at the south end, the high green headland at the north, the Seniors dotted all about in shorts and swimsuits, wading, sunbathing, playing volleyball.

He found himself a hollow in the dunes from which he could just see the ocean, but not the beach. Shouts and laughter from afar mingled with the soft thunder of the breakers. It was incredibly hot in the hollow, though the sea-wind blew over it, making the feathery heads of the dune grass nod. After twenty minutes he knew he had to get either some sunblock or a hat.

He had noticed a little pharmacy on Spruce Street. He climbed back over the dunes and walked along the wide, sandy road between them and the front row of houses. A beachfront property was the most desirable, but even in a place like this the price would be pretty stiff. A good investment, though, now that Californians were buying up the south coast. Actually he liked some of those little houses on the other side of Main better, but they were pretty much retirement-income-type places. It was too bad.

The girl behind the counter in the small drugs and souvenirs and postcards and taffy shop was beautiful: a dark-eyed redhead, luminous. She did not speak, but he was aware of her presence as he looked over the terrible terry-cloth hats by the door and then idled along the shelves, reading the protection factors on tubes of sunblock, glancing at her now and then. When at last he brought his selection to the counter she smiled at him, and he smiled back. She wore a black plastic tag with her name in gold: Irma.

"You people are really having a time of it!" she said. "I think it's just wonderful."

Warren's heart seemed to drop or sink physically, an inch or more, inside his chest.

"I work in Salem," he said.

It sounded strange.

"This is a nice town," he said.

She knew something was amiss, but didn't know what. "It's real quiet," she said. "And four makes ten. Have a good day now! Take care!"

I'm only fifty-two! Warren cried out to her in despairing silence.

The sunblock in its little paper bag was in his hand,

but he could not go back to the beach with the frolicking Seniors. He struck out north up Lewis Street, then along Fir Street to Clark Street. There was a little park back in here, he had noticed after lunch. He would sit in the park and put sunblock on his forehead and nose.

He did so, sitting on a bench in the dappled shade of the big, black, droopy trees that grew around here. He was unaccountably tired, even sleepy. But that was what he'd come here for, to relax, after all. Gulls yiped, crows croaked, children's voices called across the sunlit, weedy grass of Klatsand City Park. An intermittent droning, bumping noise must be the sound of the ocean coming and going on the wind. Above a vast bank of rhododendrons with purple flowers a small child appeared, flying. Presently it appeared again, flying, in the same direction. It was such a pleasant sight, a flying child, that Warren in his hebetude of weariness and sunlight simply accepted it.

A second and larger child in a red-white-and-blue-striped rugby shirt flew over the rhododendrons in the same direction, with the same rise and dip, like a swallow.

Warren sighed a little, getting up. He did not hurry. A third child soared past as he crossed the grass and walked around the thicket of rhododendrons.

The City of Klatsand had built for its children a skateboard rink—an oval of cement with a steeply slanted wall shaped like the figure 3—and the children of Klatsand flew about that wall and up into the air, with a light drone and clap of wheels, one after another, like swallows from a cliff.

Warren watched them with the earnest, stupid absorption of a sleepy man. They were beautiful and almost entirely silent. They flew, came down, came around on the grass with skateboard under arm, and waited in line to fly again.

Near Warren one boy stood, skateboard under arm but not in line.

"Looks like fun," Warren said, unsmiling, softly.

"Kids," the boy said.

He was, Warren realized, a couple of years older than the flying children. Maybe more, maybe four or five years older. Maybe a teen-ager.

"They don't like it when we take over," the boy said, tolerantly. He had never looked at Warren. He did not have to. He said nothing more. In the shade of the rhododendrons sat several other boys his age, waiting to take over.

Warren stood and watched the children flying until the heat of the sun beat in his temples. He went back then to the motel. Mrs. Brinnesi was out front, pulling up tiny weeds from the boxes of marigolds. "Too hot down on the beach for you?" she said with her vindictive smile, and he said, "Guess it is," though she must have seen that he wasn't even coming from the beach.

The nice lady, the one who had invited him to join her table, was letting herself in at No. 16. She smiled at him. "Well, hi there! Have you been enjoying yourself?"

"Yes," said Warren, surrendering. "Have you?"

"Oh, yes! But the beach is so hot today."

"I went to the park. Watched the kids skateboarding."

"Oh! Yes, they are so bad, those skateboards!" she said with hearty assurance of their being in agreement. "Come up behind you before you know it and could just knock you off your feet! They ought to be banned. Illegal."

"Yes," said Warren, "well." He unlocked his door. "Have a good day," he said.

"Oh, I will!" she said. "Take care, now!"

In and Out

From the quarter-inch-thick sheet of clay Jilly cut the oblong side walls and the square, peaked front and back walls. The texture of the clay was like butter when you're working sugar into it, stiff and grainy, or like boiled tongue. The clay-knife looked small in her fat fingers. It moved with a satisfying clean cut along right angles, exact, exacting, but not hard.

With the point of a paring knife she cut out a window low in one side wall, a small window high in the back wall, and the front door. She pinched and pressed a piece of clay to make it into a bit of uneven ground, the base on which she erected the walls one by one, joining the corners after running a water-dipped finger along each edge, and sealing the join the same way. The front wall went on last, fitting the edges of the side walls precisely. On the clay-daubed turntable now stood a roofless house three inches long and two inches high.

Her nieces had left some modeling clay, the oily kind, in a desk drawer. She had pinched out little animals, grotesque heads, from the greasy stuff and then mashed them back into the lump. She felt ashamed of playing like a child, of making ugly childish shapes. She hated sewing and got sick of reading. She kept thinking about some tiny houses she had seen once in China-town, made of brown clay, very delicate.

Kaye Forrest came in to sit with Mother one day, and after shopping at Hambleton's Jilly went by Bill Weisler's and asked him what kind of clay she could buy to just fool around with. Bill gave her an incredibly heavy little paper sack of dry dust. He gave her two clay-knives and an old turntable, and told her he'd bake whatever she made in his kiln, which he called "kill," so long as she'd hollow out the thick pieces so that they wouldn't explode in the heat in the kiln. She kept trying to get away and he kept telling her how to mix the clay and how to make slip and what to use it for and that she should cover the clay and the pieces with damp cloths at night, and when she drove off he was yelling that if she wanted to try bringing pots up on his wheel she could come over any evening, which left her really wishing she was at the office where she could tell somebody. "He said, 'Come over and bring pots up on my wheel!'"

Mother wouldn't enjoy it. Men were allowed to make innuendo sort of jokes, but women did not under-stand them.

The idea of doing anything with old Bill Weisler was too dismaying to be very funny, actually, but it had been interesting to see the inside of his cabin, shelves and shelves with rows and rows of the bowls and pots and vases he sold in Portland, some raw and some baked and colored. She knew he made a living as a potter, but she had never considered that that meant he lived there making pots, his hands in clay all day long, all night too, maybe.

She spun the table slowly, checking the walls for fit and verticality, admiring the view of the inside through the little oblong of the doorway.

Bringing the rolled-out slab round again, she mea-

sured off the length of the house on it and added a half
inch for eaves, estimated the width with a margin for
error, marked off the oblong, and cut out the roof. She
ruled a line down the center where the ridgepole would
go, and then with an old fork and her thumbnail scored
the surface of the clay with scratches to look like straw.
She lifted the roof on a spatula and laid it on the walls. It
fit, overhanging only a little too far on the sides. She
took it off and trimmed the edges, raking them with the
fork to look more like straw, then wet the surfaces
where roof would rest on wall, added a little slip to seal
the joins, and replaced the roof, pressing it gently down
on the house. Now when she looked in through the
doorway she saw light entering the house only through
the windows. The house had an inside, a dim, eerie place
she could peer into with her enormous eye but could
not enter, even though she had made it.

She began to cut toothpicks of clay for the window-
and doorframes. The work went well, easily, because
she knew what she was doing. Her first house, squat
and sorry, sat drying up on the bookshelf. With it were
three improving versions, a small village of some very
primitive tribe. But this one was coming out right.
Almost like the ones in Chinatown.

She had been thinking, and the thought came back
like the turntable coming round, that it was hard, or
anyway she found it hard, to realize that what you did
was usually just done once. Once and for all. That doing
something wasn't just a kind of practice for something
that would keep happening, but was what would happen, was what happened. You didn't get to practice.

Of course, there was all the stuff that needed doing
over every day, housework, office work, old Bill's pots;
but you treated that like it didn't matter, even when it
was all you knew how to do well, and kept saving yourself up for the important things, and then when you did
them you didn't know how. Like when the group of sec-

retaries met to plan meetings to talk about women in the city government, and the meeting had been so terrific, people saying things they didn't even know they thought, and ideas coming up, and nobody pushing each other around. And then Jetz's exec sec told the women in her office that they couldn't go, and the group never met again. They had just been getting ready for the real meeting and they had had it, it was done. Why was it so hard to see while it was happening that that was what was happening? Even a marriage. About the time she grew up enough to realize that marriage was what she and David were doing, he had started wanting out. Maybe because he'd realized it, too. Who knows? Even just going to Chinatown. Not a tour to China or something like that that you knew would be once in a lifetime, but just a shopping trip in Chinatown, and you saw some little clay houses, but you didn't buy them, you said, "I'll get a couple of those when I come back." And then it's years later and if you did go back they wouldn't be there. There might not be the same shops, even.

So the thing about what she was doing, even if it was stupid, at least she'd practiced it, and this time she was doing it right.

She was fitting the tiny frame around the doorway when her mother came through the room.

Jilly looked around and said, "Hi!" She didn't want to look around or speak, but she had no excuse; she wasn't working, she was playing, making toy houses. Nothing she did could be anything but playing, compared to what her mother was doing. She was walking from her bedroom, past the bathroom, through Jilly's room, to the sun-room at the back of the house. She wore the kimono Jilly had bought her in a secondhand store in Portland, embroidered in jade and apricot and gold, silly gorgeous silks over the thin and swollen places. She stopped in the doorway to the sun-room and said, "The sun's got around back here now."

Jilly bent over the turntable and made a cheerful sound. She heard her mother go on after a minute into the sun-room. There she would play at reading the newspaper, which Jilly had left for her by the armchair under the south windows. There she would play at sitting in the sun. But all the time she was working herself to death.

Since the last treatment she had not been outside. She did not cook or clean or crochet or play bridge or any of the things she had practiced for a long time. She had been practicing walking even longer, and still did that. She could walk down the little hall to the bathroom by herself, and all the way to the sun-room. Jilly's father had closed in the south-facing back porch when he bought the house for their retirement home five years ago. He had had it roofed, put in windows and louvers and miniblinds, got it all fixed up "so your mother can get the sun without the wind." Then he had gone out into the front garden and taken hold of a hoe handle and thrown it from him with a shout, flinging his arms wide, and died—right then, right there, without any practice at all.

The garden he had started to put in stayed the way it was. When Ernest brought the girls for Thanksgiving he would prune the hydrangeas and cut back the laurel hedge. Jilly sometimes spent an hour on a weekend weeding around the roses, enjoying it and always sure she would do more next weekend. Now that she was staying here she hardly ever went into the garden, because Mother never did. Mother never had gone down to the beach even when she was well. She did not like the wind. And there were insects outside.

Last spring, when it was only in the lymph nodes, one of the doctors had recommended a book about imagination therapy, and Jilly had got it and read it aloud to her. The book told her to imagine armies of Helper Cells and Hero Cells winning the war. "I thought about that army, like it said," she told Jilly in the morning in her soft, flat voice. "There was a whole lot of them. With wings. Sort of transparent."

"Like angels?"

"No," her mother said. "They were like those winged ant things, the whitish ones. They were crawling all over inside. Inside me."

At first the radio played just what Kaye liked, Willie and Don and Emmy Lou, but then there were four or five songs in a row that were about bodies, your warm and tender body, they said, the word *body* with a kind of thick sound to it, and then *love,* of course, with that same thick back-of-the-throat sound, I luhrv yer buhrdy, so she finally turned it off. If they meant sex when they said love, fine, nobody knows what love means anyhow. But when the word for what you made love to was the same as for a corpse it sounded like it didn't matter whether the body was alive or dead. She sponged the counter clean, ran the disposal, wiped out the sink, rinsed the sponges, checked around with a glance, gathered up the sections of the newspaper Jack had left on the breakfast table, put them on the coffee table in the front room, and went into the empty room. The guest room.

Its windows faced east and were full of sunlight, which showed all the winter's salty, streaky grime on the glass. I can wash the windows, Kaye thought, but immediately postponed the reprieve, making it into a reward. After. She could wash the windows after.

Nothing was really dirty or even very dusty; nothing was disordered in the bright little room. But it had been eighteen months. It was time she could clean it like the rest of the house. It had been two months. Since she had dusted. At least two months. At Christmas, before Christmas. Four months. It was time. Things have their seasons. If Jack's niece really came for Easter she would have this room, the guest room. It would be her room. Karen's room. That was as it should be; people lived in rooms and left them and the rooms were still there. They were called Sarah's room, Karen's room, but they were the same place. That had to do with love. That had to do with why it bothered her when they sang about love as if they knew what it was, as if love meant anything in words at all.

Jack knew that. He never said "I love you" except when he thought he had to, and it embarrassed both of them when he did. She never said it at all. On Valentine's Day she put a valentine under his dinner plate. Red paper hearts, white paper lace, cartoon cupids, that was "I love you." That was fine. All right. But there was this other thing that was dark, that had nothing to do with talking, with words, that was here, now, in this room—that was this room in her and her in this room, the heaviness of her body, her living body in the absence of the dead. That was what they didn't sing about.

The bed should be aired. It had stood made up all winter, getting damp. She turned her back on the bad place, the shelves, and whipped the spread and blankets off the bed. Different blankets, she had given the others away. She pulled out and bundled up the sheets, took the mattress pad off, and pushed the bed out a bit so that the sunlight would fall right across it. She took the sheets to the laundry basket on the back porch and hung the mattress pad on the lines there to air out. When she came back into the room, it looked like a motel room being cleaned, torn apart, unfamiliar. She turned at once to the shelves.

She moved Sarah's toys down onto the bureau so that she could dust the shelves. She handled the things firmly. They weren't really toys. There were the two plastic horses, the Thoroughbred and the Appaloosa. When they were seven or eight Jannine would bring her horses over and the two girls would play, down in the dunes, all afternoon. Sarah had kept the horses because they were pretty. They weren't toys any more, just pretty things she had liked. They had a right to stay there. It was all right. Things that weren't pretty, that had only been toys or only been useful, not loved, those it wouldn't have been right to keep. Jack had wanted to leave everything, keep everything. He had never forgiven her for giving away the toys, the clothes, the blankets. Even though he knew they couldn't keep them, and never spoke of it, and probably never thought about it, he had never forgiven her. People never forgave you for doing what had to be done that they wouldn't do themselves. Like those caste people in India, little dark stick-people on the TV, who looked after dirty clothes and garbage and corpses. Nobody would touch them. If you got rid of dirt you got dirty. It made sense. Jack didn't want anything in the room to be treated like dirt, to be got rid of. But it had to be. Somebody had to.

The pretty, oh, the pretty little tiger, she had forgotten it—made of red and yellow and black silk and tiny mirrors sewed in—from somewhere in India, was that why she had thought about India?—Jannine had given it to Sarah the last Christmas. With its silly cat smile, and mirrors down its striped sides. She put it down. She put it down. Beside the bookend, the sailing ship.

Jack made that before they were married. What fine work he used to do, inlay and pierced carving. Maybe when he retired he would go back to work like that. Maybe she could ask him then to make that piece he had designed years ago, in the other house. He would have the designs somewhere; he never threw anything away. A chest with a design of sea creatures on the lid in inlay, and seahorses at the corners holding it up. In the drawing you thought the chest had scalloped corners, and then you saw the seahorses standing on their curled tails. Bearing that in mind, she dusted the books and set them back behind the bookend and turned at last to the easy parts of the room.

The sunlight in the windows was so bright it darkened her eyes and she felt cold through, as if the room itself were cold, and dark, and very close, too close. The telephone in the kitchen rang, and she ran.

"Have to go up to Astoria," Jack said. His husky, grumbling voice was full of his physical presence, *his* body, thick, firm, solid, defenseless. "They sent the wrong insulation. Fuck it up every time." He grumbled but forgave them. He never looked for anything to go smoothly, only to go along smoothly himself, ducking under, as he said, letting the shit fly overhead. Lessons of Nam, he said. "Anything you want there?"

"I don't think so."

"So I won't be back for lunch."

"Well, get something to eat there, then."

"OK."

"Wait. Listen, where's the stepladder?"

"At the shop."

"Oh."

"I'll bring it home this evening. Used it fixing that molding on the Martins' house. What d'you need it for?"

"Washing windows."

"Outside? Leave that to me."

"I can do the ones I can reach, anyhow."

"OK. See you."

"Take care."

She would eat lunch early, then, and go over to sit with Joyce Dant. She called the Dants. Jilly's voice, too, was full of her body, warm, fat, and soft, a bit breathless like a girl and yet retreating, not touching, not quite meeting you. "Oh, hi, Kaye!" she said warmly, but Kaye felt she was intruding.

"I'd like to come visit with Joyce this afternoon. If you have errands or anything, it's a pretty day to be out in."

"Oh, that's really nice of you, Kaye. I don't think there's anything we need."

"Well, I'll just come and sit a bit." She could feel Jilly's resistance. You always resisted; you felt like you had to be there, *you* had to be there. Somebody had to feel that way.

"I'll be over about two," Kaye said, and hung up. She knew Jilly couldn't argue with her. She knew her own authority, and its source.

Jilly was cutting posts for the roofed veranda she had decided to build on the front of her house, when her mother spoke from the sun-room. "It's lovely and warm in here," she said.

Jilly answered loudly, "Yes! I bet it is!" But she would not go in there. This was her hour. Her one hour in the whole day. She went on cutting the shred of clay. All the rest of the time she was there to do what there was to do, but this one hour she kept back, kept out, to make stupid little imitation Chinatown mud houses. It wasn't fair of her mother to try to claim this one piece of time, too. Everything else was hers. This was Jilly's time, playtime, fat mud Jilly making mud pies.

Her mother spoke again, indistinctly responding to something she was reading in the paper. Jilly did not ask "What?" She pretended she had not heard. She could not stop listening. She never stopped listening except some nights when she fell into a sleep like stone and woke appalled at her sleep, her absence, while her mother lay struggling at her work which the drugs were supposed to make easy. Was long the same as easy? But now, just now, her mother did not really need her; she was only jealous.

The pages of the newspaper rustled, turning. Relieved, Jilly shifted her weight on the uncomfortable chair and went on working on the veranda roof. It was going to have to have a thicker beam running between the posts to keep it from sagging. Once she got that right, the roofed veranda made the house complete. The glimpse of the interior through the doorway was more charming and mysterious than ever. Though if you were an inch high and could actually go inside, you'd be in a single room whose floor and walls and roof were nothing but damp, cold, bare clay. It would be horrible. It's the inside seen from the outside, Jilly thought, bringing the turntable round, that always seems so mysterious and wonderful, and that's why—

Her mother spoke again. She wasn't talking to the paper; this was a different voice. Alone in the sun-flooded room, not fully awake, since the new higher dosage caused half-states and twilights of consciousness, she was thinking aloud; her mind was working on some question or problem, working something out. She said a few more words in a murmur and then clearly, in her small, flat voice, "All right. That's it, then. All right."

Jilly knew what she had asked and answered. Why had her daughter not come at her invitation, when she said it was warm and lovely here? Because she could no longer invite. She couldn't say, "Come in." She could only demand, "Come here!" or beg, "Come to me!" And her daughter did not want to come. All right.

But it wasn't true. Her daughter wanted to come but couldn't. She couldn't go into that room. She could only look in from the outside.

She set the finished house up on the shelf to dry. She dampened the clayey cloth and laid it over the unshaped lump. Her hands were daubed and coated greyish-white, and she went to wash them. The telephone rang, and as she turned to it she called to her mother, "I'll be there in just a moment!"

Joyce wanted to watch one of the afternoon soaps. She told Kaye what the episode was going to be about, but as soon as it started she fell asleep. Kaye knitted. The afternoon sun was on the windows of the bedroom, but the miniblinds were closed tight, shutting out the sunlight and the sea. Kaye wondered, if she were dying, would she want to be in a room with a sea view. She wondered if Joyce looked out at the sea.

Joyce lay like sticks and lumps in the bed, her face half turned away.

Kaye knew little of her. She and her husband had moved here five years ago, and he had died that first year. She had stayed, quiet, flat-talking. She was from the East somewhere, Ohio, maybe. She had a way of being aggrieved, down on things, but she had a funny streak, too, a kind of prim wryness. She wore brown and navy skirts, tan cardigans. Jilly would have given her the beautiful, brilliant housecoat that lay across the foot of the bed. Jilly was a good daughter, coming over from Portland every weekend when Joyce was newly widowed, and now staying here full time. She had a job at City Hall that she must have given up or got leave from. It would be hard to ask her about it. Jilly was much more open and easy than her mother, but she held back, too. Kaye had told her to go out and have a walk on the beach, it was so beautiful out, but Jilly said she wanted a nap and was in her room now, the blinds drawn. The three of them shut indoors with the windows covered, and outside the April sunlight pouring down on shore and sea, and the wind as warm as summer.

"Where's Jilly?"

"Having a nap," Kaye said in a murmur, knowing Joyce was less than half awake.

"She never comes."

"Oh, now, now," Kaye soothed, cajoling, dismissing. Joyce slipped further back into sleep. Did she "love" her daughter? Kaye watched her bony, swollen hand lying on the blanket. Can you love people when you're dying?

Why did you have me if this was going to happen?
But she had only been fourteen.

Jilly thumped around in the hall and the bathroom, and came to the doorway of the room, flushed from sleep, a big rose-and-golden woman. Soft and tender. "How's about a cup of tea, you two?" she said aloud.

Joyce did not answer. Probably her sleeping and waking were not much affected by anything outside her own body now. Her body, the sticks and lumps under the covering. "A rag, a bone, and a hank of hair," Kaye's father used to sing, teasing Mother, when she'd bought a new dress or got a perm and a rinse. And so they all were, that or a little dust in the sea, the soft and tender bodies, nothing much to sing about; but so you dyed and curled your hair, to look pretty.

Jilly came back with a tray. Joyce roused up. They drank tea together.

"Well, I'd better go home and wash my windows," Kaye said. "I've dodged it long enough."

"Sun coming out makes you see how dirty they've got," said Joyce.

"Awful. And I can't do the outside of most of them till Jack brings the stepladder back. But I can do the insides, and finish cleaning Sarah's room. Jack's niece will be with us Easter week, did I tell you? Karen Jones. She's at the health sciences college in town."

"Newspaper's better than paper towels. For windows. Something in the printing, in the ink." Joyce shifted in the bed and breathed heavily. She looked directly at Kaye, one brief gaze, full of hate. Don't come here with your dead daughter!

"So, I'd better be off. Anything I can do for either of you? You know, if you need anything from Astoria, Jack's up there two or three times a week."

"Oh, no, we're just fine," Jilly said.

She went with Kaye through the front room and they stood a moment, Kaye outside on the porch, Jilly in the doorway, holding the door open. The light, sweet, moving air touched them. Kaye put a hand for a moment on Jilly's arm. She saw the nails of Jilly's hand rimmed as if she had been digging in clay. She only touched her, she did not embrace her, for Jilly did not expect to be embraced, and that made it hard, even for a mother who wanted to hold her daughter. "It's hard, Jilly," Kaye said.

"Hard work," Jilly said, smiling, already turning to go back inside.

Bill Weisler

He did not often go down on the beach. It was too big, too wide and flat, and the water worried him. Why did the breakers always come in, even against the wind? It seemed like they might go out when the tide went out and come in when it came in, but even with an east wind and the tide on the ebb the waves came straight against the land and bashed and broke themselves against it. The sound of them underlying all other sounds in his life was peaceful to him, but not the sight of them senselessly breaking. And sometimes the great breadth of the beach and the sea discomforted him. It was not the terror, the feeling he dreaded so much that his mind would touch it only with the two fingers of the two words he had for it, "falling black," but only an uneasy sense of dwindling, weighing nothing, in the great desolation of the wind. As a kid down on the beach he had enjoyed that feeling of being nothing, free, but that was a long time ago. Back then, too, sometimes there had been nobody else on the beach all day. These days there was always somebody else. Town was full of them even on weekdays. The only way to keep away from them was to stay in and work.

He had put too much sand in the bucket. It didn't look like a lot, but as soon as he started to lift it he knew the metal handle would pull right out of the plastic. He tipped the faded orange bucket and let sand well out onto sand. When it was half empty he lifted it cautiously and lugged it over the dune onto Searoad. He put the bucket on the floor of his pickup and climbed in, reaching into his right front jeans pocket for the key. The pocket was empty.

He looked around the cab of the pickup for a while and then went back up the dune, following his tracks, which were the only ones in the sand, stooping and peering around among the dune grass. On the ocean side was the little dip where he had filled the bucket with clean sand and then tipped half of it back. There he knelt and scrabbled and sifted sand through his fingers vaguely for a while. It had to be here, or else in the pickup. Didn't it?

He went back to the pickup and looked all over the seat and floor and around under the front wheels and frame. He had to tell himself that he *had* had the key. Because he'd driven the pickup here. To get sand. He always put the key in his right front jeans pocket. He felt in the empty pocket again. There was no hole in it. He felt in all his other pockets again. He did not have the key. It did not make sense. He went back up the dune again, almost on hands and knees, pushing the tough, sharp-edged grass aside. The wind gusted, blowing sand in his face.

"Are you looking for something?"

He jumped. His head jerked sideways, disorienting him for a moment. He stood up and glanced up once. Where had she come from? There had been nobody except some people way off north on the beach. She was an older woman. It was all right. He had to speak to her, though. He said, "Lost my key."

Her voice had been amused on the surface but cold underneath, as if she thought he was suspicious, a trespasser. She came from the solid white house there, the last house on Searoad, summer people, the professor, they had had the house a long time, he didn't remember their name.

She said, "Oh, Mr. Weisler," as if she recognized him all of a sudden. "Your car keys? Oh, let me help you look. What an awful bother. Do you have another set?"

"Home," he said, with a jerk of his head, and pretended to look for the key, pushing the dune grass aside. He couldn't look if she was there. She kept stooping and peering on the ground between the dune and his pickup. She said something else, but his dismay was more than he could bear. He made a break for the pickup and swung up into it while her back was turned. "Going home for the other one," he said to her startled raised face five yards away, and then realized he couldn't drive home. He got out of the pickup and walked away on Searoad, his head drumming and his legs loose at the knees. She called something but he pretended not to hear. After a while he thought she had called, "I'll drive you." But he had got away. He went the shortcut, through town, walking quickly.

He stayed around home awhile to be sure she would be gone when he went back. When he did set out, going along the creek and then taking the path across Macdowell Slough, he walked quickly again. He met nobody, though he heard some kids calling in the woods. He was nervous when he came out onto Searoad, but she wasn't in sight, nobody was. The pickup sat waiting with a sad, patient look. He slipped in and started it up with the spare key and drove off without looking again for the lost one. It was gone.

Once he was home and in his workshop he thought gratefully of the old woman trying to help him find the key and offering to drive him home. He had been startled by her appearing like that when he thought he was alone. The trouble with women was he did not know how to talk to them. Men frightened him much more than women did, but there were things he could say to men, ten or twelve things: the weather, how's business, done any fishing lately, the Blazers. They would answer back, or they would say one of the ten or twelve things to him and he would answer back, and it was done. But if there were things to say to women, he did not know them; the ten or twelve things didn't work; they wanted to talk. The woman from the square solid house had wanted to talk. But she had tried to help him, and though he hadn't wanted her to, he was able to feel her kindness, now, and to think about her kindly. He had always liked that house, and she was solid and firm-looking like it, with her greyish-white hair. She had said his name in a neighborly way, "Oh, Mr. Weisler," when she recognized him. Probably she didn't see well at a distance, and he had been bent over almost on all fours. It was nice of her to call him "Mr." Most people called him Bill, but she hadn't said "Mr. Weisler" in a stand-offish way. People of her generation called people "Mr." until they knew them better than just recognizing their face. When he had to give his own name he always said it all. If he had known her name to call her by he would have called her "Mrs." She had known he was dismayed about losing his key and had tried to do something about it right away. She was a nice woman. His gratitude towards her made him feel pleasant and solid. The loss of the key no longer troubled him, and he forgot the sense of the desolation of the wind and the sand and the bowing, sharp-edged grasses, that huge place where the key had been lost.

He had a box of rawhide thongs for hanging the little wall planters that sold well at Saturday Market in Portland, at the stall Conrad ran there. He put the spare ignition key onto a thong and tied it in a loop, then untied it, added his workshop key to it, and retied it. It would be easier to find now, two keys on the strip of rawhide, and he might as well carry the workshop key as hide it behind the loose board, since he never locked the workshop.

The sand in the orange bucket was for coating the outside of cylindrical, pierced garden lanterns for candles, another item Conrad had been selling well. Sandman's Lanterns. People would pay forty-five dollars for them. The price seemed too high for the little skill and work it took to make them, but Conrad set the prices and knew what he was doing. "They're too easy, you get bored, so you get paid for getting bored, man!" Conrad said. There was justice in that, though Bill Weisler still thought the boredom wasn't worth more than about twenty-five dollars.

He got to work, because if the surface dried much more it wouldn't hold the sand, and there were twenty lanterns to be coated with the dark grey and creamy, mica-flecked basalt and quartz milled down fine and even by the Pacific Ocean. If making sand was the purpose of the breakers always coming in and never going out, at least they were good at it. They did a good job. Even a river could make sand if it was big enough; the Columbia had sand shores, and he had seen dunes way inland along the Snake River, from the train. But mostly rivers turned out his kind of dirt, the really fine-milled stuff, silt, mud, clay. Even little Klatsand Creek had some pockets of a light-textured brown clay that he had dug and cleaned and used, now and then, for small pots and bowls, handling it like terra-cotta. The cool pierced cylinders rolled under his hands and the words in his mind rolled and stilled and vanished into the work the way streaks of color vanish into kneaded clay.

* * *

He had always lived in Klatsand, before and after four years in the Army in California, Georgia, Italy, and Illinois. His mother had been fifteen years old when he was born and he had been fifteen years old when she died. He thought about those numbers sometimes. It seemed as if they should make some sense, should add up to another number that made sense, at least, but he could not make them do it. It seemed like each subtracted from the other and left nothing. His father, William Weisler, had left town a couple of years after marrying Bill's mother and never came back. She had died of peritonitis or of a ruptured spleen, due to a fall, Ray Zerder said. Ray Zerder told the hospital people about the fall, and they did not ask what kind of fall had knocked out her lower front teeth and broken her cheekbone and turned both her arms black from elbow to wrist as well as rupturing her spleen. Since Ray Zerder had moved in, Bill Weisler had been sleeping in the old woodshed. When Ray Zerder and his mother drank and started yelling and screaming in the house he would go hang around on the school playground, sometimes with the other town boys his age. When his mother died, his father's mother, Mrs. Robert Weisler, made him move into her house. He never knew what her first name was. She got the little house out back of the lumberyard above the creek cleaned up some and rented it to summer people. Bill Weisler was drafted when he was eighteen, and she died while he was in the Army. She left him the house above the creek in her will. He got the letter from the lawyer when he was in Illinois waiting for his discharge. He came across the country on the train to Portland, came on the Greyhound bus to Klatsand, and walked out past the lumberyard and through the spruce woods to his house. The lawyer had written that it was still leased to some Portland people, but with gas rationing they never came over or paid the rent. He broke in by giving the back door a hard yank—it was always stuck, not locked—and so came home. The afghan in red, white, and blue squares that his mother had made when he was ten was still on the couch in the living room. Everything smelled musty. It was perfectly still in the woods at night, only the frogs sang down along the creek, and if you listened you could hear the steady pouring of the sea.

None of the places he had been in the Army ever came into his mind, except that for a few years he used to dream sometimes about being in a windowless room with dried blood on the stucco walls. That was in Italy, though he had never actually been in the room in the dream. He thought sometimes about some of the men he had met in the Army; some of them had been good men, and he had learned the things to say to them, but they were always being moved, so that he never stayed long in a group. He had been afraid of the colored soldiers at first, but the ones he stayed afraid of were the kind of white men who were looking for trouble. That was what his mother had said: "Oh, that Ray, he's just always looking for trouble!" Bill Weisler kept out of trouble as well as he could. One big, dark brown Negro named Sef had stood up for him in the city in Italy, he didn't know its name, where they had tried to make him go to the whores with them. "You want fuckin crabs and fuckin clap you go right on," Sef had said. "Billy and I ain't interested." None of them wanted to tangle with Sef, so they let them alone. He and Sef had talked a little that night. Sef said he had a wife and a daughter in Alabama. "I never been with a woman," Bill Weisler said to him, the only time in his life he spoke to another person about sex. He had never learned the things to say to men about women. He got by because he listened and nodded at the right times when other men talked about the parts of women. He knew all the words, but they went out of his mind as soon as he stopped hearing them. He remembered the one thing Sef said about his wife in Alabama. "She got this big laugh," he said, and laughed saying it.

The things he remembered from the four years in the Army stayed very clear, because there was nothing else ever like them in his life, but there were only a few of them, a few faces and words, like Sef saying, "She got this big laugh." The rest had not made sense to him. When he tried to make sense of some things he had seen and done in Italy he got the feeling of darkness and falling, until he quit.

In the same way he did not think about the times when he had fallen all the way into the black, because thinking about it made it happen. He knew it had happened twice. There was also the time when he had drunk too much beer at the VFW oyster feed, but that time he'd pulled out of it in just a day or two. The two times when he had fallen black had been long. If some people in town thought he was crazy, and he knew they did, they had some reason to. He knew that the second time they had sent Tom James, the sheriff, to take him to the hospital, because he was in his house and hadn't come out or eaten anything for nobody knew how long, days or weeks. It was the hospital up in Summersea, where his mother had died. He remembered leaving it, but later did not know whether that was after his mother died or after they released him, coming down the steps into sunlight.

The sheriff used to check on him every week or two for a long time after that. "Hullo, Bill. Eatin'?" He had been a good man. You didn't have to make conversation with him at all. Once after a fireman's benefit dinner old Hulse Chock, who had been sitting between Bill Weisler and Sheriff James for two hours, said, "Tom, the only trouble with you and Bill is a man can't get a word in for the flow of wit and repartee," and it still struck Bill Weisler funny when he thought of it. Old Hulse had sounded so like he meant it that it made it funny, and anyhow it was a relief to get laughed at for not talking, instead of pitied or resented.

That was what made him feel easy with Tom James,

and old Hulse, and a few other people—Conrad in Portland, and Mrs. Hambleton at the grocery, and the woman who had come out to his house that day asking about clay. They didn't take him too seriously. They weren't looking for trouble. They laughed; they cleared things up. Conrad, hippie entrepreneur, had got hold of Bill Weisler's ceramics way back in 1970 and parlayed him right out of the local garden shops where he had made a bare living for twenty years into the city street markets and fairs and boutiques and malls of the seventies and eighties, till he was working seven ten-hour days a week in his workshop to meet the demand and had an incredible eighteen thousand dollars in the bank in savings. "Man, you kill me, you crack me up," Conrad said. "You are unreal!" He laughed whenever Bill Weisler said anything, and sometimes he patted his arm or stroked his shoulder and said, "Oh, man, I love you!" Conrad had made sense to Bill Weisler from the start. Only lately there had been times when he seemed to get serious, to be asking for trouble. One time last month when they were stocking the Saturday Market stall Conrad had started a kind of speech, like somebody talking on TV, talking at you but not seeing you, and kept going on and on about how the insurance racket was ripping people off, and the IRS, and who the people were that were really running the town. "OK, Bill, look at the money that's going into this new convention center, see what I mean? Talk about a pipeline!" He talked so angrily and with so many details and names and amounts of money that Bill Weisler felt that he understood, or should understand, but kept feeling uneasy and almost dizzy, as he stacked the pots and platters and planters on the raw pine shelves.

Conrad was his link to all the people, the competent, confident customers, the shop owners, the families with children, the young men and women who threw Frisbees and made campfires on the beach, the people who were easy living in the world, and if he lost that link he would be on his own again, without any way to find out if what he thought made sense. When Conrad used to tell him, "Man, you are insane!" it set Bill Weisler's mind at ease, because Conrad couldn't say that if he was.

He couldn't test things on Mrs. Hambleton the way he could on Conrad, because he couldn't actually talk to her, as he could sometimes to Conrad; but she was reassuring, because he could tell that he made sense to her. Pretty much everything did. Nothing fazed her, nobody troubled her; she'd had a hard life, lost two sons, brought up a retarded grandson, kept the grocery going; she looked at Bill Weisler across the counter and said, "How's life treating you, Bill?" or "Selling lots of flower-pots, Bill?" and laughed, because she was easy with him. She had known him sixty years.

The woman who had come to his workshop was different. Her people had come a few years back, but she didn't live in Klatsand until she came to stay with her mother with cancer. Her father was already dead. Bill Weisler knew that from people talking in the grocery store. He didn't know who she was, exactly, when she came out to his place. She had parked on the road and started to the house and then saw him in his workshop, which was the old woodshed expanded out a good bit. She said her name, "Hi, I'm" whatever it was—he had been too surprised and confused to understand what she said. She was the color of certain roses and azaleas. After her visit he had worked on a glaze for the next set of tall flower-vases and had got pretty close to that color, a pink gold with an underlay of deeper reddish peach; on some of them he laid a streak of cobalt, a light dash down one side. She had round arms and was round and full, solid. All this he was aware of while she stood there, as he was aware of what a piece he was throwing on the wheel looked like, without any words, only clear impressions of its wholeness, its completeness, whether it was right. He thought she was right. But of course she was talking and he was not following what she said. It seemed like it had been something about making animals out of clay.

"They have some, at the junior college," he said, waving his clay-encrusted hand to the south, "classes, you know." She understood him and said she couldn't go to a ceramics class because she needed to stay at home, and anyhow she just wanted to fiddle around. "Make an ashtray, like in second grade," she said, smiling. She had what he would call a big smile.

"Well, then, you need," Bill Weisler said, and ran out of words as he turned to lay his hands on the things she would need. A few pounds of dry clay, and she'd have to have a couple of knives, and if she was doing figurines a turntable—the one he hadn't dropped worked better; he dusted it off some and gave it to her, trying to explain how to use these things, how to knead, how to make slip, there was so much she needed to know. She kept smiling and laughing and saying, "I see!" and "Got it!" and nodding, and when she repeated what he said she said it better than he did.

"I can put the, what you make, in my kiln, just bring it over," he said. "I fire on Tuesday. Usually. I could any day." She looked blank. She was thanking him and smiling and drawing away, going to her car backward like she was being pulled to it on a string. "You want to try the wheel," he said, and she looked at the little lazy Susan he had given her. "You know," he said, waving his hand behind him at the workshop. "If you want to bring up stuff on the wheel, any evening, I'm here," thinking that he would come back early when he took the next lot in to Portland, so that he would be there in the evening if she came.

She did not come. She had to stay with her sick mother. He thought of her often while he worked. He thought of her as a kind person, giving up her freedom to care for her mother, and friendly in the way she talked and laughed. It gave him pleasure to think of her. She was on the right side, like Sef and the old woman who had looked for his key and Mrs. Hambleton and Conrad. If you could keep on their side you would not fall black. They were colored tan, brown, rose, gold, and cobalt. They were solid.

When Conrad let him down it was very bad. It made everything threaten to fall. It was only something he said, which Bill Weisler scarcely noticed at first, but it was like the hairline under the glaze that you don't see because you don't want to see it but you do see it. All Conrad said was, "Don't bother sorting out the seconds."

It wasn't till he was driving back home, passing the highway sign that said OCEAN BEACHES, that he started thinking about Conrad saying that, and thought that it meant he had been selling imperfect pieces, seconds, at the same price as firsts. The idea kept coming back to him, though he could not take it beyond itself and make sense of it. Nor could he get up the courage to telephone Conrad and ask him what he had meant.

Two weeks later when he took in a pickup load of the four-foot vase-planters that were selling so well at the fancy place in the mall, Exterior Decorating, Conrad helped him unpack the pieces in the back room of the shop. They were fragile because they were so big. Bill Weisler couldn't stand handling the plastic foam bits people used now, and packed in straw he got from the feed shop. He had stuck a tab of bright orange marking tape on the six flawed pieces. Conrad was brushing straw off one of them, and flicked the tab off with his thumbnail.

"Second," Bill Weisler said.

"What's wrong with it?" Conrad said, and then, "Yeah," spotting the flaw in the glaze down one side. "That don't matter," he said.

"It's a second," Bill Weisler said.

"It's nothing. It's sound, isn't it? It'll sell as a first.

They don't notice, Bill." Conrad looked over at him. "They don't care."

Bill Weisler picked up the bit of tape from the dirty floor of the back room. He did not dare stick it back onto the big, handsome planter, with its flawed blue and white glaze.

"I'll tell the showroom people to point it out to 'em," Conrad said, "OK?" He waited a minute for an answer, glancing sideways at Bill Weisler and at the planter out of his deep-set, Indian-looking eyes, obsidian eyes. Conrad was looking a lot older. "It don't make any difference to the use, Bill. It's a desirable imperfection. Shows it's handmade, for Chrissake! We could *raise* the price for it. Listen, you seen those catalogues come all the time in the mail, talking about slubs or stubs or some kind of crap like that in these goddamn hundred and fifty dollar silk shirts, little defects so you know they're really genu-wine? So call it a slub, there. Genu-wine Weisler vase with authentic slubs in the absolutely sincere glaze made with true human spit. Orange stickers, two C's; no stickers, one-fifty. Look, Bill. Nothing is perfect. Only what we say is."

"I don't know," Bill Weisler said.

Conrad reached across the planter and patted his arm. "Oh, man," he said, "you are so unreal. I love you when you look so sad! Come on, baby, let's cry all the way to the bank."

It did not make sense, so he could not talk about it. He got afraid to say anything to Conrad. It had all worked so well for so long; now was it going to fall apart? Would Conrad be angry with him?

As he drove west past the OCEAN BEACHES sign he realized that it was worse than that. He was angry at Conrad.

At the thought, the pickup swerved. A Ford merging lanes honked at him. His heart leaped and thumped for miles. In the Coast Range there were falling places, areas of black. When he drove into Klatsand it looked unfamiliar in a strange orange sunset light full of black pits and streaks. As he got out of the pickup in front of his house his shoe caught on the rubber mat on the floor, pulling a corner of it up. The ignition key was shining there on the floorboard. He picked it up and then looked at his hands because he had a key in each hand, one on a thong with the workshop key, the other by itself. It took him a minute to understand why he had two keys.

It was the old woman who had looked for the lost key in the dunes that he thought of then, and all night as he worked, for he could not sleep; he was afraid to go to bed, to lie down and fall black. The frogs sang down along the creek, ceasing and beginning again. He worked at the wheel, bringing up a shape he had not made for a long time: bowls about a foot across, rounded in at the top. *Chalices,* a word from a ceramics exhibition once in Astoria. He worked till daylight. He slept on the workshop floor, flat out, his head under the bench, in the dust of clay.

The day was bad. He knew he must not go into the house. If he did he might not be able to come out. He needed a shower, and washed as well as he could at the workroom tap. After a while he could not work.

He could not go to the old woman because he did not know her name, but the one who had come to his place was named Jilly. Mrs. Hambleton had said, "How's it going, Jilly?" to her one day in the grocery store. He knew her house. He knew every house in Klatsand and who lived in it, maybe not by name but by their looks, by their color and shape, their form of being.

He thought about Tom James, but Tom James was dead.

He went to the grey shingle house with the added-on porch in the back and knocked on the door. He knocked very softly because the mother was sick and dying. He fell black and caught himself from falling not once but over and over, brief, deep, dizzying falls. He took a step away from the door. It opened.

The rose and azalea color was paler, puffier; the cobalt was dulled. The smile was not big. She said his name in a soft, flat voice. He held out the bag of dry clay and said his speech: "Thought you might need some more."

She reached out to take what he offered, but she said, "Oh, gee, I still have lots—thanks—see, I just made these little tiny things—" She looked down at the paper sack. "I don't have any time now to, you know, do anything much else," she said, with a different smile; then she looked up into his face. He looked down. She took the sack. "Thank you, Bill," she said. Her voice shook up and down like music. He realized she was crying.

"I wanted to ask you," he said.

She caught her breath and nodded.

"If you make something doesn't come out right," he said.

"Nothing I make comes out right," she said, and laughed on those doubled, shaking notes.

"It's wrong to sell it the same as if it was right," he said.

After a while he glanced up at her.

"I guess so," she said. "Isn't it?"

"It doesn't make sense," he said.

She nodded, then shook her head.

"I've got to go back in, Bill," she said. "You know. She's." She said it that way, "She's." He nodded. "Thank you," she said again.

"OK," he said. He turned away. She closed the door. He walked through the front yard to his pickup with its patient look parked on the unpaved street. He had left the key in the ignition. The light of day was pure, flawless, a clear glaze on the solidness of things. Inside the great bowl he could hear the sound the waves made down on the beach.

True Love

A woman unmated but contented generally learns to hide her contentment so as not to shock her friends. There's no use defying whatever orthodoxy your culture has adopted. You just end up as a witch. I realize now that that is really why I got married: better to marry than to burn. And after the divorce I had an affair or two—that is, I had two, and thus am able to say convincingly that I've had an affair or two. One was with a library systems analyst and was not successful. The other was with a bookseller, and in its way it was successful. But the fact is that sexual practice merely diverts my erotic energies into an artificial form provided for them by my civilization. For me, sex is sublimation. Left to itself, in its raw, primitive state, my libido would expend itself inexhaustibly in reading.

And since I have been a librarian ever since I was twenty, I can truly compare my life to that of some pasha luxuriating in his harem—and what a harem! Half a million mistresses, when I was at the Central Library in Portland! A decade-long orgy! And during the school year, since I teach now at the Library School, I have access to the University Library. Here in Klatsand where I spend the summers, the harem is very small, and a good many of the houris are rather out of date; but then, so am I. My lust has lessened somewhat with the years. Sometimes I imagine I could be contented with a mere shelf of tried, true, and highly selected Scheherazades, with only now and then a pretty little novel to flirt with, or a volume of new poetry to make me cry out with excess of pleasure in the heart of night.

Antal came, of course, with books; or rather the books came, then Antal. I was in the Klatsand Volunteer Free Library—two rooms above the drugstore—sorting and cataloguing, which I do once a week in summer, and sometimes oftener, if the Library League volunteers have wreaked more havoc than usual in the catalogues during the rest of the year. I enjoy the work, which is easy and often funny; I find Louis L'Amour labeled as Romance, and Lévi-Strauss among the cookbooks. That day Shirley Bauer came in, and after she had rooted in the sale bin awhile she called, "Frances, did you hear we're about to have a bookstore?"

"Here?"

"Yes. Somebody's putting a bookstore in the old kite shop."

"Next to Tom's?"

"Mhm. Mary said she had a renter for it and she thought he wanted to make it a bookshop. And then I was in the post office, and Mrs. Brown said she was holding boxes and boxes of books there, General Delivery to A. Somebody."

So the books really did come before Antal did.

When he came, he stayed at the Ship Ahoy Motel, through poverty and ignorance. He was a godsend to Rosemarie Tucket, though, since she was trying to get by after her husband's death, with the lawyers and the insurance companies fighting it out. I think Antal was the only customer at the Ship Ahoy in June. And he stayed there the whole time he was in Klatsand, only about eight months, as it turned out.

I didn't meet him until he opened the shop, though I had seen him around town, and also of course when I stopped to look in his window, every time I passed, trying to see what kind of books he had. It looked as if they were used books, real books. Not those so-called remainders, which seem to be produced by publishers who are so afraid of taking risks that they prefer to publish what there is no risk at all of anyone ever buying. I saw almost no bright dust jackets, when I leaned over the flowerless window box to peer through the unwashed display window of the ex-kite shop at the piles and stacks of seductively worn, foxed, and grubby books inside. The proprietor was visible only as a dim form, sorting and shelving; he did not have a bright jacket either. I wanted to offer to help him. There was really nothing left to do at the tiny library, and I longed to get my hands on his books. I knew I could be useful to him. I can sort and shelve in my sleep, and frequently do. And I have a knack for evaluating. But the intensity of my desire rather frightened me, and with a sense that I really must control myself, I would go on to the grocery or the beach, trying to put temptation behind me.

But the presence of books in town—books I had not seen, books I had not read—was a constant, subtle intoxication. There are not all that many books in Klatsand. Most of them belong to my friends and me, and I know them cover to cover. So I could not keep long away from the window next to Tom's Grill on Main Street; and the day the bookstore opened, I was the first customer.

I will not describe my first hours with Antal's books. Hints and omissions suggest far more than pant-and-grunt accounts, I think. Anyhow, to be candid, it was an uneven collection. At first I thought it was going to be nothing but cabin-fever novels—the kind you read when trapped by rain for a long weekend in somebody else's summer cabin—the best-sellers of 1937 and 1951, true bonfires of the vanities, self-consuming autos-da-fé on the plazas of Success. But at least the poor creatures aren't infectious any more, they can't cause syphilis of the soul, they're burnt-out cases. I passed over a couple of shelves of these old whores and was feeling discouraged, when my hands—at bookshelves, my mind and eyes are not so quick or so wise as my hands—found an early Edna Ferber. It was *The Girls*, and I desired at once, passionately, to reread it. And so from charm to charm the lover is led on, all trembling amorous, and time does not exist, and money is forgot. There's Phyllis Rose! Expense be damn'd, I'll have her!

I came to. I came to the counter with, after all, only five books.

The proprietor had been admirably invisible and inaudible; he had not even said, "Can I help you find something?" He knew his job. We had greeted each other in silence with civil smiles when I came in, and not a word since.

He was a handsome man, dark going grey, thin, with fine, strong hands; the face with its dark bright eyes looked sensitive, intelligent, and not unreasonably gloomy. He would do quite nicely on the cover of a Harlequin. We discussed the books I was buying; he had read three of them and was interested in knowing why I wanted the other two. This man was a book dealer because he liked books, a man after my own heart. His prices were fair, too. Five dollars for *Land of Little Rain* in good condition was, in fact, cheap.

Along about my third visit—I was controlling myself, allowing myself only two or three shelves a day—we got chatty over a biography of Fanny Burney. He was reading her diary unabridged; I had not read it for years. One thing leading to another, we went across the street to the Dancing Sand-Dab for lunch. He hung a sign that said BACK IN HALF AN HOUR on the door-knob. The sign was there a good deal of the time. "You need an assistant," I said.

"Who doesn't?" he said, and I tried to think of somebody who didn't need and wouldn't want an assistant; it was an interesting question. Even people who love their work as I do are glad to have assistants to do the dull bits, chop the celery, paint the background, file the correspondence. But I didn't feel I could offer him my unpaid expertise. I said, "Well, once you're well established, you'll find somebody."

At the notion of becoming well established, he looked gloomy. A secondhand bookstore in a town the size of Klatsand is a risky venture, and he had already realized that he would have been safer to set up shop in Summersea or Cannon Beach. The exceedingly low rent of the ex-kite shop had lured him. But he had been doing surprisingly well, he told me. I knew there were drop-in customers, and also some steadies besides me; Shirley had been there several times, and Virginia Herne had spent Saturday afternoon going through the shelves so methodically that I was sure she was finding treasures I had missed. He was not running behind his modest expectations. And while he was here he could be looking around for a likelier location. From the way he talked, it sounded as if he knew his trade. He knew where to go in the area to buy books, what to pay for them, and how to price them. He had worked some years, I gathered, for an estate buyer, and had made up his mind then to have a book-store on the coast. It was a romantic venture, but after all, he looked the part.

I had a little trouble in my mind concerning the Klatsand Library's ongoing sale of donated books. We always kept a bin full of culls and duplicates and grotty paperbacks, priced from a dime to a dollar, proceeds to the library. We made very little from the sale bin, but it seemed that it might undercut Antal's livelihood. When I mentioned it, he smiled a charming, good-natured smile and said, "Rival giant corporations locked in hostile takeover battle cause Wall Street panic."

"Well, I'll tell you if anything interesting ever comes through," I said. "Mostly it's computer handbooks and second-year French. But sometimes there's an actual book. We sell low, you sell high; we make a nickel, you make a nickel."

"We'll be arraigned for, what do you call it—not insider trading—when corporations collude, you know—"

Neither of us could at the moment think of the paradoxical word *trust*. This touched me, as he was no older than I, and shouldn't be forgetting words. We talked about forgetting words, and not being able to make introductions because of blocking names. Our crab sandwiches arrived. "How are things at the Ship Ahoy?" I asked.

As I tell this it sounds as if we were at ease together, which is untrue. I liked Antal and thought he liked me well enough, but we were both stiff. We were uneasy people. I was self-conscious about having lunch with him and about my unkempt hair, and afraid of boring him. I could tell he was self-conscious, too, whatever his reasons were, by the set of his body and the way his eyes flicked. I don't think there was much sexual tension in this general tension, certainly not on my part, since I go through the same strain with anybody I don't know well, including infants and toddlers. At least we seemed pretty well matched in both awkwardness and goodwill. And although he looked a bit like Heathcliff, he was really more a Mr. Rochester type, a conversable man. At my question, "How are things at the Ship Ahoy?" he laughed, put his hands in his hair, and said, "Well!"—the word saying, as they used to say, volumes.

"Sidonie calls it The Last Resort."

"Right," he said. "But Mrs. Tucket is a nice woman. And it's really not too bad—except the shower. . . . She can't make repairs or do anything, really, until her husband's will clears. He made some bank in Arizona his executor, and I think they're in cahoots with his first wife, from what she tells me. She didn't even know he'd made a will."

"He didn't leave his share in the motel to her?"

"Evidently not. She needs a competent lawyer on her side, but of course she can't afford one. She was talking about consulting Don Harton."

He was watching for my reaction and caught the wince, so I said, "Don Harton is a kind old man, but he's been retired a long time. I think people here sort of assume that anything Don does is going to take the rest of his life."

"Hardly what Rosemarie needs. She probably should sell out and get loose. But she talks about fixing the place up, if she gets anything from the will, or from the insurance settlement. What did happen to her husband, anyhow?"

"A man driving a heavy pickup drove into him in the driveway of the motel," I said, with some care.

Antal was quick; he picked up my tone and asked, "Intentionally?"

"Well, that's not clear. The man with the truck—he works out of Coos Bay—he'd been drinking, here in town, at the Two-Bit. Sidonie says he had a couple of beers and a boilermaker. He went back to the motel, he was staying there. The old man and he had had some kind of quarrel earlier, somebody told me over money, somebody else said it was about the Giants. What it sounds like—Rosemarie didn't see it happen, she was in the apartment—but it sounds like the truck driver started to leave, maybe without paying, and old Tucket tried to stop him from driving out of the driveway. And the man either didn't see him or did see him, but anyhow he drove straight into him. Maybe trying to intimidate him, or thought he'd get out of the way. But he didn't get out of the way. And the truck just pushed him down and went over him."

"Between the wheels?"

"Well, one leg got under the wheels. He died in Summersea Hospital that night."

"That's horrible," Antal said.

"Yes. I think he was a horrible old man," I said. "And the truck driver must be a horrible young man."

"But he's just getting away with it? He wasn't charged?"

"Nobody saw it happen. He says he didn't see the old man. I didn't realize how the . . . the law enforcement system works in places like this. Everybody knows everybody. And Mrs. Tucket didn't want to bring charges—or so they say. She's supposed to be contented if she gets the money coming to her from the truck driver's insurance, and doesn't want charges and a trial. Running a motel, of course, you can see why. But the insurance people are fighting paying anything, saying it was the old man's fault, he walked into the truck. Have you noticed this weird thing about whose fault things are, lately? Like all those children in Los Angeles who said they were abused by their teachers, and the jury said they were lying, and they had wasted the taxpayers' money, and so everybody is innocent, except these evil preschoolers?"

He did not respond to this, but said thoughtfully, "I'm glad to get the story straight. It's hard to ask Rosemarie directly. She pretty much avoids talking about it. I can see why."

"I'm sure she's glad to have you staying there. It's a kind of a dreary place."

"It's all right," he said. "It's not important to me where I stay. I travel light."

People mostly say these things—it's not important to me where I stay, I travel light, distrust occasions that require new clothes, etc.—out of mere puritan chic; they seldom have anything to do with how the person lives. Nobody who travels with books travels light. But, judging by the windows and floor of the bookshop, Antal was fairly tolerant of dirt, and judging by the window boxes, he was indifferent to amenity. Indeed he had never noticed and never did notice that there were window boxes under his shop window. He was a bookman, and what was important to him about where he stayed was that there be books there. We had done with the sordid little murder-mystery at the Ship Ahoy, and talked the rest of our lunchtime about Fanny Burney, Dean Swift, and a collection of early Oregoniana that Antal had discovered in Astoria and was hoping to buy.

Mysteries, however, if they're any good at all, do involve one in their plot.

I was in Hambleton's one afternoon when Antal came in. Mrs. Hambleton and Rose Ellen Sissel greeted him—"We are so proud of you!" (Rose Ellen, sweet) and "Well, here's the hero of the day" (Mrs. Hambleton, dry). When he came down the soft-drink and potato-chip aisle, I asked him what he had been up to. He looked pleased and uncomfortable. "Stupid thing last night at the motel," he said. Of course I pressed him to tell, and we ended up at Tom's, having a cup of coffee at the Seashell Booth. The tabletop of the front booth is a thick slab of translucent blue-green plastic with shells, corals, fan-sponges, and a tiny crab or two embedded in it. You look down into mysterious depths of plastic. All the tables were to be like that one, but the man who made it gave up after making the one, saying it was too much work. He took his payment in six-packs and grass, Tom says—this was back in the seventies—and went to Tillamook to sand-cast candles. His master-work is called the Seashell Booth at Tom's. So we sat

there, and I traced the dim fronds in the immobile cur-
rents while Antal told me the next chapter of the Motel
Mystery.

He had been down on the beach for a night walk.
Coming back to the Ship Ahoy, he saw a big pickup
standing on the drive in front of the office, and thought,
"Well, good, Rosemarie's got a customer," and headed
for his own unit, in front of which was parked his tiny
old Italian sports car (one of the distinctly romantic
aspects of Antal, hinting at some dolce vita behind him).
But something—"It was a mean-looking truck, you
know?" he said—made him turn and go across to the
office to check up on Rosemarie Tucket.

Two men in jeans jackets were standing at the office
counter. Again Antal's natural wish was to perceive the
scene as normal. But he saw that Rosemarie's head did
not turn when he came in. Only her eyes turned to him.
Immobile, she sent him one fierce glance and stared
back at the truckers.

One of them had his hand on the little princess
phone that Rosemarie kept out on the counter. His
hand was splayed out on the phone as if to squash it.
The other man, standing right beside him, had been
ringing the bell that also stood on the counter, one of
those small round bells you hit and it goes *ting!* to call
the proprietor. He had been hitting it rapidly and
repeatedly, and Antal now realized that he had heard
that faint, piercing *ting, ting, ting* from across the court.
It had ceased when he opened the office door. The
man's hand stayed poised above the bell as he and the
other trucker turned to stare at Antal.

"Big," Antal said, telling me. "Big, ugly. Big, ugly,
young."

The one with his hand on the telephone looked
back at Rosemarie Tucket and said, "OK, lady, you got
the message, OK?"

She still seemed paralyzed, Antal said, standing as

rigid as wood, but her voice came out deep and strong. "You get out of here," she said.

Antal said something on the order of "What's going on?" to Rosemarie. The trucker nearer him, the bell-ringer, looked him over again and said, "Everything's just fine. Come on," and headed straight for Antal, who was standing in the doorway. Antal stood aside with, as he said, "the natural courtesy of the rabbit," and the bell-ringer went out. The phone-squasher stood as if indecisive or unsatisfied. "You got the message, lady?" he said again to Rosemarie, and she said again, "You get out of here!"

"Sure," the man said in a sneering, false-laughing tone, "sure. We'll come back, though. Want to be sure you got the message." He turned and without looking at Antal walked out—bulldozed out, Antal said. The instant his hand was off the little phone, Rosemarie's hand shot out to it. "Get their license!" she hissed at Antal.

"I stood there," he told me. "I couldn't get my head in gear. They'd already gotten into their truck and started it up before I understood her. So then I ran out to try to get the license number, and they saw exactly what I was doing. They gunned the truck right at me, so I jumped back up on the office porch. Then one of them said something and they ran the thing—it was a big mother, one of those high-riding pickups—in reverse, right at my Fiat. I heard a sound like metal screaming. It was awful. Then they gunned forward again past me, and the one driving leaned out and yelled, 'Oh, hey, sorry about that!' and gave me a big grin and the finger, going by. And I couldn't read the goddamn license plate—it was all smeared up with dust and grease, and there's not much light there at the entrance. I was angry, that's really all I know, I was angry. I was in my car and the key in the ignition and out on the loop road, almost like I was watching somebody else doing it. The car ran fine. They'd just done a couple hundred dollars cosmetic repair type damage, Tim says, if he can get the headlight replaced. Anyhow, I caught up with them before they got back up to the highway."

As he told his story his dark face was bright, his dark eyes flashed.

"Oh, my God," I said, "you chased them? In that little car?"

He laughed again. "I tell you I wasn't thinking. Pure mindless rage. I was going to get that license number, that was absolutely all I had in my head. And I did. The funny thing was when they saw me coming up behind them in the Fiat, they took off—bucked that big thing up the curve onto 101 and lit out. No car duels. I guess it's easy to intimidate one old woman, but anybody else gets involved they get cold feet. Anyhow, at the light there at the curve, I got the number. So I hung a U and came back, and Rosemarie phoned it in to the sheriff's office. She'd called them the moment those guys were out of the office, and stayed on till I got back. Rosemarie is a cool lady."

"And not old," I said, which was a strange thing to say, but his calling her an old woman had stuck in me, somehow. I thought Rosemarie Tucket was probably in her fifties, like me, like Antal.

He merely nodded, not noticing, so that I could repair my omission quickly and say what I also felt—"But you were pretty cool yourself! To chase a truck with a Fiat—right after they'd used the truck as a weapon—and on that south loop where there aren't any lights and nobody ever comes—!"

"I wasn't thinking. It was a stupid thing to do," he said honestly, but he was honestly pleased with himself and with my praise.

Race, the sheriff, knew who the two men were, of course. Nothing visible was to be done. "It won't happen again," according to the deputy who had visited the Ship Ahoy in the morning. "We've talked to those boys," Race told Rosemarie on the telephone. She was apparently satisfied.

"I wouldn't be," I said to Antal when he told me this. I thought of being a woman alone, at night, in that sad place between the marshes and the dunes.

"Well, personally, I'd like to see them drawn and quartered," Antal said. "Tim thinks he may not be able to beat the fender out, and the nearest place he could get a replacement would probably be San Francisco, if he can get in touch with his friend in used Italian parts there. But Race assures me whatever it costs will come out of their insurance. Just consider it an accident, he says. Since taking it to court would be what he calls tarsome. And I don't intend to contradict the sheriff. But I have boyish daydreams. . . . I'd like to make life really tarsome for those two shits. . . . Why . . . ?"

He left it there, with a gesture of his open hands. Why do the bullies always get away with it? Might doesn't make right. It makes wrong. But he didn't bluster or whine about it. I admired Antal as much for his patience as for his courage. I said so. He looked at me across the blue-green depths of the Seashell Booth table, a long, shadowy, questioning look.

So it was that night that he came to dinner at my little house on Clark Street, and we drank a bottle and a half of the Barolo I had been keeping in the pantry for two years for an occasion, and we soon began, tentatively at first but then decisively, to make love.

He did not stay the night. There is the notoriety problem in Klatsand. And although we did not say so, we were both used to being alone. What he said was that he felt uneasy about leaving Rosemarie Tucket alone all night, and I did not try to talk him out of it. No doubt the thugs would not return so soon, if ever (and indeed

Race's deputy, Antal told me later, lurked in his old Ford on the loop road and the dunes road near the Ship Ahoy every night that week). But we agreed that Rosemarie should be able to depend on Antal. He left my house about one in the morning, with my copy of *Evalina*. I stood in my doorway and watched him walk off down Hemlock Street, for of course he was on foot till his Fiat could be repaired, and I felt the most wonderfully satisfying, warm, romantic love for him, a good man who had done a brave thing, my hero. He walked under the light of the streetlamp at the corner of Hemlock and Main, and on into the summer darkness. The sea made its long, long sound over the dunes. My heart was as full as a fifteen-year-old's. True love is truly beautiful.

Our true love lasted for several weeks, as long as summer. After that first night, what I remember with most pleasure is the evenings we spent in the bookstore. I now had the right to arrange his books, to sort and shelve, sometimes to evaluate. I started at it at once. Not every night, but at least twice a week, when he closed the store I would arrive with a picnic supper. He would provide the wine, not Barolo, but a nice, cheap Chianti or Frascati from Mrs. Hambleton's surprisingly savvy wine bin, and we would eat off the counter, and sort books, newly bought hopefuls and old unsalables, and read passages aloud to each other, and argue over books, and agree about books, and shelve books. Then we would go quietly to my house two blocks away in the long twilight of the summer night. Usually Antal would leave before the early twilight of the summer dawn.

Once instead of picnicking in the bookstore we took hotdogs down to the beach and made a driftwood fire and sat by it listening to the sea; but the next time we were back among the books, among the words, in our own element.

We never made love in the bookstore. Both of us would have found it unseemly.

Along in late August the weather came in from the northeast, making the sea in daylight flat blinding blue and the night sky heavy with great stars. I got the feeling I get at that time of year, as if I were looking back, seeing summer, bright and small, an island behind me, and looking forward to the cloudy, chartless seas of autumn. And my mood then is of wanting to be done with what's done. It was probably with that unconscious desire that I came out to visit Antal at the Ship Ahoy. I have often sought closure, not knowing that I'm doing so till I stand outside the door and see that I have shut it.

I had told him I was coming, of course. It was a Wednesday, which is a sort of secular Sunday in a beach town. I had thought we might walk down the beach to Wreck Point. But he was sitting out, with Rosemarie Tucket, in the marvelous, hot, sea-cooled sunlight. The motel garden was an oval of weedy gravel encircled by the driveway on which Bob Tucket had been run over and Antal's Fiat assaulted. There were two ratty old slat loungers and two plastic-coated chairs. Antal lounged and Rosemarie sat. I had not seen him before in dark glasses. He looked saturnine and Leonard Woolfish. Rosemarie looked her age, which, I soon realized from what she said about social security payments, was older than I had thought; she was over sixty. She dyed her hair, which always fools me. She was rather stocky, with a hard-bitten look, and a pleasant, commonplace, sensible manner. Her eyes were very light and clear, with a look in them that made me think of cowboys I used to know when I was growing up in Klamath Falls, of the way cowboys look past you.

Her business had been picking up, she said; she'd had "a good crowd" the last few weekends. A "nice family" was staying the week in Unit 3. (I was sitting in the lounger next to Antal, and saw him roll his eyes under the dark glasses.) She thought she could keep the place open and get by until the insurance settlements. After that she'd see. What would be wonderful would be if she could hire somebody to help her with the work and the repairs. There was a life insurance policy of Bob's he had told her was settled on her, and she was trying to find out about that, too. She spoke of these matters with a mixture of competence and wishfulness. She had that cowboy look, dreamy, as if she were looking a long way off, across deserts and mountains.

"All this stuff has kept me so busy," she said apologetically, "I haven't ever even been in Antal's store. I do like to read."

"I bring her anything with a spaceship on the cover," Antal said. She laughed and looked at him. A flush and thrill, a loosening and weakening and warmth came into me as I watched her, as if I felt my own desire; but it was not mine.

She asked us if we would like some lemonade, and went to her apartment behind the motel office to get it.

"What a nice woman," I said.

Antal nodded lazily.

Sunlight did not suit him as night and shadow did. He was sallow, and looked as if he needed dusting. He lounged in the lounge chair; what else can one do in a lounge chair? But he wore German health sandals over white socks, and there was a hole in the toe of one of the socks. There is a sort of self-assurance, a masculine carelessness of the body, which is lovable in the young because of their beauty; past youth, it becomes mere insolence and flaunting—beerbellies under unbuttoned florals, grey chest hair sticking through mesh singlets, toenails poking out of socks. Take me as I am! But why should I? What I want is hidden, is mysterious, is chaste—the shirt buttoned, the coat buttoned—shadows. There may be things amiss, grey hair, a lame leg, age and sorrow, who knows, blindness even, but such things are themselves shadows. Indeed my hero may have holes in his socks, may have holes in his shoes, may be barefoot; but he does not, in a lolling self-satisfaction, lie looking at the unshapely toenail that pokes out of the hole in his sock. Pride forbids him. The hero's quality is pride, not self-satisfaction. Pride relates to the other. Pride is Lucifer's relationship to God, and mine to my old age and death. I will not serve! says the proud devil, and I say I will not collude. So I looked away from Antal's toenail with anger. He had shamed me.

Rosemarie came out with a tray of glasses, ice, and bottles of a lemon-lime soda-pop. I looked at her to judge her pride. She wore slacks, stockings, low-heeled white sandals, a pale blue sleeveless blouse. She had dressed for us, for others. How dare he call her an old woman?

When she gave him the glass, I knew they had slept together. All the nights he hadn't slept with me? No, only some of them. She gave him the glass with a tenderness that went to my heart. I had no way to express to her what I felt, my tenderness towards her and passionate respect, my desire to laugh with her, to know her, to share her. I drank the sweet insipid fizz and smiled at Rosemarie. Between us lay Antal's legs, his white socks, his toenail.

"Do you like science fiction" I asked her, because all I can really talk about is books. And of course she couldn't talk about books. That had been knocked out of her years ago. We compromised on "Star Trek," new and old. She liked the new series as well as the old one, I liked the old one better. Antal stared, not at Rosemarie, only at me. "You watch it?" he said. "You watch *television?*"

I didn't answer. Books were all Antal and I had in

common, except a bit of sex and heroism. Whereas Rosemarie and I had everything in common, even Antal—everything except books. I was not going to let him try to shame us for our commonness.

"The one I liked best was the one where Mr. Spock had to go home because he was in heat," I said to her.

"Except he never, you know," she said. "They just had a fight over the girl, him and Captain Kirk, and then they left."

"That's his pride," I said, obscurely. I was thinking how Mr. Spock was never unbuttoned, never lolled, kept himself shadowy, unfulfilled; and so we loved him. And poor Captain Kirk, going from blonde to blonde, would never understand true love, would never even understand that he himself loved Mr. Spock truly, hopelessly, forever.

Rosemarie didn't try to answer. Antal, scornful of our media babble, lolled, eyes closed behind his dark glasses.

I sighed and said, "Only ten days—no, nine days—longer here, for me. I can't believe the summer's over," though I could and did.

"But you come back sometimes on holidays, don't you?" Rosemarie asked. "You're a teacher?"

"Yes. At the Library School."

"That's right, you work at the library, there in town, don't you," she said, as if town were miles away. She was marginal to the little seaside community, not part of it. She lived on the edge, always looking out towards the desert, the dry mountains. Marginal, proud, a cowboy. As we sat there in the sun and sipped our fizz, I knew that, for all we had in common, she and I would not become friends. Our ways led apart. The desert was between us. That made me sad. I wished that instead of talking, to her or to Antal, whose gloom at the moment seemed mere petulance, I could sit there quietly and read a book. So presently I said, "Well," and got up, and took my leave. I walked back along the sandy road into town, and sat out in the tiny back garden of my house, and read a book till twilight.

Sleepwalkers

John Felburne

I told the maid not to come to clean the cabin before four o'clock, when I go running. I explained that I'm a night person and write late and sleep in, mornings. Somehow it came out that I'm writing a play. She said, "A stage play?" I said yes, and she said, "I saw one of those once." What a wonderful line. It was some high school production, it turned out, some musical. I told her mine was a rather different kind of play, but she didn't ask about it. And actually there would be no way to explain to that sort of woman what I write about. Her life experience is so incredibly limited. Living out here, cleaning rooms, going home and watching TV— *Jeopardy* probably. I thought of trying to put her in my characters notebook and got as far as "Ava: the Maid," and then there was nothing to write. It would be like trying to describe a glass of water. She's what people who say "nice" mean when they say, "She's nice." She'd be completely impossible in a play, because she never does or says anything but what everybody else does and says. She talks in clichés. She is a cliché. Forty or so, middle-sized, heavy around the hips, pale, not very good complexion, blondish—half the white women in America look like that. Pressed out of a mold, made with a cookie cutter. I run for an hour, hour and a half, while she's cleaning the cabin, and I was thinking, she'd never do anything like running, probably doesn't do any exercise at all. People like that don't take any control over their lives. People like her in a town like this live a mass-produced existence, stereotypes, getting their ideas from the TV. Sleepwalkers. That would make a good title, *Sleepwalkers*. But how could you write meaningfully about a person who's totally predictable? Even the sex would be boring.

There's a woman in the creekside cabin this week. When I jog down to the beach, afternoons, she watches me. I asked Ava about her. She said she's Mrs. McAn, comes every summer for a month. Ava said, "She's very nice," of course. McAn has rather good legs. But old.

Katharine McAn

If I had an air gun I could hide on my deck and pop that young man one on the buttock when he comes pumping past in his little purple stretchies. He eyes me.

I saw Virginia Herne in Hambleton's today. Told her the place was turning into a goddamn writers colony, with her collecting all these Pulitzers or whatever they are, and that young man in the shingled cabin sitting at his computer till four in the morning. It's so quiet at the Hideaway that I can hear the thing clicking and peeping all night. "Maybe he's a very diligent accountant," Virginia said. "Not in shiny purple stretch shorts," I said. She said, "Oh, that's John" Somebody, "yes, he's had a play produced, in the East somewhere, he told me." I said, "What's he doing here, sitting at your feet?" and she said, "No, he told me he needed to escape the pressures of culture, so he's spending a summer in the West." Virginia looks very well. She has that dark, sidelong flash in her eye. A dangerous woman, mild as milk. "How's Ava?" she asked. Ava house-sat her place up on Breton Head last summer when she and Jaye were traveling, and she takes an interest in her, though she doesn't know the story Ava told me. I said Ava was doing all right.

I think she is, in fact. She still walks carefully, though. Maybe that's what Virginia saw. Ava walks like a tai ji walker, like a woman on a high wire. One foot directly in front of the other, and never any sudden movements.

I had tea ready when she knocked, my first morning here. We sat at the table in the kitchen nook, just like the other summers, and talked. Mostly about Jason. He's in tenth grade now, plays baseball, skateboards, surfboards, crazy to get one of those windsail things and go up to Hood River—"Guess the ocean isn't enough for him," Ava said. Her voice is without color, speaking of him. My guess is that the boy is like his father, physically at least, and that troubles or repels her, though she clings to him loyally, cleaves to him. And there might be a jealousy of him as the survivor: *Why you, and not her?* I don't know what Jason knows or feels about all that. The little I've seen of him when he comes by here, he seems a sweet boy, caught up in these sports boys spend themselves on, I suppose because at least they involve doing something well.

Ava and I always have to re-agree on what work she's to do when I'm here. She claims if she doesn't vacuum twice a week and take out the trash, Mr. Shoto will "get after" her. I doubt he would, but it's her job and her conscience. So she's to do that, and look in every day or so to see if I need anything. Or to have a cup of tea with me. She likes Earl Grey.

Ken Shoto

She's reliable. I told Deb at breakfast, you don't know how lucky we are. The Brinnesis have to hire anything they can pick up, high school girls that don't know how to make a bed and won't learn, ethnics that can't talk the language and move on just when you've got them trained. After all, who wants a job cleaning motel rooms? Only somebody who hasn't enough education or self-respect to find something better. Ava wouldn't have kept at it if I treated her the way the Brinnesis treat their maids, either. I knew right away we were in luck with this one. She knows how to clean and she'll work for a dollar over minimum wage. So why shouldn't I treat her like one of us? After four years? If she wants to clean one cabin at seven in the morning and another one at four in the afternoon, that's her business. She works it out with the customers. I don't interfere. I don't push her. "Get off Ava's case, Deb," I told her this morning. "She's reliable, she's honest, and she's permanent—she's got that boy in the high school here. What more do you want? I tell you, she takes half the load off my back!"

"I suppose you think *I* ought to be running after her supervising her," Deb says. God, she can drive me crazy sometimes. What did she say that for? I wasn't blaming her for anything.

"She doesn't need supervising," I said.

"So you think," Deb said.

"Well, what's she done wrong?"

"Done? Oh, nothing. She couldn't do anything wrong!"

I don't know why she has to talk like that. She couldn't be jealous, not of Ava, my God. Ava's all right looking, got all her parts, but hell, she doesn't let you see her that way. Some women just don't. They just don't give the signals. I can't even think about thinking about her that way. Can't Deb see that? So what the hell does she have against Ava? I always thought she liked her OK.

"She's sneaky," is all she'd say. "Creepy."

I told her, "Aw, come on, Deb. She's quiet. Maybe not extra bright. I don't know. She isn't talkative. Some people aren't."

"I'd like to have a woman around who could say more than two words. Stuck in the woods out here."

"Seems like you spend all day in town anyhow," I said, not meaning it to be a criticism. It's just the fact. And why shouldn't she? I didn't take on this place to work my wife to death, or tie her down to it. I manage it and keep it up, and Ava Evans cleans the cabins, and Deb's free to do just what she wants to do. That's how I meant it to be. But it's like it's not enough, or she doesn't believe it, or something. "Well," she said, "if *I* had any responsibility, I wonder if you'd find *me* reliable." It is terrible how she cuts herself down. I wish I knew how to stop her from cutting herself down.

Deb Shoto

It's the demon that speaks. Ken doesn't know how it got into me. How can I tell him? If I tell him, it will kill me from inside.

But it knows that woman, Ava. She looks so mild and quiet, *yes Mrs. Shoto, sure Mrs. Shoto,* pussyfooting it around here with her buckets and mops and brooms and wastebaskets. She's hiding. I know when a woman is hiding. The demon knows it. It found me. It'll find her.

There isn't any use trying to get away. I have thought I ought to tell her that. Once they put the demon inside you, it never goes away. It's instead of being pregnant.

She has that son, so it must have happened to her later, it must have been her husband.

I wouldn't have married Ken if I'd known it was in

me. But it only began speaking last year. When I had the cysts and the doctor thought they were cancer. Then I knew they had been put inside me. Then when they weren't cancerous, and Ken was so happy, it began moving inside me where they had been, and then it began saying things to me, and now it says things in my voice. Ken knows it's there, but he doesn't know how it got there. Ken knows so much, he knows how to live, he lives for me, he is my life. But I can't talk to him. I can't say anything before it comes into my mouth just like my own tongue and says things. And what it says hurts Ken. But I don't know what to do. So he leaves, with his heavy walk and his mouth pulled down, and goes to his work. He works all the time, but he's getting fat. He shouldn't eat so much cholesterol. But he says he always has. I don't know what to do.

I need to talk to somebody. It doesn't talk to women, so I can. I wish I could talk to Mrs. McAn. But she's snobbish. College people are snobbish. She talks so quick, and her eyebrows move. Nobody like that would understand. She'd think I was crazy. I'm not crazy. There is a demon in me. I didn't put it there.

I could talk to the girl in the A-frame cabin. But she is so young. And they drive away every day in their pickup truck. And they are college people, too.

There is a woman comes into Hambleton's, a grand-mother. Mrs. Inman. She looks kind. I wish I could talk to her.

Linsey Hartz

The people here in Hannah's Hideaway are so weird, I can't believe them. The Shotos. Wow. He's really sweet, but he goes around this place all day digging in the little channel he's cut from the creek to run through the grounds, a sort of toy creek, and weeding, and pruning, and raking, and the other afternoon when we came home he was picking up spruce needles off the path, like a housewife would pick threads off a carpet. And there's the little bridges over the little toy creek, and the rocks along the edges of the little paths between the cabins. He rearranges the rocks every day. Getting them lined up even, getting the sizes matched.

Mrs. Shoto watches him out her kitchen window. Or she gets in her car and drives one quarter mile into town and shops for five hours and comes back with a quart of milk. With her tight, sour mouth closed. She hates to smile. Smiling is a big production for her, she works hard at it, probably has to rest for an hour afterwards.

Then there's Mrs. McAn, who comes every summer and knows everybody and goes to bed at nine p.m. and gets up at five a.m. and does Chinese exercises on her porch and meditates on her roof. She gets onto the roof from the roof of her deck. She gets onto the roof of the deck from the window of the cabin.

And then there's Mr. Preppie, who goes to bed at five a.m. and gets up at three p.m. and doesn't mingle with the aborigines. He communicates only with his computer, and his modems, no doubt, and probably he has a fax in there. He runs on the beach every day at four, when the most people are on the beach, so that they can all see his purple spandex and his muscley legs and his hundred-and-forty-dollar running shoes.

And then there's me and George going off every day to secretly map where the Forest Service and the lumber companies are secretly cutting old growth stands illegally in the Coast Range so that we can write an article about it that nobody will publish even secretly.

Three obsessive-compulsives, one egomaniac, and two paranoids.

The only normal person at Hannah's Hideaway is the maid, Ava. She just comes and says "Hi," and "Do you need towels?" and she vacuums while we're out logger-stalking, and generally acts like a regular human being. I asked her if she was from around here. She said she'd lived here several years. Her son's in the high school. "It's a nice town," she said. There's something very clear about her face, something pure and innocent, like water. This is the kind of person we paranoids would be saving the forests for, if we were. Anyhow, thank goodness there are still some people who aren't totally fucked up.

Katharine McAn

I asked Ava if she thought she'd stay on here at the Hideaway.

She said she guessed so.

"You could get a better job," I said.

"Yeah, I guess so," she said.

"Pleasanter work."

"Mr. Shoto is a really nice man."

"But Mrs. Shoto—"

"She's all right," Ava said earnestly. "She can be hard on him sometimes, but she never takes it out on me. I think she's a really nice person, but—"

"But?"

She made a slow, dignified gesture with her open hand: I don't know, who knows, it's not her fault, we're all in the same boat. "I get on OK with her," she said.

"You get on OK with anybody. You could get a better job, Ava."

"I got no skills, Mrs. McAn. I was brought up to be a wife. Where I lived in Utah, women are wifes." She pronounced it with the *f*, wifes. "So I know how to do this kind of job, cleaning and stuff. Anyhow."

I felt I had been disrespectful of her work. "I guess I just wish you could get better pay," I said.

"I'm going to ask Mr. Shoto for a raise at Thanksgiving," she said, her eyes bright. Obviously it was a long-thought-out plan. "He'll give it to me." Her smile is brief, never lingering on her mouth.

"Do you want Jason to go on to college?"

"If he wants to," she said vaguely. The idea troubled her. She winced away from it. Any idea of leaving Klatsand, of even Jason's going out into a larger world, scares her, probably will always scare her.

"There's no danger, Ava," I said very gently. It is painful to me to see her fear, and I always try to avoid pain. I want her to realize that she is free.

"I know," she said with a quick, deep breath, and again the wincing movement.

"Nobody's after you. They never were. It was a suicide. You showed me the clipping."

"I burned that," she said.

LOCAL MAN SHOOTS, KILLS DAUGHTER, SELF

She had showed the newspaper clipping to me summer before last. I could see it in my mind's eye with extreme clarity.

"It was the most natural thing in the world for you to move away. It wasn't 'suspicious.' You don't have to hide, Ava. There's nothing to hide from."

"I know," she said.

She believes I know what I'm talking about. She accepts what I say, she believes me, as well as she can. And I believe her. All she told me I accepted as the truth. How do I know it's true? Simply on her word, and a newspaper clipping that might have been nothing but the seed of a fantasy? Certainly I have never known any truth in my life like it.

Weeding the vegetable garden behind their house in Indo, Utah, she heard a shot, and came in the back door and through the kitchen to the front room. Her husband was sitting in his armchair. Their twelve-year-old daughter Dawn was lying on the rug in front of the TV set. Ava stood in the doorway and asked a question, she doesn't remember what she asked, "What happened?" or

"What's wrong?" Her husband said, "I punished her. She has polluted me." Ava went to her daughter and saw that she was naked and that her head had been beaten in and that she had been shot in the chest. The shotgun was on the coffee table. She picked it up. The stock was slimy. "I guess I was afraid of him," she said to me. "I don't know why I picked it up. Then he said, 'Put that down.' And I backed off towards the front door with it, and he got up. I cocked it, but he came towards me. I shot him. He fell down forwards, practically onto me. I put the gun down on the floor near his head, just inside the door. I went out and went down the road. I knew Jason would be coming home from baseball practice and I wanted to keep him out of the house. I met him on the road, and we went to Mrs.—" She halted herself, as if her neighbor's name must not be spoken—"to a neighbor's house, and they called the police and the ambulance." She recited the story quietly. "They all thought it was a murder and suicide. I didn't say anything."

"Of course not," I murmured, dry of tongue.

"I did shoot him," she said, looking up at me, as if to make certain that I understood. I nodded.

She never told me his name, or their married name. Evans was her middle name, she said.

Immediately after the double funeral, she asked a neighbor to drive her and Jason to the nearest town where there was an Amtrak station. She had taken all the cash her husband had kept buried in the cellar under their stockpile of supplies in case of nuclear war or a Communist takeover. She bought two coach seats on the next train west. It went to Portland. At first sight she knew Portland was "too big," she said. There was a Coast Counties bus waiting at the Greyhound station down the street from the train station. She asked the driver, "Where does this bus go?" and he named off the little coast towns on his loop. "I picked the one that sounded farthest," she said.

She and ten-year-old Jason arrived in Klatsand as the summer evening was growing dark. The White Gull Motel was full, and Mrs. Brinnesi sent her to Hannah's Hideaway.

"Mrs. Shoto was nice," Ava said. "She didn't say anything about us coming in on foot or anything. It was dark when we got here. I couldn't believe it was a motel. I couldn't see anything but the trees, like a forest. She just said, 'Well, that young man looks worn out,' and she put us in the A-frame, it was the only one empty. She helped me with the rollabed for Jason. She was really nice." She wanted to linger on these details of finding haven. "And next morning I went to the office and asked if they knew anyplace where I could find work, and Mr. Shoto said they needed a full-time maid. It was like they were waiting for me," she said in her earnest way, looking up at me.

Don't question the Providence that offers shelter. Was it also Providence that put the gun in her hand? Or in his?

She and Jason have a little apartment, an add-on to the Hanningers' house on Clark Street. I imagine that she keeps a photograph of her daughter Dawn in her room. A framed five-by-seven school picture, a smiling seventh-grader. Maybe not. I should not imagine anything about Ava Evans. This is not ground for imagination. I should not imagine the child's corpse on the rug between the coffee table and the TV set. I should not have to imagine it. Ava should not have to remember it. Why do I want her to get a better job, nicer work, higher wages— what am I talking about? The pursuit of happiness?

"I have to go clean Mr. Felburne's cabin," she said. "The tea was delicious."

"Now? But you're off at three, aren't you?"

"Oh, he keeps funny hours. He asked me not to come and clean till after four."

"So you have to wait around here an hour? The

nerve!" I said. Indignation, the great middle-class luxury. "So he can go *running?* I'd tell him to go jump in the creek!" Would I? If I was the maid?

She thanked me again for the tea. "I really enjoy talking with you," she said. And she went down the neatly raked path that winds between the cabins, among the dark old spruce trees, walking carefully, one foot in front of the other. No sudden movements.

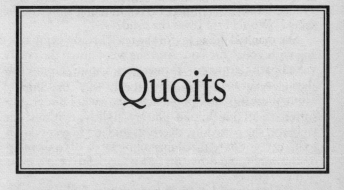

Quoits

The days after Barbara's death had not been a period of time but a place of a certain shape, a place where Shirley had to crouch down and hold still because it was the only thing to do.

On the day of the memorial service she had begun to be able to stop crouching. She found that she was with Angus and Jen, Barbara's children. But since Barbara was not there, she did not know what her relationship with them was or ought to be. Angus had behaved as a son; of course he was a son, Barbara's son—but not her son. But kind, quietly and efficiently kind, unhesitating. And now, the day after the service, he was going.

Shirley had only threadbare words. "I don't know what I would have done without you."

He had something to say, and said it: "My father should have come to the service."

"Oh—well—" In fact Shirley was glad Dan hadn't been there; but Angus was right.

"Daddy doesn't come. Daddy has back spasms," said Jen, predictably savage. "You graduate from law school, he has a back spasm. I graduate from law school, he has a back spasm. He won't come to his own funeral. Just can't move, terrible pain, you'd better bury somebody else!"

"I'm sorry he wasn't there," Angus said, direct, severe.

He kissed his sister, putting his arm around her shoulders in a reassuring, brotherly way that Shirley found pleasant, though Jen's angularity did not visibly soften to it. He kissed Shirley lightly, without an embrace; she patted his tweed shoulder. He went down to his car, got in, glanced unsmiling farewell to them up on the porch, and drove off down Clark Street in a spurt of dusty gravel.

"What a good man. A proper man," Shirley said, watching the breeze from the northwest blow the dust in a golden haze onto the Hanningers' geraniums.

"You aren't supposed to say that."

Alarmed and discomfited, a trespasser, Shirley said nothing.

Jen, who usually stooped, stood puffed up, speaking in a slow, gobbling voice: "You hate men. You want men castrated." Jen was doing an imitation of her father, Shirley realized as she went on, "Better yet, abort 'em all," in Dan McDermid's gobbling, pompous voice, but crying at the same time. Shirley looked away at once, more dismayed than ever.

"I think Angus looks like Gary Cooper," she said.

Jen said nothing, and Shirley wondered if she knew who Gary Cooper was. All the names had changed, and nobody knew the ones she knew. Since they moved to Klatsand five years ago, she and Barbara had seen no movies and watched nothing on television except what Barbara called *MacNeill and Lacey,* and had got out of touch; but surely Sean Connery was not an old man, and when she had mentioned Sean Connery the other day to little Chelsea Houk in the bakery, the girl had looked quite blank. But then, she generally looked blank, faced with anybody over twenty. Jen was going on crying, silently, so Shirley had to go on talking, trying to save face for both of them, and to hide the fact that they were afraid to touch each other.

"Angus is moral, too, the way Gary Cooper was," she said. "I mean in his movies, I suppose he was just a movie star really. But that kind of moral vulnerability. Just the opposite of all that digging in and resisting, that moral armament sort of thing. It's like rock, but it's exposed—vulnerable. What my grandmother called 'character.' People don't seem to use that word any more, do they?"

It wouldn't do. Jen continued proudly strangling sobs. Shirley set her jaw, turned to Jen, and patted the thin shoulder, muttering, "It's all right," while Jen stood rigid with resistance, gasping, "It's all right!"

In desperation, Shirley went down the two steps into the yard and began to pull up pigweed.

She wished Jen would go too, go soon. They had no comfort for each other. She was all right now, she could stand up, and she wanted to eat when she wanted to eat, and to go down to the beach alone, not leaving Jen in the house alone.

The strip of ground between the porch and the wobbly paling fence was hardly wide enough to kneel in, crammed with the fits and starts of Barbara's gardening, impatiens, lobelia, roses, tigerlilies throttled in pigweed. Shirley got down on her knees to free the lilies. As soon as her hands touched the sandy dirt, the image of the stones in Cornwall came back into her mind. She knew then that that image had been there all along, all week, that it was what she had seen listening to Barbara's long, loud, widely spaced last breaths, and that now it was the image of herself, the shape she was in her soul.

Three slabs of uncut granite, a roof weighing down on two parallel walls. Earth had been piled over that stone house, a great mound of dirt. It had blown away over the centuries like the dust from the wheels of Angus's Honda, a haze of dust in the long autumn light, in the sea-wind. Nothing was left but the stone slab walls, the stone slab roof, the wind blowing through.

She and Barbara had seen the stone places on their two-week walking tour of Dorset and Cornwall—their honeymoon, Barbara had called it once but only once, after which they had agreed not to use the wrong names just because there were no right ones. They had entered together under the roof, crouching down, between the walls. Now with her hands on the dirt she saw and felt the quality of that sea-wind, that other sunlight, and was aware of the shadow inside the walls of weathered stone leaning inward to the roof, a cold, clear darkness. The floor was dirt. They were graves, those places. Quoits, they were called, in Cornwall. They stood about on the worn slopes of the hills over the sea. They were not single graves. They had had a door, a fourth stone, pivoted; it remained on some of them. By that door, time after time, the dead had gone in and the living had come out. Like Romeo and Juliet, and Tybalt lying there keeping them company under his sheets and cerements, and older bones of older Capulets, companionable. Death used to be not a hole but a house.

There has to be some kind of companionship, Shirley thought.

Angus was probably Jen's truest companion. Her mother dead, her father a bully, her husband remarried, no kids—unless there was somebody she didn't talk about, what companion had she? With all the moving about and the breakdown of family and then of course incest being so fashionable, people didn't talk much about being brother and sister; yet Jen might well weep when her brother left.

As she rooted after a rosette thistle, Shirley thought of her own brother, Dodds. Dodds had been an insurance agent of thirty-five when hippies were invented, but he knew his hour when it came. He had put on a headband and gone to play drums and be communal in northern Maine. There he still was, Buddha-faced and beaded, drumming and farming, in his sixties, with five or was it six adopted children and a variable number of wives, or whatever they were. He raised potatoes and read *Black Elk Speaks*. Angus had called Dodds. Angus had done all that should be done, those first two days when Shirley had crouched on the floor or bed and could not talk for the great weight she bore. After she had come back out, Dodds had called twice from a pay phone in his village, with other voices faint on the crackling, roaring line, as if he were calling not only across the continent but across decades. He told Shirley to come stay on the farm as long as she liked. And she would do that. She would go be with her brother for a while. But she had to walk on the beach first, and in winter, in the dark days when you could not stand straight against the wind.

The thistle had tangled its tough roots with those of a rose. *Out of her grave there grew a rose, and out of hers a briar.* Had she done what should be done, like Angus? She need not crouch now to know the clear dark place, the shape of it. She looked up to the porch. Jen had gone indoors. The sun was cooling down in a bank of bright fog. Warmth drained out of the day like water from a tub. I kept the vigil the night she died. I called her children in the morning and they came. Then when I could come back out, the phone calls; and the notice in the papers; and the cremation and the service; and then we came back here; and wrote letters; and people called; and now. Now Angus has gone. Jen will go. Then it will all be done, won't it? And I will be alone in the house. Is there something I left out? She was sure she had omitted something, some act or obligation, but she knew also that the omission was Barbara. Barbara was what was left out, so nothing done could be complete.

Barbara's daughter had gone into the house in tears. Coward Shirley had deserted her for pigweed and thistles. She had not done what should be done. They must weep together if need be. *They twined into a true lovers' knot, for all men to admire.* She hurried up onto the porch, beating dirt from her hands, and into the house. Jen was sitting on the sofa reading the newspaper indignantly. "Judge Stevens has taken himself *out* of the case? What's *his* excuse? Back spasms? Jesus H!" Jen's vocabulary of expletives was curious; probably she had got Jesus H and Jehosaphat from her father, but Lordy Dordy was, as the *OED* would say, of unknown origin. She said it now, skipping to another column. "Lordy Dordy! what has *happened* to the Brits? If Thatcher proposed privatizing the *air,* would they all say, *Euh, how ebsolyutely syupah,* and vote for it? Privatizing water! Jesus H!"

"It is a funny word," Shirley said, much relieved by Jen's wrath. "Barbara had to explain it to me. I mean that the private sector just means business. And then the opposite of privatize ought to be publicize, but it isn't— what is it? Socialize, I guess. But nothing gets socialized anymore, does it? Except little kids in preschools."

"Socialism? Gone the way of character," Jen growled, flapping the paper around to get at the comics.

Shirley appreciated the reference. Jen was a noticer, like Barbara. But not like her, not like her at all. It was comforting to see Barbara in Angus; it was painful not to see her in Jen, to be reminded of her absence by her absence. A hole, to be talked around, not to fall into. Crouch solid, be steady, like the stone quoit, stone on earth and stone on stone, the hollow not under but within. "Wrong opposites bother me," she said, sitting down in her chair, finding that she was stiff-legged and weary. "All the pedantry I couldn't use when I was teaching takes its revenge on me. Non-opposites are even worse. When there isn't one. Like what would it be, *masculism? Hominism?*"

"Sounds like something you'd get for breakfast in Alabama."

"And a good thing too," Shirley replied darkly.

They were silent while Jen studied the funnies with the same aggressive intensity she brought to the front page. "Hah!" she said once, scornful, but did not explain.

Since she had her long-distance glasses on, Shirley tried to read Ann Landers on the back sheet of the paper as Jen held it up only the width of Barbara's little Bokhara away; but she couldn't quite get it into focus. It looked like one of those terrible poems that people were always, or so Ann Landers claimed, begging her to reprint, instead of something interesting, anyway.

"Friday," Jen said from the city desk of a newspaper in California, only it was on the edge of a forest in the twilight, something about owls.

"What?"

Jen was gazing at her over the downfolded newspaper with clear, piercing, light brown eyes. Shirley was ashamed of falling asleep and could not rid herself of the owls that stared at her through Jen's eyes.

"I said I thought I'd go back to Salem on Friday. Unless you'd like me to stay longer. Senator Bombast says I can have all next week if I want it. Or unless you want me to go sooner. I can go tomorrow. The stare continued.

"No, no," Shirley said feebly. "Whatever."

"One day will be enough to clear up whatever it is you wanted to do?"

"Oh, yes. Everything's really done. Both of you being lawyers."

"Mother had everything in order," Jen said, dry.

"It's only some little things."

"What things?"

"If you wanted them."

"Everything is yours, Shirley."

"The jewelry. And oh, this rug. And anything else—"

"She left it to you," Jen said, and Shirley felt accused, not of greed, but of cowardice.

"You ought to have some things of hers. And I can't—" Shirley held out her hand. The heavy silver ring Barbara had bought her in New Mexico was twisted on her thin, large-knuckled finger; she straightened it. "I can't wear her pieces. This, yes."

"Sell them."

"Only if you won't take them. I don't want to."

Jen drew in her breath and nodded.

"Shoes," Shirley said. "You wear eights."

Jen nodded again, morose. "I'll look at them."

"Clothes."

"I'll help you pack them up."

"What for?"

"The Women's Shelter in Portland, if you haven't got somebody here you want to give them to. I've done pro bono for them. They're effective."

Good for you! Shirley thought, seeing Jen's amber stare now as hawk not owl, the decisiveness of the day-light predator.

"Good," she said aloud.

"Anything else like that?"

"Well, anything of hers you might want. It was just that I couldn't do it while Angus was here. I was afraid he would think it was heartless—dividing the spoils—you know?"

Jen shifted her angular, spare body restlessly on the sofa. "Women should do deaths," she said. "Undertakers ought to be women. Just like midwives. Men have too many hormones and attitudes. I hated for men to touch Mother's body. Even as little as they did. I could only bear it because they were strangers. Paid. But if we could have done it, you and me—that would have been right. Appropriate. But not Angus. That wouldn't. It should be women's hands."

Shirley was taken aback. She felt an immediate agreement with Jen's idea, what Barbara called a visceral yes. But she did not like her saying *I hated for men to touch Mother's body*—it sounded glib, theatrical. Some things were truly better left unsaid, which was maybe why women should be the undertakers; or maybe not. A vague image from Dickens was in her mind, old women around a corpse, gambling—for Scrooge's bed sheets, was it? or his winding sheets, his cerements? Bed curtains, dark, wrinkled, like the weathered granite, sheltering. Old women cackling, gambling, heartless, appropriate.

"Another thing," Jen said, and Shirley found herself shrinking a little, the rabbit from the hawk—"I *hated* the thing in the paper."

"Oh. I'm sorry. I thought—"

"No, no, what you told them was fine. But what they did with it! The 'survived by' business—'Survived by a son in Portland, a daughter in Salem, and two grandsons.' Jesus H! Come *on!*"

Shirley stalled, trying to see what was tasteless or aberrant.

"What about you?" Jen demanded. "Why can't they say it?"

"Say what?"

"'Survived by her lover, Shirley Bauer.'"

"Because I'm not. I never was."

Now Jen was the daylight owl, round eyes staring unfocused.

Shirley stood up, feeling the awful electricity gather in her veins. "I wasn't her lover. She wasn't my lover. I hate, we hated, we hated that—that stupid word—'My lover!'" she crooned. "It doesn't mean love. It only means sex, an 'affair,' a liaison, it's a dirty, sniggering, sniveling word. I never was Barbara's 'lover.' Spare me that!"

After a pause Jen said gamely, though in a small, questioning tone, "Friend?"

"Spare me the euphemisms, too," Shirley said with some grandeur.

"Well," Jen said, and found no word to say, though evidently she was running through a series of them, discarding one after the other. Shirley watched her, sardonic.

"You see?" she said. "There aren't any words that mean anything. For us. For any of us. We can't say who we are. Even men can't any more. Did the paper say she was survived by her ex-husband? What about the man she lived with before she met your father, what's his label? We don't have words for what we do! Wife, husband, lover, ex, post, step, it's all leftovers, words from some other civilization, nothing to do with us. Nothing means anything but the proper names. You can say Barbara was survived by Shirley. That's all you can say."

She strode around the small room, setting items straight on table and bookcase, lightning still flowing through her, buzzing in her fingertips.

"Daughter can mean something," she said, snapping off a wilted chrysanthemum from the flowers Mrs. Inman had sent. "Son. Brother, sister. They're still worth saying. Sometimes."

"Mother," Jen said, in a voice so soft and uncertain that Shirley thought for a moment Jen was addressing her, before she understood and nodded. She was wondering if Jen would add father, when Jen cleared her throat and spoke again: "I thought at first you were saying that you and Mother, that you weren't—and I thought, I'll never forgive them!"

"Why not?" Shirley demanded, with her last unused scrap of indignation. "What's wrong with friendship?"

"Come on," Jen said, contemptuous. "You said yourself. Anyhow, what about me? Reading *Off Our Backs* and everything? All that enlightenment wasted?"

Shirley stood looking at her, and laughed. "Why, you are like her!"

Jen shook her head. "Angus is."

"All right, then, tell me," Shirley said, knowing she might transgress, but reckless, "do you know what Angus thinks, what he thought about it, about us?"

Jen went the least bit guarded. She was, after all, a lawyer. "He saw that Mother was happy," she said slowly but without apparent effort to select or invent, "and that you were nice. And respectable. Respectability matters to him."

"It did to Barbara."

"He borrowed my Adrienne Rich. But he gave it back. He said it worried him. But you didn't."

"Yes and no, maybe?"

Jen did not reject the qualification. After thinking, she added, "Angus doesn't seem to need to name things, the way I do. I wish I didn't, but I do."

"It's a hard habit to quit," Shirley said, and was suddenly so tired that she had to sit down, flop down, thump down in the armchair, all lightning spent, the respect and liking she felt for Jen puddling into sodden weariness. "Oh, what shall we do for dinner?" she said wretchedly, and thin Jen said, as she feared she would say, "I'm not hungry." She never was.

At seven-thirty, after a glass of red wine, Jen fixed them bacon and eggs.

The next day, Thursday, they "went through" Barbara's jewelry, shoes, clothes, and few pieces of furniture: the rug, the two carved chairs, the old typewriter and the new lap-computer, the immobile Volvo. Shirley had "gone through" her father's and her mother's things and knew how poor the belongings of the dead are, how little worth. She knew what Jen felt handling the odd, old, ill-kept bits of Navajo silver and Baltic amber and Florentine filigree that she had believed to be, and that had been, so long as Barbara wore them, fine and desirable. She thought of thieves rifling the hollow quoits as the earth slipped away from the granite, letting in sunlight on entangled bones, a necklace of broken amber, a twist of Cornish tin, poor gauds. She thought of the strangers in the hollow place.

On Friday at noon Jen left, fierce and tearful.

On Friday evening at last Shirley walked down Cedar Street and across Searoad to the beach, for the first walk without Barbara. Not the first alone, of course. Often each had walked alone, sometimes in a fury with the other, mostly because the other was busy or lazy or not in a walking mood. But the first walk for seven years without Barbara.

Her dinner was on the stove ready to be heated up. While setting it out she had drunk a small glass of the red wine Jen had opened, but she would eat after the walk, for sunset now in mid-October was about six-thirty, and she did not want to miss it. The wine helped a bit, but she had worked herself up for too long about the walk, and was shaky and grim as she went through the dunes. The path through them from the end of Cedar Street was almost a tunnel, the harsh dune grass meeting overhead, then opening suddenly onto the light above the sea. A fogbank on the horizon and the long clouds lying above it were a color she had never seen in the thousand or so sunsets she had watched from this beach: a greyish mauve or lilac, dull, a heavy color, but immensely quiet and splendid between the pale green of the sky and the shining, colorless water.

She trudged down to the breakers, a long way, for the tide was out. Long waves ran easily up the dun sand, and running back down left a wide rippled stretch of wet that picked up the color of the sky and intensified it to a clear jade streaked with dark lilac: colors so beautiful Shirley could not take her eyes from them. She stood with her shoes sinking in the wet sand, the color all around her, and tried to gaze her fill. She was eating the color, devouring it, she craved it, even while she was thinking that they would call such a craving soft, fanciful, unreal, denying that grief was a hollow that must be filled with the food that came to hand. They don't know what people live on! she thought. And I don't even know who they are, she thought; but she did know; they were the givers of wrong names.

She turned, the colors sliding and shining about her on the sand, and started south. She walked only half a mile or so. Wreck Point stood grey above the moving waters; the colors had gone without her noticing. She stood a minute looking back north. Fog was blurring out Breton Head and tangling in the dark hills above the small lights of town. Nobody was on the beach. There had been a young couple with a dog, she thought, while the colors were there, but they were gone. The light was lessening in the sky, and the sand lay dim. She held herself straight, planted on the sand, knowing who she was, the shape, crouched and hollow to hold the wind. The wind blew through her. Her feet were cold in their damp socks and wet shoes, and she was hungry.

Crosswords

For Keith Kroeber

I don't have much truck with spirits, ghosts, all that.
Some people like it and are full of stories of haunted
houses and the dead returning. When I was in grade
school there was a little draw out past our end of town
that the children dared each other to pass alone at
evening, and boasted about next day: "I seen the Indian!" There was supposed to be this ghost of an Indian
man, killed there way back when, would come and
stand under the trees. An easy thing to see in the twilight if you're looking for it, and they were, so as to
boast. I don't understand that triumph people take in
telling about seeing ghosts, like they were smarter than
others to have seen them, or had outwitted common
sense. The Irish beat all for that. A sensible man like
Mr. Carey would go ranting on about the second sight
when he happened to remember that his grandfather
was from Ireland. He'd tell how his mother in Oregon
had a premonition of her brother's automobile accident
in Ohio and had shouted out at the dinner table, "Oh,
John's in great danger!" And sure enough, he'd run his
car into a ditch that very day and was nearly killed.

Why he drove into a ditch wasn't part of the story.
Maybe he saw a leprechaun, though not likely in Ohio.
I am impatient with such stuff. I don't think there are
matters that are outside of nature, or that things can
happen any way different from the way things do happen. I think that things happen in nature that we don't
altogether understand, and to call them ghosts is to
make sure we will not understand. The best we can do
is not to put a name to them, but to listen. I learned that
from Terina Adams.

I met her when I was working as waitress at the
Hiway House of Waffles on the graveyard shift. As I
had no family with me at that time, it was easier for me
than for the women with children or a husband home,
and I was curious to try and see how I liked night
work. At first I liked it well enough. The work was
easy. Often there'd be a whole hour when nobody
came in, and then it would just be a trucker or a couple
driving all night, not fussy, not even talkative. Then the
day would begin to break and the pace would liven up,
but I was off at seven, just before it got heavy with the
breakfast people. It suited me fine to see the sun rise.
But I think sleeping in daylight began to trouble me
some way. At any rate, all the time I worked nights, I
was troubled by thoughts of my mother.

Thoughts of her hadn't much bothered me before. I
left home at seventeen and went to Los Angeles and got
married. After my stepfather died I did visit home in
Chico several times so that my babies could see their
grandmother and she could see them. She seemed kind
of worried and lifeless that couple of years, and I had to
try to sort out her taxes and property because she
couldn't do it, though she didn't trust my doing it,
either. She would play with the babies, though, and
made a big fuss of Joey especially. Irma was so big and
so bald, she wasn't pretty as a baby, and Mama didn't
much take to her. Anyhow, then Mama sold the house

and married that Pentecostal. He liked me about as much as I liked him, so I didn't come up to Chico again for years. She never tried to come and see the kids. We hardly even talked on the phone. I sent birthday and Xmas cards. I got divorced, and then married Tom, and divorced him, and then the kids' father suddenly wanted custody. He could afford the lawyers, so he got the kids. At that time I was drinking. I had started drinking along with Tom, and I'd had the sense to get loose from him but not from it. When I was drunk one night it seems I decided to go and see my mother. When I got sober I was two hundred miles up I-5, so I went on and drove the rest of the way to Chico. It was the middle of the day when I got there. I had to look in the telephone book, not remembering the street, and when I was in the telephone booth I couldn't think of my mother's married name. I looked up Churches in the yellow pages and started looking for Pentecostal ads that might say the preacher's name, and just then I remembered that he was called Budd, Ronald "Buddy" Budd. So I found the address, not far from where we used to live with my stepfather.

She answered the door. First she stayed behind the screen door, finally she opened it. Her hair was grey and looked like she hadn't set or even combed it, and her skin was kind of blotched with big dark spots. It was summer, hot, and she was wearing a sleeveless dress that showed her blotched arms. She weighed at most ninety pounds, I would guess. She had a look of terror in her eyes so terrible to see that I said, "Mama! What is wrong?" as if I'd seen her yesterday instead of seven years. And she took hold of me as if she was a drowning woman and I was a lifeguard. She just said my name and held on to me. Then I heard the preacher, "Who's that? Who's that?" and she clutched harder. She said, "Ailie," in a whisper, "Ailie, he *twists* me," staring at me the way a scared animal stares. Then she let go and backed away and turned to him and ducked her body and said, "It's my daughter, Ronald."

He got between us right away. He was a good enough looking man, smooth and grey and pink, but he smelled strange. I remembered that as soon as he got near me. He smelled like nail polish, like he'd been preserved.

He asked me in and we sat in the front room and talked some. He talked mostly. He asked about my children. My mother looked as if she didn't know what children. I said their father had them. She said then, "Oh, Ailie, don't let your father have them!" I said, "Their father, Mama, not my father!" She looked confused, and then she kind of laughed. She got us iced tea. I stayed about an hour, I guess. He talked about some program they had at his church.

I went to stay at a motel out on the highway. They hadn't asked where I was staying or was I on the way somewhere. When they didn't ask at first, I decided to say, if they did ask, "I'm on my way to Oregon to a job and just thought I would stop by." But they didn't ask.

I stayed at the motel that night and next day I got back on I-5 and drove up into Oregon. Why not? My car had fuel line trouble in Eugene, and while I was waiting for it to be fixed I looked at the classifieds. There was a vegetarian restaurant wanted an experienced waitress. That was me.

They were nice kids. After a month they gave me a week off to go down to LA and get my stuff. My second year there I worked in the kitchen and learned that kind of cooking. They didn't have a license at the restaurant, and I never drank from the time I came to driving the car up I-5 to Chico until I came over here to the coast, three years ago now, and began to have a glass of red wine with dinner when I feel like it. Anyhow, two years at the Dandy Lion in Eugene was enough. I came up to Portland and got the job cooking for Mr.

Carey at Pecan Pie Catering Company, and started getting lawyers lined up to get me some rights to my kids. It turned out all I had to do was ask, since their father's new wife couldn't stand teenagers. I got them back and saw them through high school.

It was hard at first. They'd been living higher off the hog with their father. And they had to leave all their friends in L.A., and Joey had been doing a lot of surfing. But as soon as I could get him the skiing stuff he started going to Mount Hood, and then he was fine. Irma held out. She had learned some ugly ways and she wasn't going to spare me one of them. Drugs was what I was afraid of, because I feel I don't understand that, but it was liquor she decided to go in for, at thirteen. I was what you could call an expert in that. We worked through it. It took a lot of work, but she got herself straight, but she overdid it. She went and became a born-again, which took her away from me in the other direction. But she was an honors student at her school.

It was in those years that my mother died. I was not notified in time for her funeral.

When Mr. Carey retired and closed the firm, Irma was working for a year-round Xmas shop over in Cannon Beach, and Joey was in the Coast Guard. I took on the Hiway House of Waffles job mostly because it was so handy to where I lived, south of Portland. I could be there in two minutes in my car. So then I went on the late shift, as I said. And after a couple of weeks, Terina Adams came on that shift too.

Terina was a very quiet person, reserved. She was proud. I thought stuck up, at first. When Yance, the night cook, would make the kind of jokes he did, she didn't smile. I always smiled. It was easier to smile. It's like there's a kind of oil that makes their wheels go round, and smiling is part of it, women smiling. They expect it, and when they don't get it they may not know what's missing but they tend to seize up and get mean, like a motor you don't oil. Well, Terina didn't give out any oil. To me either. She was civil and polite, but a mouth like a straight line. It was like she was deaf. And she looked heavy. I don't mean overweight. She was filled out, but very trim. I mean her look was heavy as if there was a weight in her, weighing down her steps and her head. She kept her eyes down, even. So it seemed like she held herself away, and if that was what she wanted, fine with me. I liked it best those nights when nobody was talking, anyhow.

I didn't use my head about Terina until when I was in the john, which had a thin wall on the kitchen side, and heard Yance say to Bert, "Tarbaby ain't here yet."

I thought, Well, you are a fool, Ailie.

She wasn't only the only black person working in the restaurant but the only black person in it ever. In Oregon the whites and blacks and Chicanos and Indians all tend to keep by theirselves, and outside Portland you could think there wasn't anything but whites. And the usual number of them are Yances. So no wonder she wasn't going around oiling anybody's machinery any more than she had to. As soon as there came a time I saw her having a cup of coffee in the back booth of her station, I went over and started asking her did she have family and so on, pushing at her, pushing at that weight in her, until she began to give a little. Like moving a stalled car. But it got going, finally, some.

Terina never wanted to talk much, but she liked me all right. It was hard for her to talk. That weight in her, she just carried it around because there was nowhere to put it down. Most of it I never found out about. Her son, who was twenty, was living with her, and she said that she could leave him nights, now, but when he got worse she would have to stop working. I was thinking how to ask what was wrong when she asked me not to say anything about her son to anybody there because she was afraid of how they would act, and Mr. Benaski might fire her if he knew. So I guessed I knew enough. "Don't tell that Yance," she said. I said that if I saw Yance's beard was on fire I wasn't sure I'd notify him. That drew that straight-line mouth out a little bit.

In fact, watching Terina, I had begun sparing the oil, saving it for when I wanted to use it. Maybe they all needed it, but not all of them deserved it, I thought. Why waste it on the Yances?

But all the time I was getting to know and admire Terina, there was this weight of my own in me. Nothing like hers, but still I kept thinking about my mother. It was as if I had something to puzzle out, kind of like a crossword, where you have a word down, say, but you haven't figured out the ones across it. I like crosswords. Often I'd do the one in the paper, those long nights. I did them to keep from thinking, because whatever I started thinking about, it would end up with my mother.

If she was the puzzle, then the word down I had was what she said: "Oh, Ailie, don't let your father have them!"

She didn't mean my real father. He was killed in the South Pacific when I was three. She meant her second husband, my stepfather, Harold. She always called him "your father" to me. Whatever "your father" did was wonderful. If it wasn't wonderful he hadn't done it. That was the rule. That's where I learned to think like that. But where did she learn it, why did she learn it? What she said, don't let him have them, sounded like she knew about the feel-good games, but if she did know, if she had known, why did she let him have me? Maybe she thought then that they were all right. Maybe they were all right. It was only his fingers. When I try to think about it, it always seems like I didn't exactly mind, because if I had I would have got away, somehow. Or I would have told her. But I did try to tell her, once. That's why I still don't know what she knew and what she thought, because all she said was the rule. "Your father loves you and would never hurt you." And it was true it didn't hurt. He kept saying, "Doesn't that feel good, now, doesn't that feel good," kind of crooning, and I didn't know if it did but I knew it was supposed to. She must have found what I called the shaving cream in my bed, but what did she think about it? I kept thinking about that—what did she think about it? Did she think I'd wet the bed, or spilled something? She never asked. What did she think when she washed the sheets? Where did she learn to think what she thought?

My stepfather sort of tapered off in my life when I started having my periods and getting my growth. I got tall all in one year, between twelve and thirteen, and I got wise, too, at least for a kid that age, and it was like I began to scare Harold off. He couldn't come at me with his feel-good games when I was nearly his size. I think my big figure did frighten him, because he got prim and prissy. He was always after my mother to make me "dress decently," not to wear shorts or halter tops, when it was 103 or 104 degrees in Chico. I had turned into a big woman, and he was a little man. He was suited that way to my mother, who wasn't short but was very fine-boned. As I look back I think they weren't a bad match, as marriages go. But what about Ronald "Buddy" Budd? That was a whole other part of the puzzle, and I didn't seem to know any of the definitions.

Was she maybe sick, that last time I saw her? When she died they said pneumonia, but maybe she had had a cancer, to pull her down like that into a concentration-camp person, a little bent stick. Was that what she was so terrified of? But then why did she say those words I couldn't make sense of at all, "He twists me"? I kept thinking that it meant something that he was doing to her mind, like they say that people have twisted minds.

I was in the john at about three in the morning, a long, cold night in November, some ice on the roads, hardly anybody in the restaurant since eleven. I had washed my hands and was straightening my uniform blouse, smoothing it down, because it wasn't cut full enough for me. Those words came into my mind again, and I felt them. I knew exactly what they meant. I knew they meant exactly what they said. My hair raised up and a kind of sick flush ran all over my face and body. I wanted to throw up for a minute. Then it passed and all I wanted was to get out of that john with its poison smell of sweet cherry disinfectant. I came out. Terina was just going into the kitchen. I thought she looked startled, but my mind was not on her.

A couple of fellows came in from the semi that had just pulled up, and I gave them the red carpet. They were nice men, from the San Joaquin Valley, had been in before on their Seattle run, and I just poured out the oil. I wanted company, I wanted to laugh at some jokes, I wanted to like them.

I kept them an hour. When they left, Terina came over, and we went to the back booth and had a smoke.

"Who is the woman, Ailie?" she asked.

"What woman?" I asked her.

She looked at me, lifting up her eyes under their heavy lids. Terina was dark-skinned, with eyes a color lighter than her skin.

"She's shorter than you, about my height, and her hair's white and kind of tufty like. She has on a blue and white housedress. She's real thin. Her arms are like sticks, and sort of bruised-looking, like leukemia, you know? I saw her with you once before. Tonight I saw her instead of you. Coming out of the ladies' room. I saw her first, and then I looked twice and saw you."

"It's my mama," I said.

"I thought maybe," she said. After a minute she asked, "Is she alive?"

I shook my head.

Terina didn't ask anything more. I said, "I have been carrying her around lately."

"We have that to do," she said, and after a while, "Trying to listen."

"That's it," I said. "Trying to listen to what I didn't hear."

Terina nodded, and that was all we said.

That afternoon when I woke up, I went to the telephone before I was hardly awake yet, like I was obeying orders. I called up the drugstore in Klatsand where my daughter had started working last summer. The owner put her on the phone, and I said, "Hi, this is your mother," without any idea what else I was going to say. She said, "Hi, Mama! I was thinking about you." The way she said it gave me the next word.

I said, "I was thinking I wanted to see you. And maybe move out to some town out there on the coast for a while. I'm fed up here."

"There's three waitress wanted signs on Main Street," she said. "But you know, Mama, they don't pay shit."

I knew then that she had made her own arrangements with Jesus. I was so relieved about that that I said, "Well! I'll be over next week. Wednesday, maybe. Can you find me a motel till I get settled?"

"I got a couch," she said.

I said, "Irma, do you remember my mother at all?"

She laughed. "No," she said. "Do I have to?"

"No," I said, "but I'll tell you. When I get there."

But I never did. It didn't seem necessary.

Texts

Messages came, Johanna thought, usually years too late, or years before one could crack their code or had even learned the language they were in. Yet they came increasingly often and were so urgent, so compelling in their demand that she read them, that she do something, as to force her at last to take refuge from them. She rented, for the month of January, a little house with no telephone in a seaside town that had no mail delivery. She had stayed in Klatsand several times in summer; winter, as she had hoped, was even quieter than summer. A whole day would go by without her hearing or speaking a word. She did not buy the paper or turn on the television, and the one morning she thought she ought to find some news on the radio she got a program in Finnish from Astoria. But the messages still came. Words were everywhere.

Literate clothing was no real problem. She remembered the first print dress she had ever seen, years ago, a genuine *print* dress with typography involved in the design—green on white, suitcases and hibiscus and the names *Riviera* and *Capri* and *Paris* occurring rather blobbily from shoulder seam to hem, sometimes right side up, sometimes upside down. Then it had been, as the saleswoman said, very unusual. Now it was hard to find a T-shirt that did not urge political action, or quote lengthily from a dead physicist, or at least mention the town it was for sale in. All this she had coped with, she had even worn. But too many things were becoming legible.

She had noticed in earlier years that the lines of foam left by waves on the sand after stormy weather lay sometimes in curves that looked like handwriting, cursive lines broken by spaces, as if in words; but it was not until she had been alone for over a fortnight and had walked many times down to Wreck Point and back that she found she could read the writing. It was a mild day, nearly windless, so that she did not have to march briskly but could mosey along between the foam-lines and the water's edge where the sand reflected the sky. Every now and then a quiet winter breaker driving up and up the beach would drive her and a few gulls ahead of it onto the drier sand; then as the wave receded she and the gulls would follow it back. There was not another soul on the long beach. The sand lay as firm and even as a pad of pale brown paper, and on it a recent wave at its high mark had left a complicated series of curves and bits of foam. The ribbons and loops and lengths of white looked so much like handwriting in chalk that she stopped, the way she would stop, half willingly, to read what people scratched in the sand in summer. Usually it was "Jason + Karen" or paired initials in a heart; once, mysteriously and memorably, three initials and the dates 1973–1984, the only such inscription that spoke of a promise not made but broken. Whatever those eleven years had been, the length of a marriage? a child's life? they were gone, and the letters and numbers also were gone when she came back by where they had been, with the tide rising. She had wondered then if the person who wrote them had written them to be erased. But these foam words lying on the brown sand now had been written by the erasing sea itself. If she could read them they might tell her a wisdom a good deal deeper and bitterer than she could possibly swallow. Do I want to know what the sea writes? she thought, but at the same time she was already reading the foam, which though in vaguely cuneiform blobs rather than letters of any alphabet was perfectly legible as she walked along beside it. "Yes," it read, "esse hes hetu tokye to' ossusess ekyes. Seham hute' u." (When she wrote it down later she used the apostrophe to represent a kind of stop or click like the last sound in "Yep!") As she read it over, backing up some yards to do so, it continued to say the same thing, so she walked up and down it several times and memorized it. Presently, as bubbles burst and the blobs began to shrink, it changed here and there to read, "Yes, e hes etu kye to' ossusess kye. ham te u." She felt that this was not significant change but mere loss, and kept the original text in mind. The water of the foam sank into the sand and the bubbles dried away till the marks and lines lessened into a faint lacework of dots and scraps, half legible. It looked enough like delicate bits of fancywork that she wondered if one could also read lace or crochet.

When she got home she wrote down the foam words so that she would not have to keep repeating them to remember them, and then she looked at the machine-made Quaker lace tablecloth on the little round dining table. It was not hard to read but was, as one might expect, rather dull. She made out the first line inside the border as "pith wot pith wot pith wot" interminably, with a "dub" every thirty stitches where the border pattern interrupted.

But the lace collar she had picked up at a second-hand clothing store in Portland was a different matter entirely. It was handmade, handwritten. The script was small and very even. Like the Spencerian hand she had been taught fifty years ago in the first grade, it was ornate but surprisingly easy to read. "My soul must go," was the border, repeated many times, "my soul must go, my soul must go," and the fragile webs leading inward read, "sister, sister, sister, light the light." And she did not know what she was to do, or how she was to do it.

Hernes

To Elizabeth Johnston Buck

Fanny, 1899

I said we had the same name. She said she had had
another name, before. I asked her to say it. She wouldn't
say it. She said, "Now just Indun Fanny." She said this
place was called Klatsand. There was a village here, on
the creek above the beach. Another up near the spring
on Kelly's place on Breton Head. Two down past
Wreck Point, and one at Altar Rock. All her people.
"All of my people," she said. They died of smallpox and
consumption and the venereal disease. They all died in
the villages. All her children died of smallpox. She said
there were five women left from the villages. The other
four became whores so as to live, but she was too old.
The other four died. "I don't get no sickness." Her eyes
are like a turtle's eyes. I bought a little basket from her
for two bits. It's a pretty little thing. Her children were
all born before the whites settled here and all died in one
year. All of them died.

* * *

Virginia, 1979

I wanted to walk down to Wreck Point, late this afternoon, I wanted a walk after writing all day. I put on my yellow slicker and went out in the winter wind. All the vacationers are gone at last, and there was not another soul on the beach. The storms have brought in an endless scurf of trash, a long, thick line lying from the foot of Breton Head to the rocks at Wreck Point. Seaweeds and litter of waterlogged twigs and branches, feathers of seabirds, scraps of white and pink and blue and orange plastic that from a distance I take for broken seashells, grains and lumps of dirty Styrofoam, worn-down bits of plastic floats and buoys, clots of black, tarry oil from one of the spills they don't talk about or a tanker release, all thrown up together on the sand in the yellowish foam the storm waves leave.

It began to rain, beating down out of the dark ceiling of clouds. I put up the oilskin hood, and the hard rain on the south wind deafened my ears, hitting the hood over them. I couldn't look up into the rain, only down at the water floating and sheeting on the brown sand, wind gusts sending cat's-paws wrinkling across it towards me, and the myriad rain hitting it, becoming it. I opened my mouth and drank rain. It increased, increased, increased, it was hard and thick, thick as hair, as wheat, no air between the lines of driving rain. If I turned left, east, I could look up a little, and I could see how the rain came, not only in waves as I often see it from the windows of the house, but spaced and crowded together to form columns, like tall white women, immense wraiths hurrying one after another endlessly northward up the beach, as fast as the wind and yet solemn, processional, great grave beings hurrying by.

There was a gust of wind so hard I had to stand still to stand against it, and another even harder. And then it began to end. It quieted. A spatter of raindrops, then none. No sound but the breakers. A faint jade blue gleamed out over the sea. I looked inland and saw the clouds still dark above the land, and the tall figures, the rain women, hurrying up the dark clefts of the northern hills. They faded into wisps, shreds of white mist in the black trees. They were gone.

As I came back towards Breton Head the light of the sky shone placid pale blue and pink on the low-tide lagoons at the mouth of the creek. The tideline of scurf and filth and litter had been scattered and blurred away by the rain. In the quiet colors on the pools and shoals of the shallow water hundreds of gulls were standing, silent, waiting to rise up on their wings and fly out to sea, to sleep on the waves when darkness came.

Fanny, 1919

This is the influenza. I know where I took it. In Portland, at the theater. People were coughing, coughing and coughing, and it was cold, and smelled of hair oil and dust. Jane wanted Lily to see the moving pictures. Always wants to get the child into the city. But the child kept fidgeting and coughing. She was cold. She didn't care for the moving pictures. She never hears a story. She doesn't put one thing to the next to make the story. She will not amount to anything. My people were no great shakes, any of them, and all of them dead now, I suppose. There might be cousins yet in Ohio, Minnie's family. Jane asked me about my people. What do I know, what do I care for them? I left them, I came west. With Jack Shawe. With Mr. Shawe. I came west, in '83, to the Owyhee. The sagebrush in the snow. I left them all there where I grew up. The cow, the white cow down in the pool like silver in the evening. No, that was later, on the dairy farm, on the Calapuya. It was mother's red cow that bawled and bawled, and I said, Why is the cow

crying, Mother? And she said, For her calf, child. For
Pearlie. We sold the calf, she said. And I cried for my
pet. But I came out with Mr. Shawe and left all that. We
had our honeymoon in the sleeping car on the train. A
bedroom. The Honeymoon Suite, ma'am! that porter
said, laughing, and Mr. Shawe tipped him five dollars.
Five dollars! We got on the train in Chicago, in Union
Station, how often I have thought of it, the high marble
walls, the trains east and the trains west, the smoke of
the trains, the voices of men calling. The cold wind blew
in Union Station. And cold, cold when we got off the
train in the sagebrush in the snow. Evening, and no
town. No railway platform. Five houses on the sagebrush plain. I never will be warm again, I think. Mr.
Shawe came back from the livery stable with the buckboard to me where I waited with our trunks, and we
drove out to the ranch across the blue snow plain. How
cold it was! How Jack Shawe did laugh when he beat me
at cribbage, nights! He always beat. How his eyes shine!
And he coughs, coughing and coughing. And my son,
and my son is dead. Coughing. There were five villages.
Owyhee was five houses and the livery stable. We were
thirty miles from town on the buckboard through the
sagebrush, through the snow. What a fool Jack was to
take on that ranch. It killed him in five years. His bright
eyes. He could have been a great man. My people never
amounted to anything. Little sister Vinnie died of the
whooping cough. Coughing, and the red cow bawling.
The white cow stands in the evening pool, water like
quicksilver, and I call her, Come, Pearlie, come! The
pet, the one I hand-reared when the mother died. And
Servine and I were fools to take on that dairy farm, I
guess. Though he did know something about dairying. I
wonder what that land on the Calapuya would sell for
now. I wonder had Servine lived would I have lived
there all these years and never come here to the coast, to
the end of things. Would I be there now in the valley

with the hills all round? Pretty country, like Ohio. It's the promise land, Fanny, it's the promise land! Poor Servine. Him and Jack Shawe both, both those men worked so hard. Worked so hard to die so young. They had hope. I never had much, just enough to get by, to go on with. Don't you hope in Jesus, Fanny? Servine asked me that when he was dying. What could I say? Little sister Vinnie is with Jesus now, Mother said, and I said, I hate Jesus. Why did you sell her to him? You shouldn't have sold her! Mother stared at me, she stared. Not a word.

Oh, I am ill. I smell dust.

The markings on the basket are like a bird's feather. Light brown and dark brown, light brown and dark brown, I can see it clear. I'd like to see it, to hold it. It's a pretty thing. It's on the chiffonier in Lily's room. The child keeps shells in it. I'd like to hold a shell, cool and smooth. Light brown and dark brown in rows, neat and firm, the marks on shells, on the wings of birds. Orderly, like writing. That was the only pretty thing I had then. Charlotte said she'd send me Grandmother's opal brooch when I got settled in Oregon, but she never did. She wrote that the jeweller in Oxford said it was just glass, not real opal, and she would be ashamed to send it, not being real. I wrote her to send it, but she never did. Fool woman. I'd have liked to have it. I think of it, after all these years. Fool woman. Oh, I ache, I am aching ill. She'd come by, Indian Fanny, when it was all trees down to the dunes. Before the loggers before the houses before the roads. When the dark hills came down to the dunes and the spruce trees dropped cones and needles on the sand, when the elk walked and the heron flew, when I brought the children here because baby Johnny was choking on that valley dust, that farm dust, breathing dried cow dung, and I didn't want any more farms any more ranches any more cattle any more coughing, and I sold the place and the stock to Hinman and took the children here west to the dark. Under the trees. Looking out to the bright water. I saw my daughter running on the sand. Away and away down the beach, running on the sand. And she'd come by, not often, the old woman, Indian Fanny. And I went that time to her shack down behind the Point, and we talked. I bought the basket for two bits. Not for the children. I kept it for myself, kept my hairpins in it, on the shelf in the little shack. What are you going over there for? Ada Hinman said. Henrietta Koop said, Whatever are you going to do over there on the coast? Why, it's the end of the world! Not a road! Johnny's lungs, I said. Why, there isn't a church nearer than Astoria! I said not a word. The dark trees and the bright water and the sand nobody can plow, nobody can graze. I have lived at the end of the world. I have the same name as you, I said.

Lily, 1918

Dead is a hole. Dead is a square black hole. Mother got up from the table and said, Oh, Bruv, oh, Bruv. Grandmother didn't say anything. When I listened to Mother crying, lights went up and down behind my eyes. Grandmother said I could go and play, but she didn't say it nicely. Lots of people came over. I played with Sammy and Baby Wanita, and Dicky and Sammy were playing cowboys and Indians and kept running through where we were making a house under the rhododendrons. Then I could go to Dorothy's house for dinner, but I couldn't stay over. I had to come home and go to bed. First the room was dark, but then it got whitey and turned solid and pressed down and squashed down all over me so that I got all narrow inside, and everything was white, so I couldn't breathe. Mother came, and I told her it was the Gas. She said, No, no dear, but I know it was the Gas. Dicky Hambleton says the men with the Gas in the War make yellow froth like Mr. Kelly's horse did when it was dying, and Dicky held his neck and coughed, groke, groke, but he doesn't know anything about it. His uncle didn't die. It was in the *Astorian* about it. Pvt. John Charles Ozer A.E.F. Oregon Hero Falls. A black square hole with green grass all round it. I'm afraid of the Gas in my room now. In bed it begins to get white and narrow every night, and I call to Mother, and she comes. It's all right when she comes. I want Mouser to sleep with me, and Mother would let him, but Grandmother says he can't because of my breathing. Maybe she'll die now. I have a dead uncle. I know a dead man. He Died for his Country. I hate Dicky Hambleton.

Jane, 1902

I write my name in the burning sand. The wind will blow it away, the sea will wash it away, and I like that. I like to write my name. I like to sign my schoolwork: Jane S. Ozer, Jane Shawe Ozer. Servine Ozer wasn't my father, only Bruv's. My father was Jack Shawe, and I remember him: the stove was going red-hot, and he stood tall and thin, with snow in his hair when he bent down to me, and he smelled like cows and boots and smoke. His breath smelled like snow. I like that, and I like my name. I like to sign my name: JANE. Plain Jane, plain Jane, loved a Swede and married a Dane, plain Jane, plain Jane, swallowed a window and died of the pane. Ha! I like signing things. I signed the beach. My beach. Private Property—Trespassers Will Be Prosecuted. This is Jane's Beach. Recoil, profane mortals! Tread not here! Do I wish Mary was here with me? No, I don't. It is entirely my beach alone this day. My ocean. Jane alone, Jane alone, run on sand, run on stone. Bare feet. I never will marry. Mary can marry, Mary be

merry. I'll marry a Dane. I'll marry a man from far, far,
far away. I never will marry, I'll live up in the shack on
the Kelly place, the property Mother bought, the Property on Breton Head. I'll live alone and be old and
scream at night like gulls, like owls. My Property. My
beach. My hills. My sky. My love, my love! Whatever is
to come I love. I love it here, I love my name, I love to
love. My footprints on the burning sand, on the cool
wet sand, write a line behind me down the beach, running in love, writing my name, Jane running alone, ten
toes and two bare soles from Breton Head to Wreck
Point and straight out into the sea and back with drip-
ping skirt. You can't catch me!

Fanny, 1906

I put in to change the name as soon as they said we were
going to get a post office at the store. Will Hambleton
wanted it to be Breton Head, for the fancy sound of it,
to bring the summer people over from Portland. Old
Frank and Sandy would have gone on with Fish Creek.
I said, That's no name, every creek in Oregon's a fish
creek. This place has a name of its own. Don't your own
dad call it Klatsand Creek, Sandy? And he's lived here
since the year one. So Sandy starts nodding that's right,
that's right. He says old Alec has it written down on a
map he has as "Latsand." But she told me the name. It
was the name of her village. I said, Well, Fish Creek is
no name for this town, with its own P.O., and that big
hotel going up. So Will started right in again saying we
need a dignified name that would attract desirable resi-
dents. I said, I guess I just assumed the new P.O. was to
be Klatsand, since all the real old-timers call it that. So
Frank starts nodding like a china doll. They all fancy
themselves mountain men, here since Lewis and Clark.
Will Hambleton's the newcomer and they like him to

remember it. I just thought that was its proper name, I said, and Will laughed. He knows I get my way.

When I came here from Calapuya, Janey was ten, and Johnny was two. We lived in that shack off the Searoad that first winter. I have saved. I have worked at the store eight years and saved. When the Hinmans finally paid off the farm, I bought that land up on the bluff, old Kelly's place on Breton Head. That property. Fifty acres for fifty dollars. The old man liked me. Said anyhow he wanted fifty dollars more than he wanted a piece of rock. It's all been logged, but they left the little stuff, it's coming back. There's two good springs, one developed. I want to take the old shack down, it's rubbish. I own that land and I own a half interest in the store and I don't owe anybody anything. If Servine had lived I guess I'd have been slaving debts out till I died. I'd like to put up a house, up there on the property. It's going to get crowded here in town, with that Exposition Hotel going up, bringing people in. Two houses going up on Lewis Street. I might could put up a house in town myself to rent or sell. Will Hambleton's taking out all those old trees down along the Searoad, and he's buying land. There'll be houses everywhere soon.

That shack, that winter, I couldn't stop the leaks. Tarpaulins on the roof blew off, pans and buckets every time it rained. And it rained, land! I never knew rain till I came here. When the sun came out baby Johnny would try to pick up the sunshine from the ground, didn't know what it was. But you walked under the trees, dark old spruce trees that kept it dark underneath them, and then one step more, and it was all the light. Even in the rain the beach is light. The light comes back from the sea. I have seen the rain fall between the cloud and the sea in lines like the pillars of a house, and the sun strike through them. I would call that the house of glory.

The elk would come out on the beach, that first

year. They don't do that any more. I see the herd inland, going through the marshes by the creek, but those days they'd walk down the dunes like a line of cattle, only tall, and looking with those bright eyes.

Well, old Frank says, siding with Will because Will's the rich man, well, what does it mean, anyhow? It don't mean nothing. I said, It means this place. It's its name. There isn't any other place called Klatsand, is there? That made them all laugh. So I got my way. The petition to change the name was already in, anyhow. I had sent it on Tuesday.

Lily, 1924

When I get married I'll have four attendants in pink and white organdie. My dress will be white lace with silver lace insets and veil, and my bouquet will be pink rosebuds and white rosebuds and baby's breath. My shoes will be silver kid. I'll throw the bouquet so Dorothy can catch it. The car will be a white roadster, and we'll drive to Portland after the ceremony and have the honeymoon at the Multnomah Hotel, in the Honeymoon Suite.

Maybe it will be a blue and white wedding and my attendants will wear blue organdie with puffed sleeves and white sashes and white shoes. Marjorie and Edith and Joan and Wanita will be my attendants and Dorothy will be the Maid of Honor with a silver sash and silver kid shoes. The wedding dress will be white lace and silver lace with a tiny stand-up collar like Mary Anne Beckberg's new dress, and silver kid shoes with those cunning little undercut heels, and the bouquet will be white rosebuds and some blue flowers and baby's breath, with a silver bow and a long silver ribbon.

We could all go to Portland on the train from Gearhart and have the wedding there, in that stone church with the tower. It would be in the Portland papers. Miss Lily Herne of Klatsand Weds.

Dorothy's mother has that old lace veil that's been in her family for hundreds of years and they keep it in the camphor chest wrapped up in old yellowy tissue paper. She showed it to me. I will be her Maid of Honor when she gets married. We promised. I wish we had an old lace veil. Grandmother never had anything pretty. She wore those awful old boots and lived behind the grocery store. All she left Mother was this house and the one the Browns live in and that land up on the Head that's all wild forest. I wish she'd bought the Norsman house instead and then we could live in it. Mr. Hambleton said to Mother, "That is a real mansion, Jane. I'm surprised your mother didn't buy it when she bought up the half-block." If the porch was fixed and it was all painted white with shining parquet floors it would be a real mansion, and we could have the wedding there with the wedding party coming down the stairs, and a long lace train on my wedding dress, and a cunning little flower girl in pink, and the little boy ring bearer in blue short pants could be little Edward. They play "Here Comes the Bride" as I descend the shining curving stairs.

I could go to Portland to the girls' school there and make a dear friend and be married in her house in the exclusive West Hills with parquet floors and landscape pictures in the wallpaper, and as I walk down the shining curving stairs in silver and white lace a bevy of beautiful debutantes watches and the orchestra plays "Here Comes the Bride." My friend's father gives the bride away. He is tall and distinguished with iron-grey hair just at the temples. He takes my arm. My bridal attendants arrange my train of white and silver lace. Miss Lily Herne of Klatsand. Miss Lily Frances Herne of Portland Weds. The bride's bouquet was of orange blossoms shipped from Southern California. I would still throw it to Dorothy.

Jane, 1907

This is why I was born:

    I wear the black skirt, the white shirtwaist, the white apron, and I pin the white cap on my hair. I wear my hair teased out, combed over itself, pinned up, and piled high. I take their orders, smiling. I carry trays of food. The women approve of me, watching me move so quick and neat. The men admire, looking away, looking back. I have seen their hands tremble. I pass behind them, a breath on the red nape of the neck above the celluloid collar. Thank you, Miss. I pass in and out the swinging doors between the hot shouting kitchen and the cool murmuring dining room of the Exposition Hotel. I carry trays that bear plates of food, plates of crusts and bones and smears, glasses full, glasses stained and empty. I set down the hot dish, delicately arranged and colored, odorous, appetizing. I lift up the cold, streaked, and greasy dish. I set down the wineglass and I carry it away. I am neat and light and quick and sweet, and I give food to the hungry. I leave order and plenty where I come and go. I content them all. But it is not for this that I go among the tables, brushing like a breath of wind behind their chairs. This is not why I was born! I was born because he stands a little to the left of the desk, his dark head bowed, his hands in the light of the lamp holding the register; and looks up; and sees me. I was born so that he might see me, he was born so that I might see him. He for me and I for him, for this, for this we have come into the daylight and the starlight, the sea and the dry land.

Fanny, 1908

She was always a good child, a bright child, her father's child. She did well at school. The spelling prizes and the composition prizes and the mental arithmetic. She was the Spring Princess in the pageant at Union School. She was the heroine of the Senior Girls' Play at the High School in the Finn Hall in Summersea. She carried flowers, a sheaf of calla lilies in her arms, and stood and sang that song:

> I don't care what men may think!
> What care I? What care I?

She swept her skirts up like a queen and bowed. Where do they learn? How do they know? Running on the beach like a sandpiper, and the next day, "What care I?" so high and strong and sweet, standing like a queen in the lights on the stage, everybody clapping their hands for her. I couldn't clap. I couldn't unclench my hands until the curtains came together. Why did I fear for her? Why do I fear for her? She never got into harm. She always did well. Oh, your Janey! they say. Janey waited on us at the Hotel. What a beauty she's grown! When Mary ran off with that worthless Bo Voder, not even married, I did feel for Alice Morse, but what did she expect, letting Mary paint her face and drive out with every lumberjack and longshoreman? Jane was always friends with Mary, but she never would go out with her with that crowd. I never once was afraid for her that way. She knows her worth. She is a fine girl. Like Jack Shawe, tall and fine, bright eyes and a ready laugh. But proud. Johnny's going to be like Servine, easy and sweet, easygoing. I'm not afraid for Johnny. No harm will come to him. What is it I fear for my girl? I fear even to say that: "my girl." Too much at stake.

I hate a low-stakes poker game, Jack Shawe used to say. Dollar a point, Fan? he'd say, setting out the cribbage board, nights on the Owyhee ranch, dry snow ticking at the walls. I owe you ten thousand dollars already, Jack Shawe! Come on, Fan, dollar a point. No use playing for low stakes.

It isn't Lafayette I fear. I believe he's a good man for all his city ways, and I know he is in love with her. They are in love. Is it just that that I fear? What is being in love? Jack Shawe. My love's Jack Shawe. From the moment I saw him standing at the harness counter in the store in Oxford. I knew then what I was born for. It all seems so plain and clear. Everything in the world, all life at once, all in one body and one mind. All the promises kept. And all the promises broken. In love you stake it all. All the wealth of the world, all your life's worth. And it isn't that you lose, that you're beggared, so much as that it melts away and melts away into this and that, day in day out wasted, work and talk, getting cross, getting tired, getting nowhere, coughing, nothing. Nothing left. No game. What became of it, of all you were and all you were to be? What became of the love? of the promises? of the promise?

That's what I fear for her, maybe. That she'll be thrown away, like Jack. That she won't amount to anything, won't come to be who she is. What woman ever did? Not many.

It's some easier for a man. But there aren't many of much account to start with. Of either sex.

Lafayette Herne, I don't know, he might amount to something, he might not. I feel afraid for him, too. Why is that? Have I come to love the boy? Yes, I am part of their love, caught in it; I have called him son.

He carries his head well. A city man, with his fine clothes and narrow shoes, his thick dark hair well combed. I like the way he turns his head and smiles. He's full of confidence. Competent. Assistant manager of the Exposition Hotel, and he's sure he'll have the managership of that new hotel he talked about in San Francisco. He's marrying on that expectation. High stakes. But he's doing well, at thirty. There is a brilliance in him, a promise. Women see it. And he sees women. Even me, he sees me; I know that; some men see all women. But he's mad for Jane. It will be a strange life for her, wife of a hotel manager, people coming and going, all strangers all the time, the fine food and drink and clothing, the fast living in the city. Is that what I fear for her, for them? What is it I fear? Why does my heart beat heavily, why are my hands clenched, as I wait here in the hotel room in Astoria, dressed for my daughter's wedding?

Lily, 1928

What oh what oh now oh now that's blood, there's blood. I am bleeding. I am blood, blood. I am dead. Oh let me be in the black dark underground, under the roots of the trees. Go away, go away, he

He took me in his car so far, his father's car in the dark so far away from the party, far away, go away. Go away now so I can hide the blood.

Maybe it was the curse. Maybe it was the curse come early. Maybe it came in the car in the dark in the road in the forest. After the dance is over how the road turns and twists in the darkness, and on every branch of every tree of the forest an angel sits wearing white shining clothing and crying out. I knew that then, but I can see them now. Then all the angels let down drops and spots of blood. Their white what oh their shining clothes have stiff brown spots on them between the legs and there is something on the skirt that smells. The color of the old tub out behind the store, by Grandmother's stairs, it was rusted through, flaking red-brown, spotted brown, touch it and your finger's dirty red. Don't suck it, Dorothy said, you'll get poison rust, the lockjaw. Maybe it was the curse. All the angels nesting netted in the trees the stars and the huge shadows and then he

I came in and Mother called, Is that you dear? and I said yes. Last night. Now it's light I see the blood.

He turned off the switch no headlamps all dark and the engine silent and I said, Dicky, we really should be going home, and oh there's oh there's the bluejay, the jay yelling, but so far away now from the sunlight. That was so dark. Please go away. Oh please oh please oh please go away leave me be. Please stop. The blood began as just a little spot but now it will run out of the pores of my fingers and legs and arms and make spots on all my clothes, on the sheets. The spots dry stiff and brown like poison rust. I smell of that smell. I don't dare wash. I should not wash. Water is clean. If I wash the water will turn red-brown and smell like me. I'll make it stink. That's not a word for nice girls to say, Miss Eltser said, but I but I oh but I am not oh I am not a

What did I do? What has happened to me? I did what has happened to me. It is what I did. Nice girls

But I said, Why, that was the turn to Klatsand, wasn't it? Dicky

Dicky Hambleton is a college man. He went to California to college, he'll go back again in the fall. I am in love with him. We have to be in love. He said, Well, little Lily, so tenderly when I came into the living room in my new dress for the party. Lily so tenderly.

Dorothy left the party. She came and said she was going, but she had Joe Seckett to take her and I was with Dicky so how could I go with her? She said Marjorie said all the boys were going out to Danny Beckberg's car and he had bootleg and they were drinking and she had seen Dicky Hambleton there with them. But I was waiting for Dicky to come back to dance. I had to wait for him. I have to be in love. That is all tiny and bright and far away at the other end of the road, the band and the dancing and the fairy lanterns and the other girls. Dicky came back, Let's go, let's go, Lily, let's go for a picnic in the woods. But it's night, I said, I laughed. I wanted to dance, I love to dance. My white skirt was so pretty, shining in the fairy lantern light when I whirled, when Dicky whirled me dancing, and my white shoes on the floorboard of the car but the angels lean out of the huge trees and bleed the darkness and it smells of iron, and the bar of iron Oh! Oh stop! Stop! Stop! Stop! Stop! Stop! Stop! Stop!

SAN FRANCISCO, SUMMER OF 1914

The summer fog lay on the sea. Tendrils of fog reached up the bare hills; fog massed and moved through the Golden Gate, erasing the islands of the bay, the ships on the water, the dark mountains of Marin. Lights lay in faint lines and curves like jewellery along the East Bay shore under hills distinct against the blue-green sky. A ferry coming in to the towered building at the foot of Market Street moved splendid over twilit water.

A man and a woman in evening dress came out of the Alta California Hotel and paused a moment on the steps. Streetlamps and the glowing windows of the hotel behind them broke the dusk into brilliances and shadows. Facing the street full of voices and movements, the stepping of horses, the roll of high, light wheels, the woman drew a deep breath and held her white silk shawl a little closer. The man turned his head to look at her. He smiled.

"Shall we walk?"

She nodded.

A clerk ran out of the hotel, deferent but urgent: "Mr. Herne, sir, the wire came in from Chicago—" Lafayette Herne turned to speak to him. Jane Herne stood holding the fringed shawl loosely, aware of her own elegance and of her husband's black-clad, slender, angular body, his low voice speaking; aware also of being posed, being poised, as if on the low, wide steps of the hotel she stood aloof, solitary as a seabird on a wide shore, facing darkness.

He took her arm very firmly, possessing it. She came, compliant, gathering up her skirt with her free hand to descend the steps, and gathering it up again as they crossed the street littered with horse dung and straw. Through the flare of streetlamps and carriage lamps the wind flowed cool and vast from the sea.

"Are you warm enough?"

"Yes."

She turned to look into the window of a jeweller's shop as they passed it, black velvet knobs and satin nests emptied for the night. He said, dryly, as if her distraction annoyed him, "I have thought about what you said."

"Yes," she said, looking straight before her, stepping out, although her stride was shortened by the fitted evening skirt.

"I've decided that you should go to your mother, as you wished, with Lily, of course, for the rest of July and August. You can go whenever you like. Take a bedroom on the Starlight. I'll come up in September if I can for a day or two, and we can travel back together. I've been working very hard, Jane, and I realize I've let my concerns prevent me from paying enough attention to your wishes."

"Or my concerns," she said, smiling.

He made a little, impatient, controlled motion of his head in response, and was silent for a minute as they walked. "You've been wanting to visit your mother. I see my selfishness in keeping you here."

"You asked me to stay, and I stayed. You weren't keeping me."

"Why must you quibble over the words? All our quarrels start with that. However you want me to say it, I'm saying that I was selfish to keep you here. I'm sorry. And I'm saying go, as soon as you like."

She walked on, and he glanced sidelong at her face.

"It's what you said you wanted," he said.

"Yes. Thank you."

He drew her arm closer in his, with a movement of relief. He began to speak, and she made a little noise, perhaps a laugh of incredulity, at the same moment.

"I don't see the joke."

"We're play-acting. If we could talk, instead of fencing—"

"I tell you that you can do what you said you wanted to do, and you say I'm play-acting, fencing. Well, what is it you want, then?"

They walked on a half block before she answered. He had shortened his stride so that they went pace for pace, their heels striking the pavement smartly. They had turned north on a quieter street, less brilliantly lighted than Market.

"To be an honest woman," she said, "married to an honest man."

A dray loaded with ten-gallon cans, hauled by a powerful team of Percherons, rumbled and clattered beside them the length of the block. They crossed a street, Lafayette Herne looking left and right and holding his wife's arm close.

"So," he said lightly, "you're going to keep on making me pay."

"Pay? Pay what?"

"For that whole misunderstanding."

"Was it a misunderstanding?"

"The business with Louisa? Of course it was. A mistake, a misunderstanding. How often do I have to say so? How often do we have to go back to it?"

"As often as you lie to me. Do I make you lie?"

"If you keep going back over the same thing, if you have no belief in me—what am I to say, Jane?"

"You want me to believe you when you lie," she said, as if asking his confirmation of the statement.

"How can I say anything you will believe while you keep nursing this grudge, this spite? You won't let me make a fresh start. You said"—and his voice shook, plangent—"that we were beginning over. But you never let me begin."

After a few more steps she drew her arm out of his and caught up the trailing corner of her shawl. The fog was thickening, turning the light of the streetlamps milky in the distances.

"Lafe," she said, "I have thought about it a lot, too. I have truly tried to begin from where we—from after you left off seeing her. I know it is true that men, that some men, have this need. It seems to me kind of like a drunkard needing whiskey, but I know that's not fair. It's more like being hungry. You can't do anything about it, I guess, any more than you can keep from getting hungry and needing to eat. And I guess I do understand that. But what I can't understand is that you make it my fault. I won't let you begin again, you say. But you know that isn't fair. You've begun again, only not with me. And you want *that* to be my fault. Maybe it is. Because I don't satisfy you. But you always deny that."

"Because it's false, it's stupid! You know it's untrue!" He spoke with passion, rounding on her; she saw tears shine in his eyes. "I love you!"

"I guess you do, Lafe. But that isn't what we're talking about."

"It is! Love is all we're talking about! Our love! What does anyone else matter to me, compared to you? Don't you see, can't you believe, that you're my wife, my world? That nobody matters to me but you?"

They had stopped and stood facing each other. Beside them was the high front porch of a frame house standing among bigger, newer buildings built since the earthquake. Tall shrubs leaned out over the wooden steps, seeming to offer them a place, a protection from the publicity of the street, as if this were the porch and garden of their own house. It was nearly dark, and the chill of the air was deepening.

"I know you mean that, Lafe," she said in a timid, rueful voice. "But lying makes love worthless. It makes our being married worthless."

"Worthless? To you!" he said, fiercely accusing.

"Well, what's it worth to you?"

"You are the mother of my child!"

"Well?" Then, with a half laugh, "Well, *that*'s true enough." She looked at him with a frank puzzlement that was a bid for frankness. "And you're the father of mine. So?"

"Come on," he said, taking her arm again and setting off.

She looked back at the steps and shrubbery of the house as if reluctant to leave them. "Aren't we a block too far already?"

He strode on, and she kept pace with him.

"It's past eight," she said.

"I don't care about the play."

At the corner he stopped. Looking away from her, he said, "Your belief in me is the foundation of everything, for me. Everything. To violate that, to say as you did that I wanted you out of town, out of the way, so that—for my convenience—"

"If I was wrong, I'm sorry."

"If you were wrong!" he repeated, sarcastic, bitter. She said nothing. He went on more gently: "I know I hurt you, Jane. I hurt you badly. I make no excuse for myself. I was a fool, a brute, and I'm sorry for it. I'll be sorry the rest of my life. If you could only believe that! We put it behind us. We started fresh. But if you keep going back to it, if you won't believe in my love, what can I do? Whose fault is it if I can't put up with this sort of thing indefinitely?"

"Mine?" she asked with simple incredulity.

His hold on her arm tightened, enough that she said

after a moment, "Lafe, let go." He did not let her go, but relaxed his grip.

She looked into his face in the pale light of the lamp across the street.

"We do love each other, Lafe. But love, being married, even having Lily—what good is it, without trust?" Her voice, growing shrill, broke on the last word, and she gave a sharp cry, as if she had cut herself. She freed her arm and raised her clenched hands to her face.

He stood alert and uncertain, facing her on the narrow sidewalk. He whispered her name and put up his hand to touch hers, tentative, as one might reach to touch a wound.

She brought her hands down to hold her white shawl at the breast. "Tell me, Lafe. What you believe, truly, is that you have a right to do what you choose to do."

After a pause he said, gently and steadily, "A man has the right to do what he chooses. Yes."

She looked at him then with admiration. "I wish I was the kind of woman who could leave it at that."

"So do I!" he said with humor, and yet eagerly. "Oh, Janey, just tell me what it is you want—"

"I think the best thing for me to do is go north. Go home."

"For the summer."

She did not answer.

"I'll come in September."

She shook her head.

"I'll come in September," he repeated.

"*I'll* come when and if *I* choose!"

They stared at each other, startled by the leap of her anger. She drew her arms close to her sides for warmth under the shawl. The silken fringes flickered in the foggy wind.

"You're my wife, and I'll come to you," he said calmly, reassuring.

"I'm not your wife, if your wife is just one of your women."

The words sounded false, rehearsed.

"Come on. Come on home, Janey. You got yourself all keyed up to this. Now you're worn out. Come on. It wasn't the night for a play, was it?" His handsome young face looked weary. "You're shivering," he said with concern, and put his arm around her shoulders, turning her to fit her body against his, sheltering her from the wind. They started back the way they had come, walking slowly, entwined.

"I'm not a horse, Lafe," she said after a couple of blocks.

He bent his head down to her in query.

"You're treating me like Roanie when she shies at cattle. Gentle her down, talk a little nonsense, turn her round home. . . . "

"Don't be hard, Janey."

She said nothing.

"I want to hold you. To protect you. To cherish you. I hold you so dear, I need you so. You're the center of my life. But everything I do or say you twist around wrong. I can't do anything right, say anything right."

He kept his arm around her shoulders and his body inclined towards hers as they walked, but his arm was rigid, weighing heavy.

"All I have is self-respect," she said. "You were part of it. The best part of it. You were the glory of it. That's gone. I had to let it go. But it's all I will let go."

"What is it you want, for God's sake, Jane? What do you want me to do?"

"Play fair."

"What do you mean?"

"You know what playing fair means."

"Driving me crazy with hints and suspicions and accusations, is that playing fair? Is that your self-respect?"

"Sallie Edgers," she said in a whisper, with intense shame.

"What," he said flatly, and stopped. He drew back from her. After a long pause he said rather breathlessly, "I can't live with this. With this hounding jealousy. With spying, sparring for advantage. I thought you were a generous woman."

She winced, and her face in the foggy pallor of the streetlamp looked drawn and shrunken. "I did too," she said.

Presently she began to walk forward, pulling the fringed shawl close about her arms and up to her throat. She glanced back after a few steps. He had not moved. She paused.

"You're right," he said, not loud, but clearly. "It's no good. I don't know what you want. Have it your way!"

He turned and walked away from her, the clap of his shoes quick and quickly fading. She stood irresolute, watching him. His tall, straight figure blurred into the blowing fog.

She turned and went on her way, hesitantly at first, looking back more than once. The fog had thickened, dimming lights to blurs of radiance, turning buildings, lampposts, figures of people, horses, carts, cars, to bulks and wraiths without clear form or place. Before either had crossed a street the husband and wife were lost to each other's sight. On Market Street the lights of carriages and cars, brighter and more frequent, made a confusion of turning shafts and spokes of shadows in the half-opaque atmosphere, and through this beautiful and uncanny movement of wraiths and appearances the voices of children were calling and crying like seabirds. War, the young voices cried, war, war!

* * *

Virginia, 1971

Gobs and hummocks, rims and forms of foam are run in by the November breakers and driven up the wet beach by the wind. Luminously white out on the water, the foam is dingy as it lies on the sand. When the great kelp trees of the sea-floor forests are battered by deep waves in storms, broken fronds and stems churn and disintegrate into a froth, whipped by wave and wind into lasting foam, that rides the combers and is thrown ashore by the breakers. And so it is not salt-white, but oxidizes to dun or yellowish as the living cells decay. It's death that colors it. If it were pure foam of water the bubbles would last no longer than the bursting bubbles of a freshwater creek. But this is water of the sea, brewed, imbued, souped up with life and life's dying and decaying. It is tainted, it is profoundly impure. It is the mother-fluid, the amniotic minestrone. From the unmotherly sea of winter, the cold drowner, the wrecker, from her lips flies the mad foam. And on the lips, on the tongue, it does not taste pure and salt, but bursts like coarse champagne with an insipid, earthy flavor, leaving a tiny grain of sand or two between your teeth.

Crosswaves pile the foam into heaps like thunderclouds and then, receding, strand the heaps, one here one there along the beach. Each foam-billow, foam-pillow shivers under the wind, shakes, quivers like fat white flesh, inescapably feminine though not female at all. Feeble, fatuous, flabby, helpless mammocks of porous lard, all that men despise and paint and write about in woman shudders now in blowsy fragments on the beach, utterly at the mercy of the muscular breakers and the keen, hard wind. The foam-fragments shatter further. Some begin to scud with a funny smooth animal motion along the wet slick of the sand; then, coming to drier sand, they stick and shake there, or break free and begin to roll over and over up to the dunes, rounding and shrinking as they go, till they stick again, quivering, and shrink away to nothing.

Whole fleets of foam-blobs slide along silent and intent under a flaw of wind, then rest, trembling a little, always shrinking, diminishing, the walls of the joined bubbles breaking and the bubbles joining and the whole fragile shapeless structure constantly collapsing inward and fragmenting away, and yet each blob, peak, flake of foam is an entity: a brief being: seen so, perceived, at the intersection of its duration and mine, the joining of bubbles—my eyes, the sea, the windy air. How we fly along the beach, all air and a skin bitter wet and whitish in the twilight, not to be held or caught, and if touched, gone!

Jane, 1929

I am looking, looking, I must look for her. I must find her. I did not watch as I should have done, and she is lost. My watch was lost, was stolen. I must go to little towns hidden deep in the folds of bare, dark hills, asking for the jeweller's shop. The jeweller receives stolen goods, and will know where my watch can be found. I drive the Ford up roads into canyons above invisible streams. Above the rim of the canyons is that high desert where my mother lived when I was born. I drive deeper into the clefts of the high, bare hills, but it is never the town where the jeweller lives. Men stand on the street talking about money. They glance at my side long, grin, and turn away. They talk low to one another and laugh. They know where it is. A child in a black crocheted shawl runs away down the dirt street between the hills. I follow her, but she's far ahead, running. She turns aside into a doorway in a long wall. When I come there I see a courtyard under shuttered windows. Nothing is in the courtyard but a dry well with a broken coping and a broken rope.

Sewing brings the dream back. I sit at the machine and the rattle of the needle is like the rattle of the car on those roads in the canyons of the dream.

Lily, did you drink your milk this morning?

She went to get the milk from the icebox. She is obedient. She was always obedient, always dreaming. But I was not always kind, or patient, or careful, as I am, as I try to be, now.

Sewing, I dream awake. I take her down to California on the train to Stanford, where the boy is. I find him there on the green lawns with his rich boy friends, and I say to Lily, Look at him, look at the lout, with his thick hands and his loud laugh, Will Hambleton's prize bull-calf! How can he shame you? How could his touch be more to you than a clod of dirt touching you? Then I say things to the boy that make him shake and stare, and I strike his face with my open hand, a hard blow, and he cries and crouches and blubbers, abject. Abject.

Then we're in San Francisco not Stanford and it's Lafe standing before us. This is your father, Lily, I say to her. She looks up. She sees him. He's gone grey, half bald, he's lost his supple waist, but a fine man still, a handsome man, wearing his years well. He looks at Lily the way he did when she was a baby, when he used to rock her on his knees and sing, Hey, Lillia Lillia, hey Lillialou. But his face changes. He sees her. His eyes grow intent. What happened to you? he asks.

A dry well with a broken rope.

It was Lafe who named her. I wanted to call her Frances or Francisca, for Mother and for San Francisco. Francisca Herne. It would have been a pretty name. But Lafe wanted his Lily.

They say they're going to build a bridge across the Golden Gate.

Lily silly Lily little one, don't go down in the well in the dark, come up, look up. You're not the first girl Lily nor the last to Oh! but that she let him in! The second time! She let him in, let him in the house, our house! That she knew no better! What did I not give her, not teach her? How could I raise such a fool? Alone, in the woods, in the car, what could she do, his thick hands, his big thick body. She stayed in her room all day, she said she felt sick. I thought she had her period. I didn't look at her. I didn't think. I was busy at the post office. I didn't look at her. And he came in the night, that night, scratched at her window, whined like a dog, and she let him in. She let him in. I cannot forgive her. How can I respect her? She let him into my house. She thought she had to, she thought he loved her, she thought she belonged to him. I know, I know. But she let him in, into this house, into her bed, into her body.

He ought to marry her, Mary says. Face up to those damn Hambletons, she said. Face up to them? Make her marry him, make her lie down every night for him to rape her with his thick body with the blessing of the law? No. They bundled him back to his rich boys' school. Let him stay there. He can boast there how he raped a girl and she liked it so much she let him into her room the next night. They'll like that story, they'll believe it. He's where I want him, gone. But I don't know where Lily is.

Eyes say what's the girl doing still in town. Showing already. Flaunting. Common decency would have sent her away. Christian morality. Child of divorce. Only to be expected.

She walks among the eyes as if they did not see her, like a wraith. She is not there.

She sent herself away, is that it? Is that where she is? Maybe she's only staying away for a while. Maybe she's hiding, hiding down inside, in the dark, where the eyes don't see. But not forever. Maybe when her child comes out into the light she'll come with it. Maybe she'll come out with it. Maybe she'll be born alive, and will be able to talk then. Maybe she'll stop pulling out the hairs on her fingers and arms and thighs, the tiny, silky, hardly-there hairs of a girl of seventeen with blond hair and fine, fair skin, one by one, till her skin is like a sponge damp with bloody water.

There's a bridge across the Golden Gate, a bridge laid down on fog. I follow a child, a girl running, out onto that bridge. Wait for me! Wait! I follow my daughter who was taken from me into the dark, into the fog.

Lily, 1931

This is my house. Mother owns it, but she says it's mine forever. This is my room, with the window looking out into the big rhododendron bushes. That's where he came in. The branches of the rhododendrons rushed and rattled around him, and he broke them, and my heart thumped so that I saw it moving under my nightgown like an animal. He tapped on the sill and tapped on the glass. Lily, Lily, let me in! I knew he truly loved me then.

In the car in the forest in the night, that was a mistake. An accident. He was drunk, he had been drinking, he didn't know. But when he came next night to the house, to the window, it was because he loved me. He had to go away because his father is hard and cold and ambitious, but he truly loved me. It was our tragedy. I love my room. I love to put fresh sheets on the bed.

I don't like to let Baby into my room. Angels come in with her. They stand at the window to deny my comfort. They stand at the door to deny his love. The angels won't let me have my tragedy. They deny it all and drive him out of the room with their bright swords. Out the window he goes, scrambling, because he thought he heard Mother coming, and the last I see of him forever is one leg, one foot, the sole of his shoe. He didn't lace up his shoes because he was in such a hurry, and the sole of his shoe gets pulled over the windowsill after the rest of him, all in a hurry because he thought he heard Mother, but it was only the cat in the hall, and the dawn had come with its bright swords across the sky. Into the rhododendrons he goes scrambling and breaking the branches. They'll never let him back into the garden.

I watch Baby Virginia with the angels in the garden. They're often with her when she's awake. I'd like to see one watching over her when she sleeps in her crib. It would be a tall guardian in the shadows watching her with a brooding face. I saw a picture like that in a magazine. When she's running about the garden in the sunshine, when she goes out like a little soft bundle in the rain, then they're there with her. She talks to them. Yesterday she said to one of the angels in the garden, looking up, her little face so puzzled, "What Dinya *do?*" I never hear them answer her. Maybe she does.

We were sitting on the porch in the warm evening and the angels gathered and clustered so thick in the lower branches of the big spruce that I whispered to her, "Do you see them, Baby?" She didn't look at them. She looked up at me. She smiled the wisest, kindest smile. The angels never smile even when they look at her. They're stern. I took her on my lap, and she fell asleep with her little head on my arm. The angels left the tree then and walked away across the lawn, towards the hills. I think they come up from the sea, and go up into the hills. The light of their swords is the light above the mountains, the light across the sea.

One leg, one foot, the sole of a dirty shoe thrown out of heaven's window. There's no heaven I don't go to church. Only when I'm tired of the angels, then I go to church with Dorothy to get away from them. Dorothy lets me have my tragedy. She is my true friend. If there was a heaven I could go there and be forgiven, all washed and washed away, and then I could have my tragedy. But the angels won't let me, so I go to my room.

No, Baby, not in Mama's room. Let's go to the kitchen, shall we, and make the pie for dinner. Would

Baby like a blueberry pie? Would Baby Dinya like to help her Mama?

"Boolybelly pie!"

The angels won't laugh. They won't cry. I hide my tears for Dicky's love from them, because they would throw my precious tears out the window like trash, like old shoes, to rattle in the rhododendrons. I save my love from them. My love, my love! A kicking foot on a windowsill.

Last night Mother came into the room when I had done singing Baby to sleep, and I remembered how she was there in the room when Baby was born, standing so tall in the dimness, silent. But I never speak of the angels to her, that tall woman standing in the shadows with a brooding face.

Jane, 1926

After all these years. Poor Lafe, it sounds like he's in over his head this time. I'd like to see this Santa Monica woman. He never had much sense picking women, except for me. And didn't have the sense to hang on to me. At least he had the luck not to get tangled up again, till now. I liked thinking of him free. It wasn't much, compared to what we had, but it was something. Now it's nothing. I can't live without her, he writes, besotted. How can a man like that be a slave to his penis?

It's queer that I think words, now Mother's dead, that I didn't often use even in my mind, before. She wouldn't have wanted that said. Not that she was prissy. It's queer how the words change and change the world. When I left Lafe she didn't approve, but she never said I should go back to him. You did what you could, she said. But she'd be ashamed of a divorce. That wasn't one of the words she wanted said.

I'm not ashamed, but I don't want it, that sour end.

Now I know I hoped for more. No more daydreams now of us both old, him falling sick, coming here, coming back. I'd give him the south room, and care for him, bring him soup and the newspaper. And he'd die, and I'd cry, and I'd go on just the same, but it would have come round again, come whole. But it doesn't do that. It doesn't come round.

He didn't think even to ask about Lily. Forgot he had a daughter.

So I'm to be a divorcée. Stupid fancy Frenchy word. Why's it only for the women? Isn't he a divorcé? With his woman who owns "beachfront property in Malibu," but I'll bet she doesn't. I'll bet she wants to own it. I'll bet there's some kind of dealing going on under the table, finagling, and Lafe fell for it, the way he always did. A taste for high meat. Poor Lafe. Poor me. I'll never be a widow. I'll never know where he's buried.

After his letter came I needed to walk, down on the beach, get the sky over me. The waves were like pearl and mother-of-pearl, coming in out of a sunlit fog. I had my walk down to Wreck Point. When I came back there were some summer people on the beach, there's always people now. That family staying at Vineys' and some from the Hotel. There was a thin boy who made me think straight off of Lafe. Twelve or thirteen, still just a child. He ran out into the water where the creek goes out to sea, the low-tide pools and shallows, such a handsome boy, kicking his feet up high, his cap pulled way down over his eyes and his nose in the air, splashing, prancing, clowning for his family, light as light. I thought, Oh, what happens to them? My heart wrung itself like a dishcloth—what happens to the lovely boys?

And then another boy, a little one. A whole family was going in a line, dragging along, worn out, been on the beach all day, it's their holiday and they can't waste it. So they were trudging along up to the dunes, and the littlest one was behind them all, standing crying. He'd dropped his collection of gull's feathers. He stood with sandy feathers all around his feet, crying, Oh, I dropped all my feathers! Tears and snivel running down his face, Oh, wait! Wait! I have to pick them up! And they didn't wait. They didn't turn around. He was six, maybe seven, too big to be crying for feathers. Time to be a man. He had to run after them, crying, and his feathers lay there on the sand.

So I came home thinking about little Edward Hambleton. They all call him Runt. The three big boys, and that mincing Wanita cadging candy every afternoon, Will of course, even Dovey calls him Runt. Dovey's afterthought! Will says, sneering, as if he'd had no part in him. Edward's no afterthought, they just never thought at all. Maybe that's why the child's not like them. Little bright fellow, he's taken a shine to Lily, follows her around, calling her Willy. Bright and sweet, and they never turn around to him. Never hear a word he says. Will pays the child no attention at all except to hit him. All in play, he says, toughen the boy up, he says. And I saw Dicky terrify the child, Get your hand out of there! What d'you think you're doing here! An eighteen-year-old bullying a child of five. Well, no doubt they'll manage to make a man of Edward. According to their lights.

Sometimes I wonder about myself as if I was another person I was looking at: Why did she come back to Klatsand? Why ever did she bring that child back here to raise? And I don't know. I loved California, I loved the city. Why did I hightail it right back here to the end of nowhere as soon as the chance came? Running home to Mother, yes, but it was more than that. When I was up there on the Property yesterday, walking the fence line against that lumber company cutting the east side of the Head, I was thinking about how I could start putting up a house there, like Mother and I used to talk about. How many times have I thought of that? A thousand times. And I thought, If I sold out my half-interest in the store to Will Hambleton, like he's been hinting at for a year now, I could put that money into real estate. I could buy that land off Main south of Klatsand Creek; there'd be ten house lots there. And the easternmost end of it would be a prime location for that lumber and supply yard Mr. Drake was talking about in Summersea last month. Jensen owns the land. He'd sell to me. If I had the cash. I'll never have it postmistressing. And it would be a relief to quit being a partner to Will Hambleton. Between keeping an eye on his hands and keeping an eye on his accounts, I told Mary, it's like doing business with a bull elephant, you have to watch both ends. If he can't snake his trunk around you, he'll sit down on you.

But it's all here, my life's all here. I take Lily in to Portland as often as I can, I don't want the child benighted. If she marries away from Klatsand, I'll be glad. There's nobody here for her; maybe when she begins to go out with the high school crowd, she'll meet some nice young people. I've thought I should send her to St. Mary's in Portland for her last year or two. Mary talked about sending Dorothy. I'm not sure about that. Only I know that I'm fixed here. My soul goes no farther than Breton Head. I don't know why it is. All I ever wanted truly was my freedom. And I have it.

Virginia, 1935

I always liked what I drew before, and everybody liked it. But today I tried to draw the elk for Gran. I could see it, just like we saw it up on the Property, and like the elk on the cup in the window. I wanted to make it for her birthday. I drew it, and it was this thing like a cigar with sticks coming out of it. I went over the lines, and then I took black and made the lines thicker. It was so bad then I scribbled it out, and took a new piece of paper, and I drew really, really light, so if I got a line wrong I could erase it, but it was just the same. I could see the elk but all I could draw was a big stupid ugly nothing. I tore it up and tried again, and it was worse, and I began crying and got mad. I kicked the table leg and it fell over, the stupid old card table in my room, and all my colors got broken, and I began screaming, and they came.

Mother picked up the colors, and Gran picked me up and made me sit on her lap till I stopped yelling. Then I tried to tell her about the elk and her birthday present. It was hard, because I couldn't breathe right from crying, and I felt sleepy with her holding me. I could hear her voice inside her saying I see and That's all right then, and then Mother came and sat down on the bed too. I leaned on her to find out if I could hear her voice inside her too. I could, when she said, Time to wash your face now, Dinnie.

But I didn't have a present for Gran's birthday, so I told her about the cup. I told her I tried to make an elk like the one on the cup at Viney's store. So after lunch she said, Let's go see that cup. We went to Viney's and it was still in the window. The elk has what Gran says is a wreath around it, and looks majestic. Why, I think that is a majestic elk, Gran said. We went in, and she bought it for herself with a nickel, but she said it was her birthday present from me, because if I hadn't found it for her she never would have owned it. Mr. Viney said it was a shaving mug. I guess it is for shavings. I said maybe she could use it for her coffee and she said she guessed she'd rather keep it for show on the chiffonier beside the Indian basket and the ivory mirror from San Francisco.

Lily, 1937

I was sitting on the couch in the front room, mending, an hour after sunrise of the clear winter day. The sun struck in through the east window straight across my work. It freed itself from the spruce branches and struck my face a blow. I closed my eyes, blind with the beating of the light. Warmth shone itself through me, clear through soul and bones. I sat there, clear through, and I knew the angels. I was pierced with light and made warm. I was the sun. The angels dissolved into the radiance of the sun. They are gone.

After a while I could open my eyes. The warmth was my own breast and lap, and the piercing brightness had gone into a beam of light that struck across the air. Dust motes drifted in the beam, moving silently like worlds in space and shining like the stars they say are suns, all of us drifting together and apart, the shining dust.

Virginia, 1957

A strong woman whose strength is her solitude, a weak woman pierced by visionary raptures, those are my mothers. For a father no man, only semen. Sown, not fathered. Who is the child of the rapist and the raped?

They never tell if Persephone had a child. The King of Hell, the Judge of the Dead, the Lord of Money raped her and then kept her as his wife. Did she never conceive? Maybe the King of Hell is impotent. Maybe he is sterile. Maybe she had an abortion, there in Hell. Maybe in Hell all babies are born dead. Maybe in Hell the fetus stays forever in the womb, which they say is Heaven. All that is likely enough, but I say that Persephone bore a child, nine months after she was raped in the fields of Enna. She was gathering flowers there, spring flowers, when the black chariot came up out of the ground and the dark lord seized her. So the child would be born in the dead of winter, underground.

When the time came for Persephone to have her half-year with her mother, she climbed up the paths and stairs to the light, carrying the little one well wrapped up. She came to the house. "Mother! Look!"

Demeter took them both into her arms, like a woman gathering flowers, like a woman gathering sheaves.

The baby thrived in the sunshine, grew like a weed, and when it came time for Persephone to go back down for the autumn and winter with her husband, her mother tried to convince her to leave the child with her. "You can't take the poor little thing back to that awful place. It's not healthy, Sephy. She'll never thrive!"

And Persephone was tempted to leave the child in the big, bright house where her mother was cook-housekeeper. She thought how her husband the Judge looked at the child with his white eyes like the eyes of a poached trout, his eyes that knew everybody was guilty. She thought how dark and dank it was in the basement of the world, cramped under its sky of stone, no place for a child to run, nothing to play with but jewels and silver and gold. But she had made her bargain, as they called it. Betrayed, she had eaten the fruit of betrayal. Seven pomegranate seeds, red as her own blood, she had eaten, betraying herself. She had eaten the food of the master and so she could not be free, and her child, the slave's daughter, could not be free. She could only ever be half free. So she took the baby in her arms and went down the dark stairs, leaving the grandmother to rage in the great, bright, empty house, and the rain to beat on the roof all winter.

Sky was Persephone's father and uncle. Hell who raped her was her uncle and husband. There was another uncle yet: the Sea.

The years passed, and Persephone and her daughter came and went between the dark house and the light. Once when they were upstairs in the world, Perse-phone's daughter slipped away. She needed a light foot and a quick eye, for the mother and grandmother never let her out of their sight; but they were busy in the garden, in the kitchen, planting, weeding, cooking, canning, all the housekeeping of the world. And the girl slipped away and ran off by herself, down to the beach, to the shore of the sea. Running like a deer, the girl—what was her name? I don't know Greek, I don't know her name, just the girl, any girl—she ran to the beach and walked along beside the sea. The breakers curled over in the sunlight, white horses with their manes blown back. She saw a man driving the white horses, standing in his streaming chariot, his sparkling salt chariot. "Hello, Uncle Ocean!"

"Hello, Niece! Are you out alone? It's dangerous!"

"I know," she said, but did she know? How could she be free, and know? Or even half free, and know?

Ocean drove his white-maned horses straight up on the sand and reached down to seize her, as Hell had seized her mother. He reached out his large cold hand and took hold of her arm, but the skin sparkled, the bone was nothing. He held nothing. The wind blew through the girl. She was foam. She sparkled and flickered in the wind from the sea and was gone. The King of the Sea stood in his chariot staring. The waves broke on the sand, broke around the chariot, broke in foam, and the woman was there, the girl, the foam-born, the soul of the world, daughter of the dust of stars.

She reached up and touched the King of the Sea and he turned to foam, sparkling white, that's all he ever was. She looked at the world and saw it a bubble of foam on the coasts of time, that's all it ever was. And what was she herself? A being for a moment, a bubble of foam, that's all she ever was, she who was born, who is born, who bears.

"Where's the child got to, Seph?"

"I thought she was with you!"

Oh, the fear, the piercing fear in the kitchen, in the garden, the cold clutch at the heart! Betrayed again, forever!

The child comes sauntering in at the garden gate, tossing her hair. She'll be scolded, grounded, given a good talking-to. Aren't you ashamed of yourself? Shame on you! Shame! Shame! And she'll cry. She'll be ashamed, and frightened, and consoled. They'll all cry, in the kitchen of the world. Crying together, warm tears, women in the kitchen far from the cold sea coasts, the bright, salt, shining margins of the universe. But they know where they are and who they are. They know who keeps the house.

Jane, 1935

I've built the house, Mother. On your land, our land, the old Kelly place, the Property on Breton Head. Money goes a long way these days, and I've saved for ten years now. Burt Brown was glad to get the work, because nobody's building much. All the frame is lumber from the old hotel, the Exposition, where I waitressed, where I met Lafe. John Hannah had it taken down last year. Take what you want, he said, and he built two houses and I built one with the lumber, the fine clear fir, the paneled doors, the white oak flooring. It's a good house, Mother. I wish you could have seen it. You kept the houses and farmed the farms your husbands bought, you bought and sold properties, you gave me the Hemlock Street house, but never had a house of your own. Lived upstairs behind the grocery. But you always said, I'd like to put a house up there on Breton Head, up there on the Property.

Last night I slept in it for the first time, though the walls aren't finished upstairs, nor the water connected, nor a thousand things yet to be done. But the beautiful wide floors lie ready for the years, and there's a cedar shake roof, and the windows look out to the sea. I slept in my room above the sea and heard the waves all night.

In the morning I was up early and saw the elk come by. The light was just enough to see them cross the wet grass and go down into the woods. Nine of them going along, easy in their majesty, carrying their crowns. One of them looked up at me as it stepped on towards the dark trees.

I got creek water, and made coffee on the fire, and stood at the window of the kitchen to drink it. The sky turned salmon red, and the great blue heron flew over, coming up from the marshes of the creek. I never know the heron as it flies, at first. What is the slow, wide-winged figure in the sky? Then I see it, like a word in a foreign language, like seeing one's own name written in a strange alphabet, and recognizing it I say it: the heron.

SUMMERS OF THE FIFTIES, SUMMERS OF THE SIXTIES

Summer visits, visits home, college vacations, taking the train clear across the continent from those eastern shores heavy with history and industry, heavy with humanity, those old cities, ancestral, self-absorbed. Home from the college they called nourishing mother, alma mater, though to Virginia it seemed an old man, rich, famous, a grandfather, a great-uncle preoccupied with great affairs, scarcely aware of her existence. In his generous, opulent mansion she learned to live quietly, a poor relation, a good girl. Getting better all the time. But summers the train went home, across the prairies, through the mountains, away from his world, west.

She and Dave were married by a justice of the peace. "You're sure you don't want to ask your mother to come?" he said earnestly. She laughed and said, "You know we don't go in for weddings much in my family." They honeymooned in New Hampshire and Maine, at summer houses of his parents, his cousins. His fellowship paid his tuition, they lived on what she earned typing and editing theses and term papers. Dave's first visit west was the summer he was finishing his dissertation.

Gran moved down into the Hemlock Street house with Mother so that the young couple could have the house on Breton Head to themselves, no old women in the way, she said. So that Dave could work without being distracted. Men can't work in holes and corners, he needs a place to spread himself, Gran said. After a day or two he moved Gran's oak worktable from the west window downstairs and put it against an inner wall. He said it distracted him to see the sea when he looked up from his writing. It disturbed him to see the sea in the wrong direction, he said. The sun doesn't set in the sea, I'll be glad to get back to reality, he said. Great scenery out there, he would say when he was back in his world. Wide-open spaces, right between the ears. My wife comes from Ora-gahn. He said it as if it were a foreign word. It was funny, endearing to her, that he could not pronounce the name of a state of the union. I thought it was Shenek-toddy till I went east, she said. He was incredulous. Anyone knew how to pronounce Schenectady. It was not funny.

Summer, summer mornings waking in the wide bed at the wide window of the west bedroom, the first thing this side of sleep was the sky above the sea. And all through sleep and waking was the sound of the sea hushing and lulling away down at the rocks under Breton Head, the unceasing and pacific sound. Dave wrote late, stayed up always until two or three, for it wasn't real work to him unless it turned night into day, rearranged the world to suit. He would come to bed in the dark, keyed up from his writing, full of a dry, electric tension, rousing her. In the dark, roused, Virginia would pull him into the beat of the sea, the tidal swing, and then the long lulling and hushing into sleep, sleep together, together. Birds would wake her with insistent choruses at dawn. She would go out into the first light. Twice that summer she saw the elk go by between the forest and the house. The sun came up late above the blue Coast Range from the deserts, the prairies, the old cities. Later, at ten or eleven, Dave would come down, sit mute with coffee cup in hand, wake slowly, get to work at the table facing the wall, writing and rewriting his dissertation on "Imagery of Civilization in Pound and Eliot." Telephone calls to his thesis director, hours long, a panic over a lost footnote. She was lazy, giving herself up to the sun and the wind, walking down on the beach, making jelly of wild plums, playing at housekeeping in her grandmother's house. When she wrote something she put it aside unfinished. It was disloyal to write. Her work would sap and drain the energy that must be his for his hard, his important work.

It was three years after that till the next summer home. Dave had taken the job at Brown, turning down the better-paying one at Indiana. I don't want to get on a side track, he said, and she agreed, though when they visited Bloomington for his interview her heart had yearned to the place, the high groves of the campus where fireflies flickered in the sweet inland darkness. It remained a dream. Reality was east. But he knew she was homesick.

"How about that hike around Tillamook Head this summer?"

"Over it. You can't go around it, you'd fall in the sea."

It was the hike they had kept saying they'd take, the summer of the dissertation.

"Come on," he said. "Ora-gahn or bust!" And they drove west from the old cities, all across the prairies and the deserts and through the mountains, west with the sun, in the secondhand Mustang, that good little car. Gran stayed up in her own house, this time, to be visited, cooking magnificent dinners for them, poached salmon with dill mayonnaise, boeuf bourguignon, trout caught in Klatsand Creek one hour and fried the next. "When my husband managed the hotel in San Francisco," she said, "I learned to cook from the French chef."—"God, she's wonderful," Dave whispered. They slept in the little house on Hemlock Street, in the little room that had been Virginia's room all her girl-life, where an Indian basket and an ivory-backed mirror and a green glass net-float lay on the marble-topped chiffonier. They walked the beaches and hiked every trail in the Coast Range. Dave studied maps, set goals. No way down that side of Saddle Mountain, they told him, so he found a way. He triumphed, he conquered, he won the West. She followed, Sacagawea.

"I haven't seen the elk once this summer," she said the week before they left.

"Hunters," Gran said. "And logging."

"Elk?" Dave said. He asked the boys at the service station where the elk were. He drove her all over the back roads they had told him about. He drove over Neahkahnie Mountain and down Nehalem Spit until the road ran out. They walked the long dunes above the marshes between the river and the sea. "There! There!" he cried, exulting, as the crowned shadows rocked away into the shadowy marshes. He had caught the elk, he had given them to her. They drove home in the good little grey Mustang over Neahkahnie Mountain, the road turning above the twilit sea. Her mother had kept supper out for them, cold ham and three-bean salad.

"Tell me about fireflies," her mother said to Dave. He treated her as if she were a child, and she spoke to him as a child might, trustingly.

"We called them glowworms," he said. "If you got a lot of them in a jar, after a while they used to start going on and off all together." He spoke of his childhood as if it had been very long ago, as if there were no more glowworms.

Lily listened with her sweet docility. "I only knew the name," she said. "Fireflies."

"They never made it across the Rockies," Virginia said, and her mother said, "Yes. That's in your poem."

"'Sparks,'" Virginia said, startled. She hadn't known if her mother had read the book, which stood crisp and new on the bookshelf in the parlor. It had been awarded the Yale Younger Poets prize. "Yale, eh," Dave had said.

The summer home a couple of years later, the summer when she cried. That was all she had of that summer, tears. Tears wept alone in the little dark bedroom, her room. Tears wept alone on the beach at evening, swallowed while she walked. Tears wept alone as she washed steamer clams at the sink in Gran's house, tears swallowed, hidden, dried. Invisible tears. Dry tears, evaporated down to crystals of salt, stinging her eyes and tightening her throat to an endless ache. Mouthfuls of salt. Silence. The summer of silence. Every night Dave called from Cambridge to tell her about the apartments he had looked at, the apartment he had found, how his book was going, the book on Robert Lowell. He had insisted that she spend the summer in the West. He had given her Ora-gahn. She needed a rest, cheering up. Summer in Cambridge was terrible, hot, muggy, he said. "Are you writing?" he asked, and she said yes, because he wanted so much to give her her writing, too. Every night he called and talked and she hung up and cried.

Her mother sat in the little back garden. Between the big rhododendrons under the bedroom window and the paling fence held up by a wild old rambler rose there was a strip of weedy grass, and on it Lily had set two lawn chairs. The evening air was fragrant with the roses. The wind blew warm from the northeast, from the land.

Inland it was blistering this week, they said. Even here it was hot inside the house. "Come out and sit," her mother had said, so when she finished crying in her dark little room she washed her face, washed the salt away, and came outside. Her mother looked like her name, dim white in the dusk between the rosebush and the dark rhododendrons. There were no fireflies, but her mother said, "There used to be angels. Do you remember them, Virginia?"

She shook her head.

"In the grass, in the trees. You talked with them. I never could."

The land-wind carried the sound of the sea away. Though the tide was in, just over the dunes down Hemlock Street, they could hardly hear the waves tonight.

"Once you asked them, 'What Dinya do?'"

She laughed. Tears started, but freshwater tears, flowing, profuse. She drank them. "Mother," she said, "I still don't know."

"Oh, well, yes," Lily said. "Why don't you stay here in Oregon? Dave could get a job at one of the colleges, I'm sure."

"He's an assistant professor at Harvard now, mama."

"Oh, yes. You haven't called me 'mama' for years, have you?"

"No. I just wanted to. Is it all right?"

"Oh, yes. I never did feel 'mother' was right."

"What did you feel was right?"

"Oh, nothing, I suppose. I never was really a mother, you know. That's why it was so wonderful that I had you, had a daughter. But I always felt a little uncomfortable when you called me mother, because it wasn't true."

"Yes, it was true, mother, mama. Listen. I lost a baby, I had a miscarriage, early in June. I didn't want to tell you. I didn't want to make you sad. But now I want you to know."

"Oh, dear," with a long, long sigh in the dusk. "Oh, dear. Oh, and they never come back. Once they're gone."

"They can't make it across the Rockies."

Summer in Vermont. The air a warm wet woolen blanket wrapped closed about the body, folded over mouth and nose, soft, suffocatingly soft and wet as sweat. A blanket of sweat. But no tears, wet or dry, salt or sweet.

"It's the self-centeredness that troubles me," Dave said. "I thought we had a partnership, a pretty extraordinary one. Suddenly there seem to be all these things you want that you haven't had, but I don't know what they are. What is it you really want, Virginia?"

"That is what we shall never know," she quoted unkindly; she had become unkind, unfair. "I want to finish my degree, and teach," she said.

"Are you giving up the idea of writing, then?"

"Can't I write and teach? You do."

"If I could take off time just to write—! It seems that you're trying to throw away what most writers would kill for. Free time!"

She nodded.

"Of course, poetry doesn't take the kind of time professional writing does. Well, I suppose the thing for you to do would be go over to Wellesley and take some courses."

"I want to enroll in a degree program, I'd like to do it," it was impossible, of course, it was impossible to say it, she said it, "in the West."

"A degree program? Out West?"

She nodded.

"You mean go to some college out there?"

"Yes."

"Virginia," he said with a bewildered laugh, "be rational. I teach at Harvard. You don't expect me to give

that up. But you want to go to a graduate school somewhere out West? What happens to us?"

"I don't know."

Unkind, unfair. The round, close hills huddled over
the cabin. The damp sky lay on the hills like a wet blanket, an electric blanket. Heat lightning flickered and
flared in the clouds. The thunder never spoke.

"You're willing to simply throw away my entire
career?"

Unkind, unfair. "Of course not. Anyhow your
career doesn't depend on me any more."

"When did it ever depend on you?"

She stared. "When you were in grad school, when I
worked—" He looked blank. "You just said we were a
partnership! I worked. I was in the typing pool, I edited
theses—"

"That?" He paused a moment. "You feel that that
hasn't been repaid you?"

"No! I never thought of it like that. But you finished your degree. And now I want to. Is that unfair?"

"Pound of flesh, eh? No, it's not unfair. I just didn't
expect it, I guess. I thought you took your writing more
seriously. Well, listen. If this is really so important to you,
at this stage, I can look into the chances of getting you
into the Radcliffe graduate program. There might be a little static, but so long as I don't get any danger signals—"

"What can I say that you can hear?"

He finished his beer and set the can down on the
cabin floor, keeping silence. At last he spoke measured-
ly, thoughtfully, patiently. "I'm trying to understand
what it is you want. What you've always said you wanted was time for writing. You have it now. You don't
have to work, we're past that stage. We certainly don't
need the money you'd make teaching, if you did get a
degree. And you won't get much poetry written in
graduate school, you know. But I think I do see why
you think you ought to finish. A kind of moral point, a

kind of closure. But isn't it really the suburban house-wife syndrome? Women who don't have anything to do, going back to school for 'self-improvement' or, God help us, 'self-expression.' All that's rather beneath your level, you know. And to use the doctorate as a time-filler before having children—" He shrugged. "So, what I suggest is that you take a month this autumn, at the beach, in Maine. Take the whole semester, if you want. Do your writing. I can visit weekends. But don't just play with graduate work, Virginia! Women keep doing that, and it—I'm sorry, but it degrades the work. Schol-arship, the university, isn't a sandpile, a playground."

She looked down at the beer can in her hand. "More like a battleground," she said. "Red in tooth and claw, the professors."

He smiled. "If you see it that way, why do you want to join the fray?"

"To get my union card."

"The Ph.D.? What for?"

"So I can get a teaching job."

"You can teach creative writing without the degree, you know."

"You don't respect creative writing courses. You've said so often. Why do you say I could teach them?"

"Because they're playschool courses," he said, and got up to go to the refrigerator in the other room of the cabin. While he spoke he opened the refrigerator, took out a can of beer, opened it, and came back to sit down in the wicker chair by the screen door. They had not lighted a lamp, and the room was nearly dark. Mosquitoes whined at the screens.

"If you want to play, fine. But you're not going to make it on the grown-up side of the fence, Virginia. The rules are different. You've had it easy. The Yale prize dropping in your lap. And then, as my wife, certain doors have been opened for you. You may not want to acknowledge just why certain reviewers have taken your work so seriously, why some editors are so receptive. You don't have to. You can write your poems and fool around with reality; that's your privilege as an artist. But don't try to bring that attitude out of the kindergarten. Where I have to live, success isn't a matter of a prize or two. It's a lifetime's hard work. Nothing, nothing is just handed to you. You earn it. So please, don't start messing around with everything I've built up for us, out of some kind of restlessness or feeling 'unfulfilled.' I've heard your artist friends going on about what they call 'the Eastern Establishment.' That's babytalk, you know. If I weren't part of the real establishment of letters, do you seriously think you'd have got your last book published where you did? You're involved in a network of influences. Success depends on it, and to rebel against it, or deny it, is simply childish irresponsibility. Toward me."

"My last book," she said in a low voice, without enough breath, "was a failure. A miscarriage, propped up in a, in a perambulator. I'm not denying anything. I just want to stop going wrong. To go right."

"'R' or 'wr'?" he asked gently, quizzically, cocking his head. "You're all worked up, Virginia. You're letting dissatisfaction with your work, and this bad luck with the miscarriages, get you down. I don't like seeing you make yourself so unhappy. Try my idea. Go to Maine, go write, go rest!"

"I want to work for a degree. On the West Coast."

"So you said. I'm trying to understand, but I don't think I do. The idea is that I'm supposed to quit a tenure-track position in the English Department at Harvard to go teach freshman comp at some junior college out in the cactus, because you've got a whim to take a doctorate at Boondock State? How am I supposed to understand that? Have you been talking with your mother lately? This sounds like one of her versions of the real world! Seriously, Virginia, I think I have a right to ask you to consider what you're asking of me before you put a strain like this on our relationship."

"Yes."

"Yes, what?"

"Yes, you have that right."

"Well?"

"It goes both ways, doesn't it?"

"What does?"

"A relationship. I can't breathe, Dave. You're getting all the oxygen. I'm not a tree. I tried to breathe nitrogen in and oxygen out, like trees do, I tried to be your elm tree, but I got the Dutch elm blight. I'm going to die if I go on trying to live here. I can't live on what you breathe out. I can't make your oxygen any more. I'm sick, I'm afraid of dying, I'm sorry that puts a strain on our relationship!"

"All right," he said, like a cleaver falling.

He stood up, looking out through the screen, filling the doorway.

"All right. Without the poetic metaphors. What is it you want, Virginia?"

"I want to take my Ph.D. at a western school, and then teach."

"You haven't heard anything I've said."

She was silent.

"Just tell me what it is you *want*," he said.

Summers, pieces of summers, bits and scraps, when she would come up from Berkeley for a week or two, after summer session and before fall term, and sleep. That was all she had of those weeks, sleep. Sleep on the beach in the sun, in the hammock up on the Head in the shade, in her bed in her room. Sleep, and the sound of the sea.

And after that the summer, the long, wide, large summer when she stayed with Gran in the house on Breton Head because she was writing her dissertation. "You can't spread out all your books and papers in that poky little house. You need a place to yourself to work," Gran said. —"That's what Virginia said," Virginia said. But she slept three or four nights a week down with her mother at Hemlock Street. She got up early those mornings and went down to the beach to walk down to Wreck Point and back, walking by the waves thinking about *The Waves*, walking through the morning thinking about *The Years*, singing nonsense to the sea. Then she walked or drove up the dirt road to the house on Breton Head, the wide-floored house, the wide oak table under windows that looked over the sea where the sun went down. She wrote her dissertation. She wrote poems in the margins of the notebooks, on the backs of file cards.

"It's not Dave's child, then."

"I haven't seen him for three years, Gran."

Gran looked uneasy. She sat hunched in the Morris chair, squirmed, picked at her thumbnail like a teenager.

"Lafayette and I lived separately for twelve years," she said at last, sitting up straight and speaking rather formally. "He asked for a divorce when he wanted to remarry. But I think if there had been another man, I would have asked for the divorce myself. Particularly if there was to be a child."

"Dave doesn't want a divorce. He's been sleeping with a girl, a student, and I think he thinks if he gets divorced he'd have to marry her. Anyhow, if I'm still married when I have it, the baby is 'legitimate.' Unlike its mother. I don't mean to be flip, Gran."

"It makes a difference," her grandmother said without any particular emotion.

"I met the . . . the father this spring at Fresno. He lives down there. He's married. They have one child, she was born damaged, it's called spina bifida. It's pretty bad. Taking care of her is full-time for both of them. They don't want to institutionalize her. She's emotionally responsive, he says. His name is Jake, Jacob Wasserstein. He teaches modern history. He's a nice man. Very gentle. He has a lot of guilt about his daughter, and his wife. He's a guilt specialist. He teaches World War II, the concentration camps, the atomic bomb."

"So he . . . "

"He knows I'm pregnant. I saw him in June just before I came up home. He's very guilty and very happy, just what he likes best. I don't mean it was intentional. My diaphragm leaked." She stopped speaking, feeling her face and throat throb red. False, flip, all of it. She felt her grandmother's deep resistance, not disapproval, not judgment, but resistance: a wall. She felt herself outside the wall, flimsy and wordy, cheap. Nothing in Jane Herne's life had come cheap, she thought.

"So," Jane Herne said, seeking words. "How will you . . . will your teaching in Southern California . . . "

"I've discussed it with the chairman. They're giving me the spring term off. They're being really nice about it. This is where being Mrs. is helpful. Is necessary, actually. But I can get a divorce afterwards. Talking with you, I guess I see what I ought to do is tell Dave I do want a divorce. And file for it if he won't agree. Oh, God. I hope he agrees."

"That's all right," her grandmother said stiffly. After a pause she added, with more ease, "You generally get what you want, Virginia. Make sure you want it."

She thought that over for a while. "The baby. And the job at UCLA. That's what I want. And the next book of poems. And the Pulitzer Prize. All right?"

"Well, you'll earn what you get. You always did."

"Not the baby. I guess I kind of got him free. What do you think, is it time for a boy in this family?"

Jane Herne looked out the west window to the sky above the sea. "You don't earn them," she said. "They don't belong to you."

* * *

Fanny, 1918

My fat easy baby, my sunny Johnny, good child, safe child, never did any harm. Never a worry to me, and I never worried over you. My boy's not in trouble. A kind, steady fellow, and they all know it, they all like Johnny Ozer. Even when I saw the terrible pictures in the magazine I only thought of those poor foreign men. So far away. All the smiling faces in the Portland station, the young men in the train windows smiling, waving their hands, waving their hats, all the pretty girls waving. The stories about the doughboys, and the jokes, and the jolly songs, over there, over there, the drums rum-tumming over there. It'll be good for Johnny, a year or two in the Army, see the world. Toughen his hide a bit, Will Hambleton said, you've got a mama's boy there, Fanny, let him go, make a man of him. A man in a ditch in the mud choked to death by poison gas. I never said don't go. I never said don't go. I didn't know, but why didn't I know? Why didn't I fear for him? Why didn't I fear evil?

I lost my son. So they say. She lost her son. As if he was something I owned, a watch. I lost my watch. I lost my son. I was careless, I was a fool. But you can't keep him. You can't put him in your pocket, pin him to your dress. You have to let them go. With little sister Vinnie down by the pond, in the hot morning, making mud-pies, we called it, shaping the sticky clay of the pond bank into figures, horses, houses, men. Set them on the muddy bank to dry. Forgot them, and they picked up the water, they slipped back into mud. I came again in the evening and there were only lumps and smears of mud on the mud, shapeless, not men any more. Make a man, make a man of him. Fool woman, you didn't lose your son. You threw him away. You let him go, you sent him, you forgot him and he turned to mud.

The knuckly red hands, the way he ducked his

shoulder. His soft voice. He was a bright, soft boy. He would have made himself a man, a good man, a real one.

Oh, Servine, I am sorry. I am sorry, Servine, he would have done you proud.

He was crazy to get into that uniform. He thought that would do it. That's what they all said. How could he know? At twenty years old? I should have known. But I didn't fear evil. I didn't say to him the uniform won't do it, you do it yourself, John Ozer. I feared for his lungs, there in the dusty valley, on the dairy farm, that's why I ever came here to Klatsand. When he was a tiny boy he'd laugh and cough and cough. I feared for his lungs, and I let him go breathe poison gas. I cannot breathe now. I want to tell him to fear evil, fear evil, my good son, too late.

Jane, 1967

I watch the light on the ceiling, the moving light that shines up from the sea. I lived my life beside the sea, that great presence. All my doings were here, my business among the others in the world, but all along it was beside me, that other world.

I did what most of us do, pretending to keep our own world out, wrapped up in our skin, keeping ourself safe, thinking there's nothing but me. But our world goes through and through us and we through it, there's no boundary. I breathe in the air as long as I live, and breathe it out again warmed. When I could run, I ran down the beach and left my footprints behind me in the sand. Everything I thought and did the world gave me and I gave back. But the sea won't be taken in. The sea won't let tracks be made on it. It only holds you up if you flail your arms and legs till you're worn out, and then it lets you slip down as if you'd never tried to swim. The sea is unkind. And restless. All these long

nights I hear its restlessness. If I could get to the east
windows I could look out to the Coast Range, the blue
mountains always shaped the same. They let the mind
follow their curves against the sky just as they let your
feet walk on them. And lying here I watch the clouds,
and they're not restless, they're restful. They change
slowly, melting, till the mind melts among them and
changes as silently. But the sea down there bashes its
white head against the rocks like an old mad king, it
grinds the rocks to sand between its fingers, it eats the
land. It is violent. It will not be still. On the quietest
nights I hear the sea. Air's silent, unless the wind blows
hard, and earth's silent, except for the children's voices,
and the sky says nothing. But the sea yells, roars, hisses,
booms, thunders without pause and without end, and it
has made that noise since the beginning of the world
and it will go on making that noise forever and never
pause or stop until the sun goes out. Then will be death
indeed, when the sea dies, the sea that is death to us, the
uncaring otherness. To imagine the sea silent is terrible.
It makes me think that peace hangs like a drop of spray,
a bubble of foam, in the tumult of the waves, that all the
voices sing out of the unmeaning noise. It is the noise
time makes. Creeks and rivers sing running to the sea,
singing back into the unbroken tuneless noise that is the
one constant thing. The stars burning make that noise.
In the silence of my being now I hear it. The cells of my
body burn with that noise. I lie here and drift like a drop
of spray, a bubble of foam, down the beach of light. I
run, I run, you can't catch me!

Lily, 1943

When Edward Hambleton was a little boy he loved me
and I loved him, little Runt, running to me red-faced
and smiling, yelling, Hi, Willy! at the top of his voice.

He thought my name was Willy. Because of hearing his father called Will, I guess. I called him Little Buddy. And he is my brother truly.

May and the Hambletons call his baby Stoney, but his name is Winston Churchill Hambleton. When he came early, they telephoned Edward at Fort Ord, and he said, Name him Winston Churchill. A boy needs a good name in times like these, he said.

These are the dark times. When Mother and Mary and Lorena Weisler and Hulse Chock sit talking after the newscast about the Pacific Theater, the cities in Italy, I think we live in a world that has all gone dark so that there's only the radio connecting people, and we here away out on the edge of it, on the edge of the sea where the war is. With the blackout, the town is as dark at night as if there were only forest here again. As if the town had never been and there was only the forest at the edge of the sea.

These are the dark days. Mother said that once about the other war, about my uncle John who was killed in France. Those were the dark days, she said. I can't remember him, only a shadow between me and the west windows in somebody's house, tall and laughing. And I remember riding on a horse with somebody walking along beside holding me, and Mother said that would have been Uncle John, because he worked at the livery stable for a while, and would give me rides on an old pony around the yard. And he would ride like the wind down the beach, she said. He was twenty. He was in the trenches, that was how they said it then. Edward is twenty-two now. In the South Pacific Theater. Like an actor on a dark stage. He hasn't seen the baby. I wonder if he is dead. They say it can be weeks before you hear. They say letters come from men that are dead, sometimes after they have been dead for weeks or months.

There is no use loving him. It's like a letter from a

dead man. There's no use my loving anybody but Mother and Dinnie and Dorothy. I know Dovey Hambleton hates me for living here. We say good morning, Lily, good morning, Dovey. All these years. She never speaks to Dinnie. Dicky's other children are in Texas, she was talking about them to Lorena in the store, but she stopped when I came in. They are Dinnie's sisters, her other granddaughters. Those words are like knives: daughter, granddaughter. I don't say them. They cut my tongue. I say Mother, but often it cuts my tongue when I say it. Only there is Dorothy, my friend. She was never not my friend. That is a word as sweet as milk.

Dorothy's hair is turning blond, so she dyes it back to red now. Since she had her babies her neck and ankles have got thick. She doesn't move the way girls move, light and free, the way Dinnie goes down the street all legs and ponytail. Dorothy was like that when we used to play down by the creek, playing house all afternoon, playing weddings with our dolls. Now she's heavy and open and slow, like a red cow, beautiful. She knows everything. She doesn't worry. It doesn't worry her that Cal and Joe are in the war. With her the war isn't like a black empty theater but more like a construction site, men in trucks, busy. Cal's in a lot less trouble now than he was with that logger's wife in Clatskanie! she says. Army's the safest place for him! And Joe's driving a laundry truck at some base in Georgia. My war is with a million dirty skivvies, he wrote Dorothy. She reads me his letters. They're funny, he is a kind man. She misses him but she doesn't really miss him, she doesn't need him. She is complete. Like a round world. I love her because she looks at me out of her round whole world and brings me in, so that I'm not out at the edge, under the open sky. I can't walk on the beach, under the open sky, by the sea, not since the war started. Not since the angels. They're gone, but I still fear their wings, out there. Oh, Lily, she says, stop mooning. Oh, Lily, if you aren't the craziest!

What do you think, Lil, is that baby of mine cute or is he cute? Lily, will you keep the kids this afternoon, I have to go up to Summersea. Lily, is that daughter of yours bright or is she bright? Dorothy can say all the words. She's not afraid. She is my true love.

Jane, 1966

"Angel child," Lily says when Jaye runs to her with a question or a flower. "Come to Lily, angel!"

Her arms are thinner than the child's arms.

I'm seventy-nine years old and I have no idea what love is. I watch my daughter dying and think she never was much to me but heartbreak. But why does the heart break?

I don't understand it. I don't know right from wrong. I thought Lily was wrong to stay home and not have the treatments. I thought Virginia was wrong to come here to be with her. Leaving everything she's worked for, the university, throwing it away. She says they'll take her on full-time at the community college in Summersea next year. She says she wants that. Wants to stay here. I thought she was wrong to have that child, some man's child she didn't even want to marry. It all seemed wrong to me. What do I know? I couldn't have managed without her. I can't look after Lily. Can't lift my arms. Can't pick up the cat, have to wait for him to jump in my lap, come on, old Punkin, and he teases me, sits and washes his face first. And that nurse. The cancer nurse.

They say the word right out, now. Never had it in the family, save for that thing Mother told me of: her mother in Ohio had what looked like a little seed stuck to her toe, and flicked it off without much thinking, and it bled all night long so the sheets were ruined. But she never got it, nor Mother, nor I.

I can't abide the woman. "The medicine makes them dopey," she says, or "They don't know what's best for them," right in front of Lily, as if Lily were a baby or an idiot! But she's strong and knows her business, I guess. And Lily is patient with her. Patient with everybody, everything. Always. Lily shames me.

I breathe free when Virginia comes in with the child, and the nurse goes. Evenings, the four of us, Jaye asleep and Lily drowsing along, Virginia and I sit and talk, or she grades her papers, or we play cribbage. I win, generally. It's one thing Virginia's no good at. I told her the other night, you win the prizes for poetry, but don't ever take up cards for a living.

Lily was right to want to die in her own house; Virginia was right to let her. I didn't want her here. I didn't want my daughter here to die. Or live. But she didn't want to come here. She was born in the City, but her life has been in the house on Hemlock Street. She never was away for as much as a week, but for that one trip to the World's Fair, before the war. But her daughter will live here, in this house, my house. The daughter conceived in the bed the mother is dying in. In that little room. The rhododendron bushes outside the window. Virginia answered me straight, the way she does: Yes, she said, yes, if you leave me the house on Breton Head I will live there. She said, I love Los Angeles but I have work to do, and I do it better here. What about your teaching? I said, and she said, I will do it as well here as I would there, and she laughed. If you leave me the house, she said, I will live in it and Jaye will grow up in it.

That gives me pleasure. She gives me pleasure. She looks like Lafe, the way she carries her head. She glances sidelong, her eyes flash. I thought she was wrong to let Lily have her way, wrong to have the child, wrong to come here to live, but I guess we think when a woman's free she's wrong.

I miss my freedom. Running down the beach, clear to Wreck Point, barefoot, alone.

When Edward came yesterday, I thought while we were talking, this is the nearest I come to running down the beach these days. Talking with Virginia, talking with Edward. When we talk I'm still on the move. As if the mind were a beach, the long empty sand, the waves, the sky. Virginia and I talk about people, students and teachers at her college, writers she meets when she travels to her prizes and meetings, people in town here, people I used to know. She likes to hear about the town back when I was growing up, and the San Francisco years. But that's a fairy tale to her. Edward's not all that much older than her, but he's got an old mind. Maybe it was being in the war. But even as a boy he was thoughtful. Virginia flies, flies like a heron, often I can't follow her. Edward plods along trying to see his way, trying to think things out, trying to know what's right. She's free; he seeks his freedom. I admire that in him. And a man that a woman can talk honestly with is a rare man. Edward got all the honesty in the Hambleton family.

Now and then I do stop and say, in words, in my mind: Edward is Virginia's uncle by blood. And I wonder if he ever thinks about that. We've never talked about it.

I never spoke to Will Hambleton from that day on. The day she told me.

Twenty years. Passed him ten thousand times on Main Street. Passing a dog, nothing.

He learned soon enough to send somebody else to the post office, Wanita or Edward or one of the grocery clerks, for the mail or to buy stamps or send parcels. I wouldn't wait on him. If he came in, I went to the back till he was gone. Stood there. At first my face would burn, then it was nothing to me. I'd find something to do till he was gone. Sometimes other people would come in while he stood there, and I'd speak to them, ask them to wait or come back later. I know what people here thought of crazy Jane Herne at the P.O., holding a grudge for twenty years, pretending a man doesn't exist, and Will Hambleton who owns half the town at that. I don't say I was right. I don't say I was wrong. I was doing what I could.

Will Hambleton brought up his eldest son to do evil and rewarded him for doing it. I could have forgiven the boy, I suppose, if there was any reason to. But not the man. I do not see a reason to forgive him.

I did what I could, and it was nothing. What can you do to evil but refuse it? Not pretend it isn't there, but look at it, and know it, and refuse it. Punishment, what is punishment? Getting even, schoolboy stuff. The Bible God, vengeance is mine! And then it flips over and goes too far the other way, forgive them for they know not what they do. Who does know? I don't. But I have tried to know. I don't forgive a person who doesn't try to know, doesn't want to know if he does evil or not. I think in their heart they know what they do, and do it because it is in their power to do it. It is their power. It is their power over others, over us. Will's power over his sons. His son's power over my daughter. I can't do much against it, but I don't have to salute it, or smile at it, or serve it. I can turn my back on it. And I did.

Virginia, 1972

Still I elude myself. There is a shape. The sea-fog will take shape, form: an arm, the glint of an eye, footprints in a line above the tidemark. I have to pursue, for the pursuit creates the prey. Somewhere in these mists I am.

Body's not the answer. Maybe it is the question. In the fulfillment of sexual desire I have found the other not the one I seek. I believed what all the books said; though my mothers did not say it, I believed it: The other is the foundation. But I built nothing on that foundation. A firm ground it may be, but a foreign one, the country of the other. I wandered in his kingdom, a tourist, sightseeing—a stranger, bewildered and amazed—a pilgrim, hopeful, worshipful, but never finding the way to the shrine, even when I read the signposts that said Love, Marriage, and followed the highroads beaten wide by a million feet. A failed crusader, I never got to the holy place. I built no fortresses, no house even, only shelters for a night, tents of leaves and branches, like a savage. Ashamed, I left that country, his great, old country, stowed away, sailed off to the new world. And there I sought the new life.

Body's all the question. What could be more one's body than one's child shaped in one's womb, blood, flesh, being? Seeking my being in hers before she was conceived, so I conceived her, imagining the small embodiment that I could purely cherish. But when she first moved in me, I knew she was not mine. This was the other, the other life, more purely other than any other, for if it were not, if no charge were entrusted to me, how could I purely cherish it?

So she was born out of me on that last long wave of unutterable pain, and runs free now. She returns, she comes home, home at four in the afternoon, milk and a cookie, can we play by the creek, never yet gone longer than overnight or farther than a school excursion, but she runs away from me. I feel the string stretch, the fine cord of ethereal steel that she'll keep pulling out so long over the years, so fine, so thin that when she's gone I'll hardly know it's there, not think of it for weeks, maybe, until a sharp tug makes me cry out for the pain in the roots of the womb, the jerk and twist of the heartstring. I feel that already. I felt it when she took her first steps, not to me but away from me. She saw a toy she wanted, and stood up and took her first four steps to it, and fell down on it in triumph. She went where she wanted to go. But I can't run after her. I must not pursue her, making her my prey. Not even the flesh of my flesh is the one I stumble after, my soul taking its first steps and falling flat, defeated, empty-handed, bawling for comfort.

Oh, the images, how they flock and hurry to me, comforting! lifting me up in their arms to dizzy heights! murmuring like voices heard inside a breast my ear is pressed against, don't cry, my baby, it's all right, don't cry.

Are my images all body, then? Are they soul at all? What are these words to which I have entrusted my hope of being? Will they save me, any more than I can save my child? Will they guide me in my search, or do they confuse and mislead me, the beckoning arms, the glinting eyes, laughter in the fog, a line of footprints leading down to the edge of the water and into it and not back?

I have to think they are true. I have to trust and follow them. What other guide have I than my dear images, my lovely words, beckoning me on? Sing with us, sing with us! they sing, and I sing with them. This is the world! they say, and they give me a sea-borne ball of green glass reflecting the trees, the stars. This is the world, I say, but where in it am I? And the words say, Follow us, follow us! I follow them. The pursuit creates the prey. I come up the beach in the fog from the sea, into dark woods. In a clearing in the woods a dark, short, old woman stands. She gives me something, a cup, a nest, a basket, I am not sure what she gives me, though I take it. She cannot speak to me, for her language is dead. She is silent. I am silent. All the words have gone.

* * *

SAN FRANCISCO, SUMMER OF 1939

Jane

Half my life, since I saw the fog come drifting through the Golden Gate. They've put the great red bridge across the Gate, and the double bridge across the bay, and made an island full of lights and flowers and towers and fountains in the water, but the fog isn't any different. It comes in shining over the City in the sun, the crest of a great, slow wave. It breaks slowly and the bridge is gone. The City across the grey water is gone. The top of the Tower of the Sun is gone. The grey water fades away. In a luminous cold grey silence we walk, eating hot, fresh French fries from a paper cone.

I took the child to the City of Paris store to buy her a "real San Francisco dress." I had told her the ivory-backed mirror came from Gumps, and so we had to go to Gumps. I bought her a good silver-mounted brush. She'd learn to live here in no time. She flicks her eyes sidelong and sees everything. After a day at the hotel she could have been a city child, cool as a cucumber, picking up her fork in the restaurant, flirting out the big napkin on her lap, "I'll just have ice water, please!" Oh, she's the cucumber, that Virginia.

But Lily, poor Lily, to think she was born here, in the hospital right up there on the hill, my San Francisco baby, my little Francisca! She stares around her like a wild cow. Her eyes roll. And her hat, oh, land, my daughter in a hat like that. Lily isn't worldly, is what it is, and I am. I love this city.

If I saw Lafe Herne coming down the street: I thought of it when we passed where the Alta California Hotel used to be. If I saw Lafe come down the street I'd turn and go with him. Even if he had a Santa Monica woman on his arm. He has two arms. I want to tell him that I never found a man but him worth the trouble. He deserves to know that. Not that it would mean much to him. He'd be sorry for me, think I pined, think I meant I made a mistake in leaving him. I made no mistake. What's love without trust? I made no mistake, but I'd like to see him turn his head and look at me, the flash of his eyes. I'd like to see him. He's sixty now. It's all gone. It seems a world away, the Alta California torn down, all Market Street rebuilt, and it's not that I want to go back. I don't. What I'd like is to see Lafe Herne at sixty, and walk with him down the beautiful way between the fountain pools and the rainbow iceplant flowers to the Tower of the Sun. My arm in his, the way we used to walk. And watch the fireworks with him, the way we watched them on the Embarcadero, the Fourth of July, a week after we were married. But it doesn't come round like that. You don't take hands but once. And I was right to let go.

But I do get tired. In the street outside the hotel when we came back from the fair this evening, the fog was thick, and I was tired, and Lily and the child were worn out. The newsboys were calling, and my heart went cold. I thought they were calling that there was to be war.

Lily

Six days now till we go home. This time the train will be going the right direction. The Coast Starlight, that's its name, a beautiful name. And the Pullman porter was so kind, making up my berth, making jokes. He called me Missy. You all right in there, now, Missy? But when I woke in the night the mountains were turning outside the window in the moonlight across gulfs of darkness. I want to be home. Six days now. I wear out walking those long, long avenues on Treasure Island, and the wind blows so cold down the Gayway. There are great maps of the world, and a man painting a picture bigger than the side of a house, and Venus rising from the foam of the sea with the winds and the flowers about her. It is all so big, and so many people, so many many people! I can't keep up with Mother and Virginia. They want to see every sight. They wanted to see the microscopic animals and the huge horse and to go down in the mine. They wanted to see Ripley's Odditorium, but when the man blew smoke out of the hole in his forehead Mother said, Oh, pshaw, and turned away, and Virginia was glad to get out, too. But then she wanted to see the woman cut in half with mirrors. How do they bear it all? How do they step so boldly out into the street? The cars whiz, whiz by—How do they know which streetcar to take, and where to catch the bus? How do they recognize our hotel among all the other great high buildings all alike? I was walking right past it when they laughed and made me stop. How are they so brave, so at home in this strange world full of strangers?

Virginia

I will never in my life forget the beauty and the glory of the World's Fair. I know that glory is where I will live, and I will give my life to it.

The best thing of all was the Horse. We were walking to where the bus comes to take you back to San Francisco, after all day on Treasure Island. We were tired, and oh it was so cold with the wind blowing the fog in, but I saw the sign THE BIGGEST HORSE IN THE WORLD! And I said, Can we see that? And Gran never says no, except for Sally Rand. So we went in. At first the man was going to say he wasn't open, I think, but then Gran looked in and said, My land! What a beauty! And the man liked her, and let us in, just by ourselves without any crowd. He took the money and began to tell us about the Horse.

He was a Percheron, mottled grey like the sky over the sea sometimes is. His head was as big as I am. He turned and looked at us with his huge dark eyes with long dark lashes. I felt truly awed in that presence of majesty. He stood in a stall, very patiently, on straw. Beside him the man looked like a little boy. After a while I asked if I could touch him. The man said, Sure, honey, and I touched the shining mottled leg at the shoulder, and the Horse turned his head again. I touched his vast soft nose, and he breathed his warm breath on me. The man picked up one of the Horse's forefeet to show us. Under the coarse, flowing fetlocks, the hoof was as big around as a platter, with the mighty horseshoe nailed on. The man said, Would the little lady like a ride? And Mother said, Oh, no, and Gran said, Would you, Virginia? I could not speak. My heart was great in me. It swelled in my bosom. The man helped me over the fence around the stall and then just swung me up with a kind of push, and I sat astride the Biggest Horse in the World. His back was as wide as a bed, so my legs stuck out, and he was warm. I could touch his mane, which was knotted into many neat, tight, whitish knots down his great grey neck. He stood there gently. We couldn't go anywhere because he was fastened in his stall. When do you take him out? Gran asked, and the man said, Generally early, before the fair opens up. I take him on a lead up and down the avenues. That would be a sight to see! Gran said, and I imagined it: the great Horse stepping out in the silent morning like thunder, like an earthquake, arching his neck, stamping his mighty hooves.

Coming home on the bus and streetcar I thought all the time about the Horse. When I am home I am going to write a poem. I will imagine in it what I did not see, the stepping of the Great Horse in the fog on silent avenues under the Tower of the Sun, and I will put in it the glory and the majesty that I have seen. For this I was born, to serve glory patiently.

Jane, 1918

I close my eyes and see the fireworks. Flowers of fire
opening, falling like bright chrysanthemums over the
dark beach. Aahhh! everybody says. Fireworks may be
the nearest thing to perfect satisfaction in this world.

All the flags and bunting and speeches in front of
the hotel this afternoon. Brave boys, glorious victories,
Huns on the run.

I shut my eyes and saw Bruv running on the beach,
three or four years old, running ahead of Mary and me.
Mother trusted us to watch him all Saturday; it made
like a vacation for her working in the store. You girls,
keep him in sight! He'd fly along the beach like a little
thistle seed. Three or four years old. We didn't worry
about him. He was afraid of going in the water.

Every time I pass the livery stable I think of him on
that pretty bay colt he'd ride down onto the beach,
summer before last. Every time.

At the Hambletons' picnic they'd looped red white
and blue crepe paper on the fence and stuck flags in
every tree in the yard. Willie Weisler kept talking about
how he hopes the war will go on so he can enlist. "Even
if I am only sixteen I'm big enough to kill krauts, ain't I?
Ain't I?"

"Big enough fool," his mother said.

She's right, too. Talking about killing krauts, with a
name like that. And in front of Mother and me. But still
it troubled me she'd speak that way to him in front of us.
Women talk to their sons that way, like they despise the
boy for being something they expect him to be. But men
glory in it. Will took Dicky around back of the house
right at the picnic to whip him for some insolence, making sure everybody knew Dicky's so bad he has to be
whipped. Making sure Dicky knows it. Boasting.

Even Mary's always making out Cal to be a ruffian,
when the poor child's nothing but a puppy. All he needs

is a pat and a kind word. But that's just what Mary and
Bo won't give him. Like they thought it was their duty
not to. The ruffian in that family is Dorothy. I'm glad
she's taken to playing with Lily. Lily's too moony, lives
inside her head, drifts by like a little moth. "City child,"
Mother said, when we were first home. "Never gets her
little dresses dirty. As if she didn't touch the ground."

"I know I got dirty enough," I said.

She said, "You weren't any city child. Where you
were born was thirty miles to the next house."

"Born dirty," I said, but it didn't amuse her. Mother's dignity never did allow for some of my jokes. And
now she doesn't smile. She never looked tired till this
year. I know she's pleased with my taking over the
post office from her. I wish she'd go ahead with building up there on Breton Head, on the Property, like
she's always wanted to. I suggested we walk up there,
clean out the spring, but she put it off. I wish I could
hearten her. If she won't build up there I wish she'd
come live with us, but she's too independent. Those
rooms above the grocery seem so dark now. It's like
her life is dark. I feel that darkness when I'm with her.
Yet she takes pride in me, I know that. It is the ground
I stand on.

Like chrysanthemums, opening and falling in the
dark. I see the fireworks down on the beach in the night,
and the breakers gleaming for a moment under the colored sparks. I see Bruv riding in the evening, fast, full
gallop down the beach, away and away.

"Well, now, how about a toast," Will Hambleton
says, standing up at the long picnic table, "to the new
owner of the Exposition Hotel!"

No doubt now who's the great white chief in Klatsand. I've never understood how Mother gets on so easy
with him. She won't stand for any of his nonsense, and
he knows it, I guess. But the way he crowds you and
crowds you, with that barrel chest and big face and

speechy voice of his, I lose patience. And Dovey cooing. And the pushing, yelling boys, and little Wanita. Now, with her they do just the opposite from what they do to the boys: they praise her for being something they despise. A little dressed-up parrot. She's a pretty child, but land! those bows and ruffles! and stood up on a chair to recite poetry! "My Country's Flag." I got one look at Mother's face.

I caught that red ruffian Dorothy behind the rhododendrons imitating her to Lily, all lispy sweet, "my tuntwee's fwag," and I did long to laugh, but I had to hush her up. Will doesn't like fun made of him or his. And he comes it pretty high over Bo and Mary. I suppose he only had them at his picnic because Mary and I are friends. I trouble him. I go up to Portland on the train. I lived in San Francisco. Lafe managed a big hotel. I might know something Will Hambleton doesn't know. I might have an idea in my head. It makes him nervous.

Well, I know what Will would start, if I gave him one word or sign. He may yet, even if I don't. There's that look in his face, no mistaking it ever. It's like smelling something. When they get fixed on you that way, when their body's attention is on you, you know it like you know it's a warm day, without thinking. But I think of Will's body naked, like a big cheese. I think of meeting, at lunchtime? where? some bedroom with the blinds down? It turns my stomach to think of it. And then he'd go home to Dovey. Like Lafe would come home to me.

And that's why he'd be doing it. Not for love and not for desire. Those are the names they call it, the excuse. Great names, like flags and speeches. What he wants is the advantage. The power. He's got it over Mother only through his money, and never to his satisfaction. She's a partner, independent. She isn't afraid of him. If he got me to cheat with him, he'd have us both at his advantage. And the satisfaction of cheating on Dovey, too. Well, Will, it would be a nice pie if you could eat it, as the joke goes.

I dream sometimes, but there isn't a man in this county I'd look at twice. I don't know what I want; I don't know that I want anything. Only to know some soul better. I don't know anyone. I never have. Mary, of course, she's a good friend, we share our whole lives, yet something's left out. It's like there's a country in me where I can't go. Lafe might have gone there, but he turned away. And other people have that country in them, but I don't know how to find it.

Lorena Weisler—she makes me think that all I know of her is some person she puts on like a dress. At the picnic, Dovey was going on about some new kind of crochet that Mrs. Somebody from Portland had shown her that uses a special tee-tiny hook and so on, and Lorena said, "Satan will find mischief still for idle hands to do." She said it in such a mild quiet tone, it went right by Dovey and Mary, and nearly by me. I looked at Lorena. Placid as a goldfish. But there are countries in her. She is a mystery. You live your whole life around the corner from someone, talk to her, and never know her. You catch a glimpse, like a shooting star, a flicker in the darkness, the last spark of the fireworks, then it's dark again. But the spark was there, the soul, whatever it is, lighting that country for one moment. Shining on the breakers in the dark.

Virginia, 1968

Last summer, the night after Gran's funeral, Edward Hambleton came up to the house. He always used to call before he came; not that time. I was putting the coffee grounds out on the flower bed, the way Gran did, when I saw him walking up the drive in the evening light. It was a long summer sunset, pale gold deepening to orange and mauve, darkening to red.

Jaye was asleep. She'd been quiet at the funeral, watchful, a little awed. When we got home she thought she'd lost her stuffed lion, her Leo. She began crying, insisting we'd left it at the cemetery. And when I found the little lion out on the deck where she'd left it, she had a tantrum. I had to shut her in her room awhile, though I didn't want to; I wanted to hold her and cry too. At last she got quiet and we could rock together, silent. She was asleep before I got her into her bed. With Leo on one side, and the old cat on the other, old Punkin. He wanted company, he missed Gran.

So Edward came on foot, alone, and we stood in that flame-colored light in the garden, hearing the sea.

"I loved your grandmother. And your mother," he said.

He wanted to say more, but I didn't know what it was, and was not willing to help him say it. My heart was busy with grief and solitude and the glory of the evening. If he spoke I would listen, but I would not be his interpreter, his native guide. I think that it behooves men to learn to speak the language of the country we live in, not using us to speak for them.

He hesitated awhile, and then said, "I love you."

The great fires in the west made his face ruddy and shadowy. I moved, so that he thought I was going to speak. He held up his hand. I've often seen him raise his hand that way, talking with Gran, as he sought a word, an idea.

"When you were in college, in the late forties, you'd come home at Christmas, summers. You wait-ressed at the old Chowder House. You'd come into the store, shopping for your mother." He smiled, so broad-ly, so cheerily that I smiled too. "You were my delight," he said. "Understand me: there was nothing wrong between May and me. There never has been. I came out of the Army, you know, and found that I'd got me this wife, and a baby. And that was a wonder. It was amazing. And then Tim came along. And I loved running the store, the business. I didn't want anything but what I had. But you were my delight."

He held up his hand again, though I hadn't been about to speak.

"You went east, got married, got divorced, took your degree—I lost you for years. But I'd go into Dorothy's shop and see your mother, like a wild cottontail rabbit there behind the counter, making change. Or I'd get talking with Jane, after council meetings. And there it was. Not pleasure, not contentment, but delight. All I had with May and Stoney and Tim, I could hold. In my hands, in my arms, I could hold what I had. And that was happiness. But with you Hernes, I held nothing. I could only let go, let go. And it was the truer joy."

His sons are both in Vietnam. I turned away from him in shame and sorrow.

"There is the family of my body," he said, "my parents, my brothers and sister, my wife, my sons. But you have been my soul's family."

He stood looking out into the red sky. The wind had turned. It blew from the land, smelling of the forest and the night.

"You are my brother's daughter," he said.

"I know," I said, for I wasn't sure he knew I knew.

"It means nothing," he said, "nothing to him, to any of them—nothing but silence and lies. But to me it has meant that, however much I held, I had to let go, too. Not to hold. And now it's all letting go. Nothing left to hold. Nothing but the truth. The truth of that delight. The one perfectly true thing in all my life."

He looked across the air at me, smiling again. "So I wanted to thank you," he said.

I put out my hands, but he did not take them. He did not touch me. He turned away and went round the house to the driveway. He was walking down the road to town as the last colors faded and the light greyed to twilight.

I believed what he said. I believed in that truth, that delight. But I wanted to cry for him, for the waste of love.

Edward was my first love, when I was thirteen, fourteen. I knew who he was, but what did it matter, what did it mean? He was kind, thin, handsome, he joined the Army, he married May Beckberg. I was a kid with a crush. I saved the cigarette butt he put out in the ashtray in Mother's house when he came to say goodbye. I kept it in a locket on a chain, and never took it off. I worshiped May and the baby. I held them in holiness. Pure romance: to love what you can never touch. And was the love he thanked me for, his pure delight, ever more than that—a bubble without substance, that a touch would break?

Yet I don't know if anything is more than that. He held his sons, as I held Jaye that night, and tonight, close, close against the heart, safe, till sleep comes. We think we hold them. But they wake, they run. His sons have gone now where only death can touch them, where all their business is death.

If they die, I see him follow them. Not touching them, but following. And May, that strong woman, alone. She always was alone, maybe. He thinks he held her, but what do we ever hold?

Lily, 1965

When I was very, very young, Mother took me downstairs to see the candles lighted on the Christmas tree in the lobby of the hotel, the hotel we lived in before I can remember. But I remember that, now, all at once, like a picture in a book. The page has turned, and I see the picture. All around me and above me are great shadowy branches, shining with ribbons of tinsel, and in the shadows are round worlds, many, large ones and small ones, red, silver, blue, green, and candles burning. The candle flames are repeated and repeated in the colored worlds, and around the flames is a kind of mist or glory.

They must have set me down there under the tree. Maybe I wasn't walking yet. I sat amongst and under the branches, in the pine smell and the sweet candle smell, watching the colored worlds hanging in the hazy glory and the shadows of the branches. Near my face was a very large silvered glass globe. In it were reflected all the rest of the ornaments that reflected it too, and all the flames, and the shoots and tremblings of brightness down the tinsel, and the dark feathering of the needles. And there were eyes in that shining globe, two eyes, very round. Sometimes I saw them, sometimes not. I thought they were an animal, looking at me, that the silver bubble of glass was alive, looking out at me. I thought the tree was all alive. I saw it as a world full of worlds. It is as if all my life I have seen the tree, the candles burning, the bright eyes, the colors, the deep branches going round and up forever.

Do you see the angel at the top of the tree?

A man asked that. A man's voice.

I only wanted to look into the branches of shining worlds, the universe of branches, the eyes looking back at me. I cried when he lifted me up. Do you see the angel, Lily?

Fanny, 1898

We waited for low tide to ford Fish Creek. As the horses started into the water a great bird flew suddenly down the creek between the black trees, over us. I cried out, What is that! It looked bigger than a man. The driver said, That is the great blue heron. He said, I look for it whenever I cross this creek.

There is not much to the town. End of the world, Henrietta Koop said. The General Store where I will work for Mr. Alec Macdowell and his son Mr. Sandy Macdowell. One fine house belonging to an Astoria family, the Norsmans, but they are seldom here, I'm told. The smithy and livery stable owned by Mr. Kelly. A sorry farm across the creek. And fourteen houses among the stumps. The streets are laid out good and straight but are mud two feet deep.

Mr. Sandy Macdowell had me this house ready. A man's idea of ready. It is two rooms and sets by itself under the black spruce trees just behind the sand dunes. It is some south of where the platted streets stop, but a sand road runs in front of the property. Mr. Macdowell calls it the Searoad, and spoke of a stage line they hope to run along that road, when they have cut a road across Breton Head north of the town. Mail is carried up the beaches from the south, now, when the carrier can ride through. He can't when there's high tides in winter. Mr. Macdowell apologized for the house. It is just a shack, small and dark. Stove is all right, and all the wood I want to cut lying handy. The roof is bad. He said he hoped I would not feel lonesome. It was the only house empty just now till they can fit up the place upstairs behind the store. He told me ten times there was nothing to fear, until I said, Mr. Macdowell, I am not a timid woman. I guess you're not, he said.

He said there were no Indians and nobody had shot a cougar for ten years. But there is the old woman who lives down behind Wreck Point, I have seen her twice now. And this morning I was up to light the stove while the children were still sleeping. The rain had stopped. I stood in the doorway in the first light. I saw elk walk past, going south in a line along the dunes. One walked behind the other, tall as tall horses, some with antlers like young trees. I counted them: thirty-nine. Each one as it passed looked at me from its dark, bright eye.

Virginia, 1975

There's always the story, the official story, the one that is reported, the one that's in the archives, the history. Then there's the child of the story, born of the story, born out of wedlock, escaping from between the sealed lips, escaping from between the straining thighs, wriggling and pushing her way out, running away crying, crying out loud for freedom! freedom! until she's raped by the god and locked in the archives and turns into white-haired history; but not before her child is born, newborn.

The story tells how the grieving mother sought her daughter over land and sea. While she grieved and while she sought, no grain grew, no flower bloomed. Then, when she found the maiden, spring came. The wild grass seeded, the birds sang, the small rain fell on the western wind.

But the maiden no longer maiden must return for half the year each year to her husband in the underworld, leaving her mother in the world of light. While the daughter is dead and the mother weeps, it is the fall and winter of the year.

The story is true. It is history.

But the child is always born, and the child has her story to tell, the unofficial, the unconfirmed, the news.

She had done her time inside. She had held court as Queen of Hell for half eternity. She had shelved the law books in the archives and filed all the files of the firm. She had lived with her husband for the appointed time, and the season of her return was at hand. She knew it by the way the roots that hung down through the low stone ceilings of the underworld—taproots of great trees, oaks, beeches, chestnuts, redwoods, only the longest roots could reach down so far—by the way those roots sent tiny fibrils, curling split ends, growing out, groping out from the damp, dark grout between the rocks that make the sky there. When she saw the thin root hairs reach out she knew the trees were needing her to come and bring the spring.

She went to her husband, the judge. She went to the courthouse, appearing before him as a plaintiff. The uncomplaining multitudes of the dead, the shadows of life awaiting judgment, made way for her. She came among them as a green shoot comes through the sodden leaves at winter's end, as a freshet of black living water cracks the rotten ice. She stood before the golden throne of judgment, between the pillars of silver, on the jewelled pavement, and stated her case: "My lord, by the terms of our agreement, it is time I go."

He could not deny it, though he wanted to. Justice binds the Lord of Hell, though mercy does not. His beautiful dark face was sad and stern. He gazed at her with eyes like silver coins, and did not speak, but nodded once.

She turned and left him. Lightly she walked the long ways and stairways that led up. The dog barked and the old boatman scowled to see her stand alone on the dark side of the river, but she laughed. She stepped into his boat to be ferried over to the other shore, where the multitudes waited. Lightly she stepped out and ran up the brightening paths, and came through the narrow way at last into the sunlight.

The fields were dun and sodden after long snow and rain. Her feet, that stayed so clean in Hell, were black at once with mud. Her hair, always so dry and neat in Hell, was windblown and wet at once with rain. She laughed, she leaped like a deer, she ran like a deer, running home to Mother.

She came to the house. The garden was untended,

winter-beaten. "I'll tend to that," she said. The door of the house stood open. "They're expecting me," she said. The kitchen stove was cold, the dishes had been put up, no one was in the rooms. "They must be out looking for me," she said. "I must be late. Why didn't they just wait here for me?"

She lighted the fire in the stove. She laid out the loaf and the cheese and the red wine. As evening darkened she lighted the lights so that the windows of the house would shine across the dusk, and her mother and grand-mother, trudging the road in the rain, would see the light: "Look there! She's home!"

But they did not come. The night passed, and the days passed. She kept the house, she planted the garden. The fields grew green, trees leaved, flowers bloomed: daffodil, primrose, bluebell, daisy, by the garden paths. But they did not come, the mother, the grandmother. Where were they? What was keeping them? She set out across the fields to find them. And she found them soon enough.

I don't want to tell the story. I don't want to tell that a child sees her grandmother burned to death and her mother raped by the enemy by the soldiers by the guerrillas by the patriots by the believers by the infidels by the faithful by the terrorists by the partisans by the contras by the pros. By the corporations by the executives by the rank and file by the leaders by the followers the orderers the ordered the governments the machinery. To be caught in the machinery, to fall into the machine, to be a body torn to pieces, harrowed, disemboweled, crushed by a tank by a truck by a tractor, treads and wheels smash the soft arms, the bones snap, the blood and lymph and urine burst out, for flesh is not grass but meat. I don't want to tell that a child sees the god, sees what the god does. I don't want to tell the story of the child, the child who is the spring of the world, who went out of her house and saw her grandmother doused in gasoline and burning, the grey hair all afire. She saw her mother's legs pulled apart by the machinery and the barrel of the gun pushed up into her mother's womb and then the gun was fired.

She ran, ran like a woman, heavy-footed, her breasts jouncing with each step, her breath in gasps, ran to the narrow way and down, down into the dark. She did not pay the boatman, but commanded him, "Row!" In silence he obeyed her. The dog cowered down. She ran the long ways, the dark stairs, heavily, to the house, the courthouse, the palace of precious stones under the stone sky.

The anterooms and waiting rooms were full as always of shadows, fuller than ever before. They parted, making way for her.

Her husband, her father's brother, sat on his throne holding court, judging all who came to him, and all came to him.

"Your mother is dead," she said. "Your sister is dead. They have killed Earth and Time. What is there left, my lord?"

"Money," her husband said.

The seat of judgment was solid gold, the pillars were silver, the pavements were diamonds, sapphires, emeralds, and the walls were papered with thousand-dollar bills.

"I divorce you, King of Dung," she said.

Again she said, "I divorce you, King of Dung."

Once more she said, "King of Dung, I divorce you."

As she spoke the palace dwindled into a pile of excrement, and the dark judge was a beetle that ran about among the turds.

She went up then, not looking back.

When she came to the river, great black waves beat against the beaches. The dog howled. The boatman ferrying souls across tried to turn back to the far shore, but his boat spun round, capsized, and sank. The souls of the dead swam off in the black water like minnows, glimmering.

She plunged into the river. She swam the water of darkness. She let the current bear her, riding the waves, borne to the mouth of the river where the dark waters broadened to the breakers across the bar.

The sun was going down towards the sea, laying a path of light across the waves.

Wrecked on the sand of the sea-beach lay the salt chariot, the sparkling wheels broken. The bones of the white horses were scattered there. Dead seaweed like white hair lay on the stones.

She lay down on the sand among bones of seabirds and bits of broken plastic and poisoned fish in the scum of black oil. She lay down and the tide came in across the bar. The waves broke on her body and her body broke in the waves. She became foam. She was the foam that is water and air, that is not there and is there, that is all.

She got up, the woman of foam, and went across the beach and up into the dark hills. She went home to the house, where her child waited for her in the kitchen. She saw the light of the windows shine across the darkening land. Who is it that lights the light? Whose child are you, who is your child? Whose story will be told?

We have the same name, I said.

Biographies

Fanny Crane Shawe Ozer

1863—born near Oxford, Ohio

1883—married John Shawe; came west to ranch near Owyhee, Oregon

1887—daughter Jane born

1890—John Shawe died

1892—married Servine Ozer and bought dairy farm near Calapooya, Oregon

1896—son John born. Servine Ozer died.

1898—moved to Fish Creek (Klatsand), Oregon, to work in General Store owned by Alec and Sandy Macdowell. Lived on Searoad, below Salal Street

1900–1916—Postmistress of Klatsand

1900–1919—lived in apartment upstairs behind General Store

1902—bought 50 acres on Breton Head, north of Klatsand

1904—bought General Store in partnership with Will Hambleton

1912—bought half-block on Hemlock Street and built two rental houses

1915—gave one Hemlock Street house to daughter Jane
1918—son John killed in France
1919—died of influenza

Jane Shawe Herne

1887—born at Little Owyhee Ranch, Oregon
1891–1898—lived near Calapooya
1898–1908—lived in Klatsand. Attended Union School
     and Summersea High School, 1898–1905.
     Worked in General Store, 1905. Waitressed at
     Exposition Hotel Dining Rooms, 1906–1907.
1908—married Lafayette Roger Herne, assistant man-
     ager of Exposition Hotel
1908–1915-lived in San Francisco at Alta California
     Hotel, of which Herne was manager
1912—daughter Lily Frances born
1915—separated from husband and returned to
     Klatsand
1915–1935—lived in Hemlock Street house with daughter
     Lily
1915–1916—clerk at Exposition Hotel
1916–1960—Postmistress of Klatsand
1919–1927—manager of Klatsand General Store
1926—divorced from Lafayette Herne
1927—sold her inherited half-interest in store to partner
     Will Hambleton; invested in various properties
     and developments in Klatsand
1932–1948—Councilwoman of Klatsand Town Council
1948–1954—Mayor of Klatsand
1935—built house on lower Breton Head and lived
     there 1935–1968
1960—gave 30 acres of upper Breton Head property
     adjoining state lands to form Breton Head
     State Park
1968—died of heart disease

Lily Frances Herne

1912—born in San Francisco, California
1915–1966—lived in house on Hemlock Street,
      Klatsand, Oregon
1929—daughter Virginia born
1945–1962—clerk in Dorothy's Stationery and Gift
      Shop, Klatsand
1966—died of leukemia

Virginia Herne

1929—born in Klatsand, Oregon
1935–1944—attended Union School; 1944–1947,
      Summersea High School; 1947–1951, Reed
      College, Portland; 1951–1953, Pennsylvania
      State University
1952—married David Torrance Hall; 1952–1957 lived in
      Pennsylvania, Rhode Island, Massachusetts
1954—first book of poems, *Stone Forms,* Rose Press.
      Yale Younger Poets Award
1957—*Times Out,* poems, Harvard University Press
1957—separated. 1957–1962 in doctoral program at
      University of California, Berkeley. 1962, Ph.D.
      degree in English
1962–1966—Associate Professor of English, University
      of California at Los Angeles
1963—daughter Jaye born. Divorced from David Hall.
1966—Instructor of English at North Coast Community
      College, Summersea, Oregon; 1966–1967
      Assistant Professor, 1967–1969 Associate
      Professor, 1970– Professor
1967—moved from Hemlock Street house to house on
      Breton Head with daughter
1969—*Woolf's Voices,* University of California Press
1971—*Searoad,* poems, Vashon Press

1976—*Behind the Silence,* poems, Capra Press. Western
  States Award
1978—*Severing,* poems, Harper & Row. American
  Book Award, etc.
1979—*Selected Poems,* Harper & Row
1983—*Persephone Turning,* Harper & Row. Pulitzer
  Prize for poetry

The Best in Science Fiction and Fantasy

A FISHERMAN OF THE INLAND SEA by Ursula K. Le Guin. The National Book Award-winning author's first new collection in thirteen years has all the majesty and appeal of her major works. Here we have starships that sail, literally, on wings of song... musical instruments to be played at funerals only...*ansibles* for faster-than-light communication...orbiting arks designed to save a doomed humanity. Astonishing in their diversity and power, Le Guin's new stories exhibit both the artistry of a major writer at the height of her powers, and the humanity of a mature artist confronting the world with her gift of wonder still intact.
Hardcover, 0-06-105200-0 — $19.99

L OVE IN VEIN: TWENTY ORIGINAL TALES OF VAMPIRIC EROTICA, edited by Poppy Z. Brite. An all-original anthology that celebrates the unspeakable intimacies of vampirism, edited by the hottest new dark fantasy writer in contemporary literature. *LOVE IN VEIN* goes beyond our deepest fears and delves into our darkest hungers—the ones even our lovers are forbidden to share. This erotic vampire tribute is not for everyone. But then, neither is the night....
Trade paperback, 0-06-105312-0 — $11.99

A NTI-ICE by Stephen Baxter. From the bestselling author of the award-winning *RAFT* comes a hard-hitting SF thriller that highlights Baxter's unique blend of time travel and interstellar combat. *ANTI-ICE* gets back to SF fundamentals in a tale of discovery and challenge, and a race to success.
0-06-105421-6 — $5.50

Today . . .

HarperPrism

An Imprint of HarperPaperbacks

SMALL GODS by Terry Pratchett. International bestseller Terry Pratchett brings magic to life in his latest romp through Discworld, a land where the unexpected always happens—usually to the nicest people, like Brutha, former melon farmer, now The Chosen One. His only question: Why? **0-06-109217-7 — $4.99**

MAGIC: THE GATHERING™—ARENA by William R. Forstchen. Based on the wildly bestselling trading-card game, the first novel in the *MAGIC: THE GATHERING™* novel series features wizards and warriors clashing in deadly battles. The book also includes an offer for two free, unique MAGIC cards.
0-06-105424-0 — $4.99

SEAROAD:Chronicles of Klatsand by Ursula K. Le Guin. Here is the culmination of Le Guin's lifelong fascination with small island cultures. In a sense, the Klatsand of these stories is a modern day successor to her bestselling *ALWAYS COMING HOME*. A world apart from our own, but part of it as well.
0-06-105400-3 — $4.99

CALIBAN'S HOUR by Tad Williams. The bestselling author of *TO GREEN ANGEL TOWER* brings to life a rich and incandescent fantasy tale of passion, betrayal, and death. The beast Caliban has been searching for decades for Miranda, the woman he loved—the woman who was taken from him by her father Prospero. Now that Caliban has found her, he has an hour to tell his tale of unrequited love and dark vengeance. And when the hour is over, Miranda must die.... Tad Williams has reached a new level of magic and emotion with this breathtaking tapestry in which yearning and passion are entwined.
Hardcover, 0-06-105204-3 — $14.99

and Tomorrow

WRATH OF GOD by Robert Gleason. An apocalyptic novel of a future America about to fall under the rule of a murderous savage. Only a small group of survivors are left to fight — but they are joined by powerful forces from history when they learn how to open a hole in time. Three legendary heroes answer the call to the ultimate battle: George S. Patton, Amelia Earhart, and Stonewall Jackson. Add to that lineup a killer dinosaur and you have the most sweeping battle since *THE STAND*.
Trade paperback, 0-06-105311-2 — $14.99

THE X-FILES™ by Charles L. Grant. America's hottest new TV series launches as a book series with FBI agents Mulder and Scully investigating the cases no one else will touch — the cases in the file marked X. There is one thing they know: The truth is out there.
0-06-105414-3 — $4.99

THE WORLD OF DARKNESS™: VAMPIRE— DARK PRINCE by Keith Herber. The ground-breaking White Wolf role-playing game Vampire: The Masquerade is now featured in a chilling dark fantasy novel of a man trying to control the Beast within.
0-06-105422-4 — $4.99

THE UNAUTHORIZED TREKKERS' GUIDE TO *THE NEXT GENERATION* AND *DEEP SPACE NINE* by James Van Hise. This two-in-one guidebook contains all the information on the shows, the characters, the creators, the stories behind the episodes, and the voyages that landed on the cutting room floor.
0-06-105417-8 — $5.99

HarperPrism
An Imprint of HarperPaperbacks